PROMISES, PROMISES . . .

"All I want is a wife," said the chatty, impossibly handsome king.

"She'll have the face of an angel, of course, and golden hair, and eyes as blue as the bluest sky. Or maybe brown eyes and black hair. I can be flexible," said His Majesty, to show he was reasonable.

"What I really want is someone who's *quiet*, damnit. Is that too much to ask? Is that really too much for the King of Avalon to ask? A wife who knows how to keep her mouth shut? Why is it so damnably hard to find a woman like that?

"I swear, if ever I meet a woman who doesn't talk my ears off, I'll marry her straight away. Even if she's ugly! If she can keep her mouth shut, I'll make her my queen!"

The king heaved a beleaguered sigh. "On my honor, I swear it. . . ."

The Wild Swans

KATE HOLMES

LOVE SPELL BOOKS ✦ NEW YORK CITY

A LOVE SPELL BOOK®

June 2000

Published by

Dorchester Publishing Co., Inc.
276 Fifth Avenue
New York, NY 10001

ISBN 0-505-52383-3

The name "Love Spell" and its logo are trademarks of Dorchester Publishing Co., Inc.

Printed in the United States of America.

The Wild Swans

Chapter One

Women!

James Richard Henry Michael Bledgabred Taillefer, King of Avalon, Darian, Longshore, and the Western Isles, Duke of Lemaire-over-the-Sea, Count of Borghame, Chosen of God and, by His Gracious Might, Anointed among Men—affectionately known among his people as King Jim, though he was just plain Richard to his friends—shifted uncomfortably in his saddle and glowered at the road ahead.

Women were the bane of a man's existence. From the moment he was breached until the moment he went to the grave, there was a woman around somewhere doing her damnedest to make his life miserable.

And young, beautiful women were the worst

of all. Worse than a prating priest any day of the week. Worse even than hives under chain mail—and after that bout at the tournament on St. Stephen's Day, when he'd damn near gotten killed because he was more focused on his itching than on the opponent trying to bash his brains out, he'd have sworn there wasn't anything in the world worse than hives under chain mail.

But that was before he'd met Her Royal Highness, Princess Graciella Antoinette Elizabeth de Belmaine.

Richard's glower darkened. Just the thought of the Princess Graciella gave him a pain.

Oh, she was beautiful enough—he'd give her that. Beside her, the sun grew pale, and stars turned dull. And her breasts!

At the thought of her breasts, the King of Avalon, Darian, etc., raised himself slightly in his stirrups to relieve the pressure at his crotch and shift his John Paul to a more comfortable position. He shouldn't be thinking about the Princess Graciella's breasts while he was riding—surely the resultant compression of the crown's most precious jewels wasn't good for his future as a father.

"Thinking about the Princess Graciella, are you?"

Richard sat back in his saddle and glared at the grinning, golden-haired man who'd ridden up beside him.

"Trying to adjust these damned tight hose. I swear, Harry, I don't know where Thurgood gets the damned things. He's had the dressing of me since I was twelve, and he's still finding ways to make me miserable. Said he figured these would be more comfortable than braies and laced hose." Richard's expression darkened as he slumped lower in his saddle. "Much more of this and I'm likely to be singing soprano soon."

Harry's grin widened. "Couldn't be any worse than your singing now. The only time I can bear to listen to you is when I'm too damned drunk to care"

"Hah!" said His Majesty, but his heart wasn't in it. He gloomily resumed his study of the ground in front of his horse's nose.

The two rode for a way in silence, sunk in their thoughts and as indifferent to the looming forest through which they were traveling as they were to the crowd of noblemen, huntsmen, servants, and miscellaneous retainers riding in their wake.

"Tell me, Harry," the king said at last, unable to keep his misery to himself, "how long is it now that we've known each other? Twenty years? Twenty-five?"

Harry's blond eyebrows shot up at the question. "What the devil difference does it make how long we've known each other?"

Richard's mouth thinned in irritation. He glared at his friend.

9

Harry's eyebrows abruptly reversed direction. "All right, all right. Let me think." His frown deepened. "You were seven, and I was almost nine—I remember how angry I was that you were taller than I was, even then—and I'm thirty-two now. Or am I thirty-one? So that makes it . . ."

He chewed on the corner of his mustache as he considered the question, then tried ticking the years off on his fingers. His frown turned to a scowl when he lost count for the third time. He threw up his hands, disgusted.

"Hell, I don't know how long we've been friends! Long enough for me to know there's something bothering you, and it isn't the glorious Graciella's breasts!"

"Forget the breasts." Richard waved a hand to indicate that he'd forgotten them. "In all the years you've known me, Harry, have you ever known me to be unreasonable?"

"Hmm," said Harry consideringly. "Well, there was that disagreement we had over that saucy little serving wench in—"

"Harry . . ." said His Majesty.

Harry got back to the subject at hand. "Well, then, no, I can't say I've ever known you to be unreasonable." He threw a quick glance over his shoulder at the mass of people following them to make sure no one was near enough to overhear. "If anything, you may be a little too reasonable. For a king, that is."

"What the hell do you mean by that?"

"I mean this business of letting old Archie push you around the way he—"

"He does not push me around. And that's Bishop Archibald to you."

"The hell he doesn't push you around! Just because you promised your father on his deathbed that you'd keep the peace and call a truce with his old enemy doesn't mean you have to put up with the man's arrogance. You think you're being considerate of his pride, but he just thinks you're a fool he can rule if he maneuvers things cleverly enough."

Richard shrugged in irritation. "He can't maneuver me, you know, even if he thinks he can. I won't let him."

"That doesn't stop him from trying. Your trouble is, you're too damned honorable. You're clever—smarter than Archie and all his minions put together—but you're not devious, and you're not good at spotting someone who is." Harry lowered his voice and leaned toward Richard. "I'm telling you, Archie is a devious toad, and you'd do well to get rid of him while you still can."

Richard waved away his friend's concern. "Forget Archibald. I don't want to talk about him."

Harry hesitated, as if weighing the risk of pressing further, then regretfully settled back in his saddle.

"What I need to know," said Richard, "is what I should do now. About a wife, I mean.

"You're going to give up on the Princess Graciella? You're really going to give up those incredible breasts?" Harry's mustache twitched. "You're running out of choices, you know."

"I know." Richard sighed. He seemed to be sighing a lot these days. "It's not the breasts. It's not the legs—they're perfectly reasonable legs. Really. I even like the rest of the package, you know? Boobs. Butt. Waist. Hips. Legs." He sketched an outline in the air to show what he meant.

Harry nodded. He knew. He himself had tried to look up Graciella's skirts. Twice. And that wasn't counting all the times he'd tried to look down her front.

"Trouble is," Richard continued glumly, "that package comes attached to a mouth that won't stop. You've heard her. Hell, everybody's heard her. Graciella would talk the ears off a dead man!"

That was no less than the truth. The Princess Graciella had a tongue that flapped at both ends. She got up in the morning chattering, and she went to sleep at night still chattering, and she never stopped talking in between. Not even to draw breath.

Richard was still dizzy from the battering his ears had taken. After five days of it, even Graciella's breasts had begun to lose their appeal. At last, in desperation, he'd pleaded a war on some border or other and fled.

It hadn't done his pride any good to run, of course, but he wasn't as particular about his pride as he was about his peace of mind. And Graciella had given him no peace whatsoever.

"Old King Torvan isn't going to be too happy about your leaving, you know," Harry said. "He seemed to take it for granted you'd never get past those breasts. Especially not after you turned down Princess Thessia and Princess Mirabelle and Princess Alice and—"

"I couldn't marry her, Harry. She'd have driven me mad with her constant yammering. They all would. Not one of them knows how to keep silent for longer than it takes to blink. Not one! Folks wouldn't like having a madman for a king."

"Hmm." Harry didn't look convinced.

Richard brightened, though. If you looked at it that way, he hadn't really run. He'd had to leave for the sake of his subjects, so they wouldn't have a madman for their king. Knowing he'd done it for the good of his people made him feel a little better.

"I'm not an unreasonable man, Harry," he said. "Really I'm not. All I want is a wife. You

13

know, someone beautiful and kind and sweet and clever. But not too clever, mind. It wouldn't do to have a wife who was cleverer than me."

Harry shook his head. "Wouldn't do at all."

"But clever enough. Can't have a stupid queen, either."

"Of course not," said Harry.

"She'll have the face of an angel, of course," said Richard, warming to his subject. "And golden hair down to her waist, and eyes as blue as the bluest sky."

Harry nodded in agreement.

Richard narrowed his eyes and stuck out his lower lip, considering. "Or maybe she'll have brown eyes and black hair."

"Brown eyes are fine," said Harry agreeably.

"She'll have legs that go on forever," said Richard a little dreamily. "Long, slender, shapely legs with fine ankles and a dimple at the knee, and thighs that—" He sucked in his breath. There wasn't any need to expand on the thighs. "And she'll have breasts like Graciella's."

"Mrrumph," said Harry.

Richard glanced at him questioningly.

His friend shrugged. "Not much chance she'll have breasts like that," he said with an apologetic grimace. "Stands to reason she wouldn't. There can't be another pair like 'em in ten kingdoms."

Richard considered the possibility of finding

another pair like Graciella's, then nodded regretfully. "You're right. That is asking a little much."

"It's not impossible, mind," said Harry. "Not likely, but not impossible."

"I can be flexible on the breasts," said His Majesty, to show he was reasonable.

Which didn't mean he was giving up on the breasts entirely. Even a reasonable man could hope.

"Anyway, what I really want is someone who's warm and gentle and soft and cuddly and eager and . . . and . . . and whatnot. And quiet, damn it!"

He threw up his hands. "Now, is that too much to ask? Is that really too much for the King of Avalon, Darian, Longshore, and the Western Isles—not to mention all the rest of it—to ask? Is it *really* so unreasonable to want a wife who knows how to keep her mouth shut?"

"Not at all," said Harry. "Perfectly reasonable."

Richard heaved a weary sigh. "That's what I thought. So why is it so damnably hard to find a woman like that, Harry? Is it me?"

"Of course not," growled Harry loyally.

"Well, then?"

Harry just gazed sympathetically at him.

Richard slumped in his saddle, shoulders drooping.

"I swear, Harry, if ever I meet a woman who doesn't talk my ears off, I'll marry her straight-

15

away. I don't even care if she's old and ugly or still toddling around in short coats. If she can keep her mouth shut, I'll make her my queen. On my honor, I swear it!"

Men!

Her Royal Highness, Princess Arianne of Montavia, released the shirt she was knitting to suck at the drop of blood welling at the tip of her finger. This was the third time this evening that she'd pricked herself on the nettles she was knitting, and she was getting downright tired of it, thank you very much!

It would have been easier if she could have cussed over the accident, but not a word could she say, vulgar or otherwise, and it was all her brothers' fault. All twelve of them. If they hadn't ignored everything she'd ever taught them about studying hard and minding their manners and always being polite to their elders, they wouldn't be in this mess, and neither would she.

Arianne glared at the prickly lump of knitted nettles in her lap, then sighed and leaned back in her chair.

The fire in the hearth crackled comfortably, warming the room and casting a pleasant glow that kept the night at bay beyond the cottage's curtained windows. She could hear the rain drumming on the thatching overhead, but not so much as a drop had worked its way through.

Small comforts, but she was grateful for them. Especially since she hadn't had much else to be grateful for lately.

A week had passed since all the trouble started, but she could remember every detail, right from the moment little Gunelda, the second kitchen maid, had burst into the castle still room, where Arianne was inspecting the latest batch of ale. The maid had been gabbling like a demented duck, but Arianne had had no trouble grasping the girl's point: Arianne's twelve mischievous brothers had invaded the kitchen, and all hell had broken loose.

Arianne had abandoned the gabbling Gunelda and raced toward the kitchen in the hope of stopping them. She'd been too late. By the time she arrived, the boys were long gone, and Cook was screaming for their heads, princes or no.

It didn't take long to sort out the particulars. A dozen angry people were anxious to inform Arianne—in passionate detail—of the princes' manifold sins, beginning with their tying up their tutor, then sneaking down to the kitchen to steal a dozen tarts that had been intended for the king and his guests at supper. On their way out, they'd frightened the kitchen cat, upset the scullery maid's bucket of soapy water, and startled the kitchen boy so that he dropped the load of firewood he was carrying.

The firewood had landed in the dirty water spreading across the newly scrubbed floor and splashed everyone and everything within reach—but not before one good-sized chunk had clobbered Cook's aching bunions and another had banged the shins of the undercook, who had already started after the errant princes armed with an enormous wooden turnip masher. At the sudden blow to his shins, the undercook had abandoned his quest for vengeance and grabbed for his wounded ankle—and dropped the turnip masher on his other foot in the process.

Judging from his frothing diatribe, no justice short of hanging, drawing, and quartering their Royal Highnesses would be good enough for the undercook. Cook, he'd said, could have their heads afterward.

Cook's eyes had gleamed at the prospect.

Arianne had escaped from the outraged kitchen staff only to run smack into an angry mob of castle folk intent on *their* fair share of vengeance. She'd listened with growing dismay as they'd recounted, loudly and with feeling, the continuing saga of her brothers' assault on the castle.

From the kitchens, the princes had moved to the poultry coops, where they'd snitched all the newly laid eggs, most of which they'd used as ammunition against the hulking stable boy, with whom they had a longstanding quarrel. They'd aimed the rest at the irascible old gardener whose protests over their raids on his strawberry beds had led to their incarceration in the schoolroom in the first place.

Not content with that, they'd further enraged the hen wife by kidnapping a goose and a turkey cock, then staging an impromptu race out of the coops, past the stables, and across the bailey to the main gates, which had caused the castle guards to forsake their duty posts, upset a score of passersby, frightened the horses, and spooked one of the milk cows so she broke her halter and galloped about wreaking more havoc than the boys and the goose and the turkey cock combined.

And everyone wanted to tell Arianne about it.

Princes or not, the old Master of Horse had said, he'd tan every one of their backsides—twice—if ever he got his hands on them. Terrorizing his horses like that! Why, he had a good notion to tell the king what they'd done! And if that new colt had taken hurt from Prince William trying to ride him—without bridle or saddle, too!—he'd personally make sure His Royal Highness didn't sit down for a month!

What about her cow? the dairy maid had demanded shrilly. And my pig? shouted another. And the baskets of vegetables Prince William trampled with that damned colt? the gardener had cried, brandishing a big-knuckled fist under Arianne's nose. She'd carefully refrained from commenting on the raw egg that matted his beard and stained his leather jerkin and mud-caked hose.

The guards had finally gone slinking back to their duties, and the boys had fled through the castle gates upon grasping the full extent of the disaster and the awful retribution that awaited them the instant they reappeared.

Nobody seemed to know what had become of the goose or the turkey cock.

And so it had gone, out of the castle and through the village and down the road that led into the forest. It hadn't been hard for Arianne to trace her brothers' progress—all she'd had to do was follow the trail of destruction they'd left in their wake—but it hadn't been nearly so easy to fend off the angry folk she encountered along the way, all of whom expected *her* to set things right *immediately*.

Arianne was deep into the Dark Woods before she'd managed to escape the last of her brothers' furious victims. At the time, she'd been grateful for the citizens' retreat, since she hadn't wanted anyone throttling her brothers before she had a chance to do the job herself.

Of course, that was before she'd found out just how much trouble the boys could get into when they *really* tried.

At the memory of her solitary progress through the Dark Woods, Arianne shivered, then tossed the nettle shirt she'd been knitting on top of the heap of nettles beside her. Her fingertip throbbed where she'd pricked it, but the throbbing was only slightly more noticeable than the dull aches from all the other pricks and scratches and cuts she'd acquired over the last few days.

As soon as she finished these damned nettle shirts and had everything set to rights, Arianne swore she really was going to throttle her brothers—every one of them! Even sweet little Dickie, who was only five and who wouldn't have thought of any mischief if his older brothers hadn't led him into it.

At the thought of Dickie, she blinked and sniffed—just a little sniff, because she was a princess, after all—and scrubbed at her nose with the back of her hand, remembering.

Despite the approaching night and all the frightening tales she'd heard about what could happen to solitary travelers caught in the Dark Woods after sundown, she'd forged deeper into the forest alone. She'd had to. Dickie didn't like the dark, and Tryffin was prone to catching cold if he didn't keep his head covered, and Geoffrey needed to have that bandage on his finger changed. He'd cut himself the day before trying to whittle a wooden spoon for her, and though she'd fussed at him for being careless, she'd been touched by the gesture and worried that the cut would turn putrid if she didn't watch it.

Besides, she'd hated to think what everyone

back at the castle was saying about her brothers' latest escapade. She could almost hear them, chattering in the Great Hall and whispering in the corners about how something like this was bound to happen sooner or later—all those troublesome boys, you know, and Princess Arianne spoiling them, and hadn't they always said she was too young to take on such a responsibility and couldn't be trusted to keep them in line? And now look!

No matter what everyone said, Arianne knew she couldn't have done otherwise. From the time she was little, she'd fussed over her brothers. Her father was too wrapped up in his studies to think much about them, and her mother was too busy breeding them and popping them out to have time to spend worrying about them once they were past the diapers-and-wet-nurse stage.

Arianne hadn't minded, really, even though her brothers annoyed her at times. She'd been twelve when Rheidwn was born, and delighted to have a real live baby to play with. Her mother had gotten pregnant again almost immediately. Eleven more boy babies had followed Rheidwn in quick succession. Two sets of twins and one set of of triplets had speeded up the process considerably but had been doubly and triply hard on her mother.

When her mother had died giving birth to little Dickie, Arianne hadn't hesitated; she'd taken over the job of coddling her father and running the castle and its people. Most important, she'd taken over mothering the twelve young princes. Despite the trouble they caused, they were good boys, and they were her brothers, and Arianne loved every one of them.

And that's why she hadn't turned back to the castle when the villagers had left her alone in the Dark Woods. She'd *had* to keep going. Her brothers needed her, and that was that.

After what had seemed like hours of wandering through the gloomy forest, Arianne had come at last to an ugly little thatched cottage. The cottage had surprised her, because she'd traveled through the Dark Woods before—with her father's knights and servants as escort, of course—and she didn't remember ever having seen it. But there it was, hunkered under a towering pine tree like a poisonous mushroom.

It had been grimly unwelcoming. There'd been no lights in the dusty windows, no smoke from the chimney, no sign at all that anyone was within.

Arianne had crept closer, and for some reason her heart had pounded in her chest. Her hands had grown cold and clammy and demonstrated a strong tendency to tremble in time with the quaking of her knees. She'd circled the cottage, trying to peer in the dirty windows. She hadn't been able to see anything except the squat, dark shapes of a table and chair that occupied the center of the single room. It looked as if no one had lived there for a long, long time. She'd knocked at the door. A hollow echo had been the only answer.

Cold and tired and growing more worried by the minute, she'd been about to move on when a sudden beating of wings had stopped her. Like angels in her dreams, a dozen beautiful swans had flown out of the forest to circle over her head. She'd gaped at them, startled, then shrunk back against the cottage door when they abruptly swooped down to land at her feet.

To her amazement, as each swan landed, it shed its white feathers and changed into one of her brothers. They'd fallen on her, laughing and crying and hugging her until she was breathless—but not so breathless that she couldn't laugh and cry and hug them right back.

Eventually, amid the tears and the scoldings and the hugs, she'd heard the whole story. How her brothers, not content with having upset the peace of castle and village, had wandered into the forest and found the cottage. How they'd peeked in the windows, as she had, and knocked at the door. They'd been very hungry by that time, despite the purloined tarts they'd gobbled up earlier, so when they'd gotten no answer, they'd decided to break in and look for something to eat.

That's when things had *really* gone wrong.

The cottage's owner, an ugly, ill-tempered crone, had returned precisely when they were scraping the last of the jam out of her jam jar with the intention of spreading it on the last scrap of bread from her bread box. Enraged at the princes' presumption, the crone had cursed them, turning them all into swans, then vanished.

There was one way out of the mess, her brothers had hastened to assure her when Arianne had exclaimed in horror at the tale, but it wasn't going to be easy, and she was the only one who could help them.

"Anything!" Arianne had cried. "Anything if it will set you free!"

"We can't be freed until you've knit us twelve shirts out of nettles you've gathered by the light of the full moon," Rheidwn had explained. "Donning the shirts will break the enchantment, and we'll turn back into princes."

"Nettle shirts?" Arianne had demanded, aghast. "I have to knit *twelve* shirts out of *nettles?*"

Rheidwn had nodded glumly. "And you can't go home or say a word till you're finished. Not even little bitty words like 'no' or 'yes' or 'please pass the butter.' "

"I can't talk?" She'd stared at them as if they'd gone mad.

"No, nor sing, either."

Arianne had almost choked. "I can't even *sing?*"

All twelve of them had shaken their heads.

At least they'd had the grace to look abashed. They knew how much she liked to sing.

Before she could ask another question, the little time allotted them to be in their human form had run out. In the blink of an eye, they'd magically changed back into swans and, with a great whoosh and flap of wings, disappeared into the forest. The swan that was little Dickie had looked back mournfully over its shoulder, but it had flown away with the rest, leaving her standing alone on the cottage's stone step as the evening shadows faded into night.

Arianne hadn't had any choice. She'd moved into the crone's abandoned cottage and set about trying to put things right.

Gathering enough nettles to make twelve shirts was bad enough—for boys who were growing like weeds, no less!—but the crone had made things as miserable as possible for her. The shirts couldn't be knit out of just *any* nettles. Oh, no! *These* nettles had to be gathered by the light of a full moon, which was just enough illumination to find the nettles but not enough to keep her hands from getting ripped to pieces as she picked them.

Arianne sucked at the finger she'd just pricked, which was still throbbing, and glared at the mound of nettles she'd heaped on the floor beside her chair.

She'd had to wait two days before the full moon rose. She'd used those two days to clean the cottage from top to bottom—from the look of the place, the crone hadn't used a dust rag in years—and to bake bread and make three kinds of soup so she wouldn't have to waste time cooking once she had the nettles.

It had been hard work, but she'd been grateful for the distraction. Every time she started thinking about her brothers, out in the cold and the wet and the dark without her to take care of them, or of her father, lost among his books and without her to make his coddled egg just the way he liked it in the morning, she wanted to cry. And she was absolutely determined that she would not cry. Not even a little bit.

An occasional sniff or two or a little moisture in her eye didn't count. She would *not* cry. Not even when her poor hands hurt as much as they did now—and after a night spent gathering nettles and two days spent knitting them, they hurt a lot.

None of that mattered. Feeling sorry for herself wouldn't get Rheidwn's shirt done, let alone the other eleven. She couldn't repress a slight grimace, however, as she picked up her brother's shirt, then retrieved the second set of knitting needles so she could finish off the sleeve she was working on.

She was just casting off the cuff when the silence in the cottage was broken by a peremptory knock at the door.

"Anybody home?" a deep, masculine voice loudly demanded.

Arianne started and dropped the needles she held. She barely managed to bite back a curse.

The knock came again, louder this time. "I know you're in there! I can see the smoke coming out of the chimney!"

Arianne hesitated. She was all alone here in this cottage in the Dark Woods. Who knew what kind of man might be wandering around out there, and on a night like this? Thank God she'd remembered to lock the windows and bar the door.

"Open up in there! I'm the King of Avalon, and all my followers have gotten lost, and I'm cold and wet and damn near starved. Open up, I say, and let me in!"

Chapter Two

Rain poured off the cottage eaves onto Richard's head and shoulders in gouts and runnels and drips. It dribbled off his nose and slid down his back and trickled into his sodden, muddy boots. He was cold and hungry and, obviously, wet. His shoulder ached from a spill from his horse he'd suffered when crashing through the woods, and he'd torn his best tunic, which meant Thurgood would fuss, and he hadn't the faintest idea where his people had gotten to or why they should have been so stupid as to get lost in the first place. Kings never got lost—and never needed to ask for directions, for that matter—so how could dozens of retrainers so easily lose their way? *He* knew where he was, after all—right here in the middle of the Dark Woods, soaking wet. Why didn't *they* know where he was?

All in all, he was definitely Not Pleased.

He had, in fact, been cross as a bear for hours.

He pounded on the door a third time and was rewarded with the grating sound of its bar being lifted inside. An instant later the door swung open and the welcome, ruddy light of a fire poured out, gilding the darkness and highlighting the woman who stood on the threshold glaring at him.

Deep in his sodden hose, John Paul suddenly stirred to life. Richard sucked in his breath, his misery utterly forgotten. He hadn't thought any woman could be better looking than the Princess Graciella.

He'd been wrong.

He blinked to shake the rain out of his eyes.

It was no trick of the light or his own weariness. The woman standing before him was incredibly beautiful. No, *stunning*—with delicate features and pearl-pink skin and eyes that were as blue as the bluest sky. And that hair! Gloriously long and golden, it tumbled over her shoulders and down her back in a wild, curly tangle that made his fingers itch to play in it.

His gaze slid lower.

Better and better and *better*. She didn't have Graciella's plush breasts, but what she did have were high and round and firm. More than a handful. *Much* more than a generous mouthful.

John Paul strained against the hose.

Richard's gaze dropped lower still.

Below her breasts was a waist that curved in deliciously, then flared to hips that—

He wrenched his gaze back to her face, then smiled and stepped into the cottage.

She backed up a foot.

He gave her a reassuring nod. Even an extraordinarily beautiful peasant girl would be intimidated by having the dashing, handsome, and utterly irresistible King of Avalon, Darian, and whatnot on her doorstep. No sense in scaring her witless right at the start.

On the other hand, there was a certain respect owed a king, even a wet and muddy one, though she didn't seem to realize it.

"I thought you'd never answer the door," he said, trying not to growl. "It's damned wet out there, if you haven't noticed."

She frowned at him. Her eyes narrowed.

Even frowning, she looked good. *Really* good.

Richard wrenched his gaze away to survey the cottage. It was a neat little place, tidy and sparkling clean all the way up to the rafters. The few bits of furniture—a table, one chair, a couple of chests and stools—were crudely made but serviceable. A good-sized bed stood in a far corner, half buried under a pile of quilts. The fire crackled invitingly, a welcome contrast to the gush and roar of water outside.

"Nice place."

He deliberately avoided looking at the bed.

She didn't say a word, just stood there staring at him suspiciously, one hand on the door, the other fisted on her hip.

"My friends and I were out hunting, and they all got lost somehow," he said. "I saw your light, and I thought . . . that is . . . well . . . Hmm."

She was eyeing him exactly the way Nurse used to eye him when as a lad he'd come dragging in with his hose torn and his tunic ripped and any number of bumps, bruises, and scrapes decorating his scruffy hide. He'd called it Nurse's Look, and it had inevitably presaged a scolding, at the least, or no plum tarts for a month, or something really, really horrible, like being forced to copy out his lessons five times. Neatly and without smudges or one word of complaint.

At the thought of his old nurse and her Look, the tingling and stirring in his hose abruptly stopped stirring and tingling. John Paul drooped. In fact, he deflated to such distressing proportions that he put absolutely no strain on the hose whatsoever.

King or not, Richard shuffled his feet and cleared his throat. Before he could stop himself, he hung his head, done in once more by the Look.

That's when he noticed just how muddy his boots were, and how clean her floor. Or rather, how clean it was except for where *he* stood in a spreading puddle of dirty brown water.

That explained the Look.

He hastily retreated to the stoop and scraped off the mud as best he could despite the rainwater pouring off the roof and down the back of his neck.

"May I come in now?" he asked meekly. "Please?"

Even mutton-faced nurses liked meek, he'd found. In his experience, blue-eyed angels couldn't resist it.

His blue-eyed angel was no exception. She rolled her eyes and sighed, shook her head with the weary resignation of a woman accustomed to dealing with muddy-footed males, and reluctantly gestured for him to sit on the stool in front of the hearth.

For a minute, he thought about arguing—a stool was scarcely the appropriate kind of seat for a king—then decided it wasn't worth the effort.

He sat and gratefully stretched his feet to the fire. Damn, but he was wet.

The angel grabbed a mop and made a hasty stab at cleaning up the mess he'd made, then came toward him at the hearth. As he watched her, he forgot all about stiff and sore and wet and hungry.

She even walked like an angel—gracefully,

with a provocative little swing to her hips that was tempting to watch from the front and downright blood-stirring from the rear. She stopped not three feet in front of him, put her fists on her hips, narrowed her eyes, and glared at him.

Just as if she thought he was still twelve years old and had forgotten to wash behind his ears, Richard thought, shifting uncomfortably on the stool.

Arianne sighed. The puddle in the doorway had been bad enough, but he'd trailed muddy footprints across her clean floor, and now he was making an even muddier puddle on the her hearth. And that didn't count the water that dripped off his nose and ears and elbows to splatter on the floor around him.

His black hair looked as if it might be curly by nature, but right now it was plastered to his skull like fur on a drowned cat, marring a noble-looking brow and funneling water into his dark blue eyes and down his face.

She watched, fascinated in spite of herself, as one rivulet traced its way along the side of his nose and into the corner of his mouth. It was a beautiful mouth. Firm, well shaped, and with an intriguing upward curve at either end that made her suspect he smiled often.

Which might prove dangerous if he stayed longer than ten minutes or so. When he'd smiled at her, there in the doorway, she'd felt an odd quaking sensation low in her belly. Her knees had gone weak, and her lungs had seemed too large for her chest, and she'd suddenly felt just the tiniest bit dizzy. If he hadn't stopped smiling and looked at his feet, instead, there was no telling *what* might have happened.

She suspected he had that effect on a lot of women. No female over the age of ten or under the age of ninety-eight who wasn't blind, senile, or demented would be able to resist the charm that oozed from that big, beautiful body like rainwater oozed from his sodden clothes.

It wasn't just that he was gorgeous, either. She'd met gorgeous before. Sir Reginald de Greve, one of her father's favorite knights, was gorgeous. He was also loyal, clean, brave, reverent, and thrifty, but he'd never made her knees go weak or her heart go pitty-pat. Not even once. Lord Tilbury was gorgeous, too. So was Sir Lionel, and Roger, Count of Malbourne, and Sir Tristan, and Prince Henry, and the cobbler who lived with his mother in the third cottage down from the castle, and—

Arianne cut the thought short. Suffice that there were a lot of gorgeous men around, and not one of them had ever affected her the way this bruised, bedraggled specimen of manhood was affecting her now. Thank God she'd had a lot of experience dealing with the male of the species. Otherwise, she might be in danger of losing her head, and *that* would fling the fat in the fire for sure!

Gorgeous or not, the lunk looked as if he'd taken a toss in a briar patch right before plunging fully clothed into the nearest pond. A cut over his brow oozed blood, turning the water dripping from his hair a pale pink. His cheek and chin—a fine, strongly sculpted chin with the faintest hint of an intriguing cleft—were scraped and raw, and a bruise was beginning to form at the angle of his beard-shadowed jaw.

Frowning, she moved closer. The cuts needed tending, and she hadn't been able to help noticing that he walked a little stiffly, as though he had a few more heavy-duty bruises elsewhere.

Her cheeks warmed at the thought of exactly where that "elsewhere" might be, since she'd noticed the stiffness while eyeing his derriere as he'd walked across the room.

It was a great derriere. Neat, compact, and with just enough curve—

She drew in her breath, then frowned even harder. Not by so much as a flicker of an eyelash was she going to let him know how he affected her.

Richard knew he didn't look his best, but that didn't mean she had to glare at him as if he were a hunk of rotting fish the cat had dragged in. He was a king, after all, and a damned good-looking one, if half the women from here to the southern border were to be believed. And there must have been at least a dozen of 'em who weren't influenced by the fact that he was a king and in want of a wife.

But, whether he was good-looking or not, this peasant girl was eyeing him as if he had three eyes and a wart at the end of his nose.

It wasn't at all what he was accustomed to, and he definitely didn't like it.

"What?" That came out a little more querulously than he'd intended.

She didn't say a word.

Richard shifted uncomfortably on the stool. What could he possibly have done to make her retreat into silent accusation like this? Damned unfriendly, he called it.

He'd knocked politely, hadn't he? Introduced himself before she even opened the door? Complimented her on this shoe box of a cottage? Even scraped off his boots. What more could she want?

It wasn't as if he was unreasonably demanding, either. All he wanted was some wine, food, dry clothes, and a little sympathy and tender care, though not necessarily in that order.

Not one unreasonable demand in the lot of 'em. And he hadn't even demanded 'em. Yet.

He thought of the way she'd greeted him at the door—suspicious, right from the start. Which, now that he thought about it, was downright insulting. It wasn't as if—

Of course! The puddle he'd made when he'd

walked in. How could he forget? There wasn't a woman alive who wouldn't put the state of her floor before the comfort of a man any day of the week and probably twice on Sunday.

"I'm sorry about the puddle I left at the door."

Her mouth thinned; her gaze dropped to floor. Richard looked where she was looking. It took a moment for him to realize she was staring at a large and very muddy footprint.

"*And* the tracks on the floor."

Her gaze silently rose to meet his.

"I couldn't help it, you know," he added plaintively. "It's raining out there."

The corners of her mouth quirked upward, and her lips twitched ever so slightly.

She didn't remind him of Nurse at all when she looked like that.

As quickly as it had come, however, her good humor vanished, and the frown came back. She moved closer, grasped his chin, and tilted it upward. Her blue eyes darkened. With concern, perhaps? He could always hope.

Her lashes, he couldn't help noticing, were thick and black as sable. Long, too. *Really* long.

Maybe he could induce her to kiss his hurts away. Look pitiful enough, and women always turned maternal and comforting.

He'd turned that fact to good account on more than one occasion, and right now—

He frowned. No, he didn't want maternal. Comforting would be nice. Tenderness would be better. A little lust wouldn't come amiss, either. But maternal? No, thanks.

She leaned closer, studying his battered face. Without thinking, he tilted his head and got a nice, clear view down her cleavage.

John Paul perked right up despite the damp.

A lot of lust, then.

Frowning, she jerked his chin back up, then probed at the scrape above his eyebrow.

Richard winced. "Ow!"

She ignored him and went on probing. Finally satisfied the wound wasn't mortal, she lightly traced his cheek, then the line of his jaw to the tip of his chin. The gesture might have been suggestive if she weren't following the edges of his scrapes and bruises. Her perfect right eyebrow arched in silent query.

"My horse threw me," he said. That was close to the truth, anyway.

Her equally perfect left eyebrow quirked upward to join the right. Her more than perfect lips twitched with amusement as she let go of his chin and silently stepped back, eyeing him with exactly the same expression Nurse had used whenever he'd told a fib.

Richard blushed. "All right, then. I fell off."

She smiled with an irritating trace of smugness.

"It was right after everyone else got lost, you

see, and—Well, they did!" he said defensively when her smile widened. "I'm the king, you know. They're supposed to follow *me*, not some damned big hart with as nice a rack as—What? *What?*"

She was laughing at him. Outright laughing at him!

He thought about it, then sighed. "All right, all right. I thought I was following that damned hart, too. A fellow can be mistaken, you know. Especially in this damned dark forest. Never know where you're at. Every damned tree looks just like the last. . . ."

His grumbling self-justification trailed off into silence. She wasn't laughing anymore. In fact, she looked downright sad. A little lost, even. Lost and in need of a broad chest to lean against, and maybe a little loving to—

He had to dig his fingers into his thighs to keep from pulling her into his arms right then and there.

What was he supposed to do? He thought about dragging her into bed with him and making love to her until they were both too sore to walk, but he had enough experience with females to know that that approach, which made sense to any sensible, rational male under the age of a hundred and two, wouldn't work at all with an irrational female. Not on such short acquaintance, anyway.

She gave a doleful sniff, then blinked a few times as if she had a cinder in her eye.

"Er . . . Um . . ."

Please, God, no tears. He couldn't deal with tears.

"Was it the swearing? I didn't mean to upset you. The words just sort of slipped out, and—"

She sniffed again, shot him a withering glance, then abruptly turned away to fuss over a pot hanging above the fire.

Just like a woman! Crying at the drop of a kerchief, then blaming a man if he couldn't figure out why or what to do about it.

Richard crossed his arms over his chest and subsided onto the stool, disgusted.

Arianne sniffed and stirred the pot of soup she'd set to warm earlier. Poor little Dickie. Poor Rheidwn and Tryffin and William and Benjamin John and all the rest of them. Out there in the cold, dank, dark forest in the storm, alone and with no one to care for them or feed them or make sure they brushed their teeth and washed behind their ears before they went to bed. Not that swans had teeth to brush or ears to wash behind, of course, but still . . .

And all the while here she was, thinking lustful thoughts about a bedraggled stranger instead of worrying about them.

But what could she do? They were far away, and this great lump of a fellow was here and needed her help, and she couldn't knit *every* waking minute of the day, no matter how much she wanted to free her brothers from that wicked witch's spell.

She sneaked a guilty peek at her visitor. He was slumped on the stool, arms crossed over his magnificent chest, long legs stretched out in front of him and crossed at the ankle. Fortunately, he was staring irritably into the rafters and paying no attention to her whatsoever. Waiting for the soup, no doubt, and for her to serve it to him.

She snorted and turned back to the soup. King of Avalon indeed! As if she didn't know that the mightiest king in all the land wouldn't be running around loose in the Dark Woods without even a squire to attend him. That sort of thing simply didn't happen in a well-run kingdom. Somebody as important as the King of Avalon was bound to have five dozen grooms and knights and squires and pages and fetchers of this and that following him wherever he went. Poor man probably couldn't even scratch without having half a dozen of them jumping up to offer their assistance. They couldn't *all* have "gotten lost," as he put it, not even if they'd tried.

She peeked again. He was still staring at the rafters, but now the toe of his boot was twitching back and forth impatiently, and his brow, noble though it was, had crinkled into a frown.

Probably trying to think, she decided. The effort was often more of a strain than the average male could handle.

The uncharitable thought made her blush. She wasn't usually so mean-spirited, but then, she'd never before met a man who had the kind of unsettling effect on her that this one did. She could flirt with the best of them, but this fellow wasn't wasting time on flirting. He'd skipped right over flirt and gone straight into leer with an arrogance that almost convinced her that he really was what he claimed to be.

Not that he didn't look like a king, mind you. He did. In fact, he looked exactly like the kings in the picture books she'd read as a child—tall, dark, handsome, proud, and . . . and *kingly*, despite the mud and the muck and the blood. Which just proved he wasn't one. Couldn't possibly be.

Arianne gave the soup a particularly vigorous stir. She knew a lot of kings, and not one of them looked kingly. To tell the truth, most of them looked downright ordinary. If it weren't for their fancy clothes and fine jewels and the crowns atop their heads—which were bald as often as not—there wasn't much to set them off from their lowliest swineherds. Well, that and the fact that they bathed rather more often than the swineherds, though even that wasn't always guaranteed.

Take her father, for instance. Though gentle

and kind and wise, he was also thin, stoop-shouldered, and vague, with a flyaway tangle of wispy white hair that he was always scratching in puzzlement, which made his crown tip forward over his nose in a most unkingly fashion. King Wilbert of Millersville-on-the-Marsh was a weedy, nervous little fellow who tended to giggle whenever he was embarrassed, which was most of the time. And King Bertram of Batch, which was only one kingdom over from her father's kingdom of Montavia, was fat and ugly and forever belching over his soup. But this one . . .

"That soups smells good. *Really* good."

The words brought Arianne's attention back with a snap to the matter at hand. She looked up to find her guest standing not a foot away, craning to peer at the soup, a hungry, hopeful look on his handsome face.

"Absolutely delicious, in fact," he said, clearly trying to be friendly.

She ignored him.

He gave her an encouraging little smile. "I'm very partial to soup."

She ignored the smile, too.

That surprised him. He stared at her, then glanced around the cottage, still wearing his hopeful look. "I don't suppose you'd have some wine around here someplace?"

Goaded, Arianne shook her head and thunked the spoon against the edge of the pot to dislodge a bit of onion. Good manners required that she offer him a meal and a place to sleep. If she was back home, she wouldn't have hesitated for a second.

But here, alone with him like this, with only one bed—

She blushed, ducked her head, and gave the spoon another thunk. She hadn't thought about the bed.

And then there was the matter of his clothes.

With a sigh of resignation, she set the spoon aside and turned to study him. He wasn't dripping quite so much now, but he still looked like the next best thing to a half-drowned cat.

She needed to clean that cut on his forehead and the scrapes on his cheek and chin. She needed to mind her manners and offer him something to drink even if all she had was herb tea and water. And if he didn't get out of those sodden clothes pretty soon, he'd catch his death of cold, and then she'd feel bad and just a little guilty, and that would never do. She already had more than enough troubles without adding to the heap.

Only problem was, there weren't any spare clothes to be had in the cottage, dry or otherwise.

"A pot of ale would be all right if you don't have any wine," he assured her earnestly. By now his smile was wavering a bit around the edges.

She frowned, which made him shuffle his

feet just like Jonathan James, who was nine and tended to look guilty even when he hadn't done anything wrong.

The thought of little Jonathan made her smile.

Her guest smiled back, relieved. "For a minute there, I thought you were going to toss me back out into the storm."

His smile sent shivers down her spine. She liked it better when he squinted irritably or even looked down her dress. Rudeness she could handle, but his smile—

Dry clothes. Concentrate on finding him dry clothes.

Arianne glanced around the room, searching for inspiration. Nothing in the closet. Not since she'd cleaned out all the spiderwebs, at any rate. Nothing in the chest against the wall except for a couple of pots that needed mending. The other chest held a few old towels, a pillow that was shedding feathers, and no clothes whatsoever. The little cabinet on the other side held her meager supply of flour and salt and things, but not so much as a handkerchief. Nothing under the bed, nothing—

Her gaze slid past the bed, then snapped back. A lumpy quilt, freshly washed and mended, lay folded at the foot. It was the only thing in the place large enough to wrap around that big body of his.

She smiled in satisfaction. Yes, that would

do. She could see him already, huddled under the quilt just like her brothers when they were sick and needed cuddling. There wasn't a man alive who wouldn't look silly dressed like that. Silly, she could handle. Better that than having to look at those magnificent broad shoulders or the way his wet tunic molded that nice, firm, round rump and those long, muscular thighs, and—

No, best not think about his rump or thighs or . . . or other things.

It didn't help that he was standing so close she could hear the tiny splats as water dripped off his clothes onto the stone hearth.

"Er . . . the ale? You didn't say if you had any." The glimmer of hope in those gorgeous, dark-blue eyes of his was beginning to fade, but he wasn't giving up yet.

Ignoring the faintly plaintive note in his voice, she bustled about gathering things. Two towels from the chest. She glanced at him and as quickly looked away. No, make that three, which was all the extras she had. He was big enough and wet enough to need every one of them.

She set the chipped washbasin on a stool, poured in some water, then arranged the rest of it—towels, quilt, a hard, gray lump of soap that looked as if it hadn't been used in years, and a tatty old rug on the floor to catch the spills. All she had to do was add hot water and, voilà!

She turned to fetch the kettle of water she

always kept warming by the fire—and ran headfirst into a wall of wet male chest. Clapping a hand over the curse that almost escaped her, she staggered back, heart pounding.

Automatically, he put out a hand to steady her. "Sorry. Didn't expect you to turn around like that."

Angry and not a little frightened that she'd come so close to ruining everything, she dropped her hand and glared up at him. If he made her break her vow of silence, she'd kill him, one handsome inch at a time.

"What?" He looked aggrieved. His hand dropped to his side. "I didn't mean to startle you. If you hadn't turned around so fast—"

Arianne scowled and rubbed her nose, which was wet from being mashed into his chest, then shrugged, embarrassed. To cover the embarrassment, she pointed to the basin and soap, then snatched up a towel and slapped it into his hand.

"For me?"

She nodded.

He eyed the makeshift arrangement dubiously, then gave a little sigh. "Thanks. I . . . er . . . don't suppose you have any other soap than that?"

She shook her head.

"Or any dry clothes that would fit?"

Another shake.

His shoulders slumped just the tiniest bit. "I didn't think so. And no ale, either, right?"

Since she wasn't sure if she was supposed to nod or shake her head, she simply shrugged, picked up the quilt, and mimed wrapping it around her shoulders.

For a minute, he didn't get it. "That's *it?* That's all you have?"

She nodded.

He sighed. "I was afraid of that."

Shoulders drooping, he plopped down on the stool that held the quilt and towels. Arianne rolled her eyes but didn't argue. They were his towels and his quilt. If he didn't care if they got wet before he had a chance to use them, *she* certainly didn't!

Before she realized what he was about, he tugged off his right boot and began pouring out the water in it—onto her floor. At her choked sound of horror, he froze and looked up, the shoe still dangerously tilted in his hand.

"What?"

She glared at the boot, then sternly pointed toward the door.

"What?"

Idiot man didn't have a clue, she thought with disgust. Like the rest of his breed, he thought the women around him had nothing better to do than wait on him hand and foot and straighten up the messes he left behind.

She pointed again, first to his boot, then to the door.

Grumbling under his breath, boot in hand, he stomped over to the door. With one boot off and one boot on, it was really more an undignified *stomp-plop-stomp-plop*, but he didn't seem to notice. Still grumbling, he pulled off the other boot, opened the door, and leaned outside to empty the pair of them.

The wind blew the rain into his face and onto her floor, but he didn't seem to notice that, either. He gave the boots one last hard shake, slammed the door, and *plop-plopped* back to where she stood watching him.

"There," he growled, dropping the boots on the floor. "Satisfied?"

She beamed up at him and went to fetch the hot water. By the time she came back with the kettle, he'd unbuckled his belt, pulled off his tunic, and was struggling to unlace the fine linen shirt underneath.

Arianne's grip on the heavy kettle weakened suddenly, and her knees started to buckle.

The wet tunic had been bad enough, but the shirt clung to his skin like a water weed, molding itself to every glorious curve and hollow, hinting clearly at the soft glow of bare arms and abdomen, the tangled mat of black curls on his chest. The sight was enough to make any sensible woman want to rip off the shirt so she could get to the man beneath, hot skin pressed to hot skin, with nothing in between.

If she'd had the slightest idea how to go about it, she might even have tried.

Unfortunately, she'd never so much as kissed a man—the little peck she'd exchanged with Prince James Frederick when she was nine and he was ten and his father had come for a visit didn't count—but she had a sudden, vivid sense of how it would be, wrapped in his arms, her breasts crushed against that hard chest, the soft black curls tickling her skin, his hands flat against her bare back, sliding down her spine—

With an effort, she sucked in air, tightened her grip on the kettle, and forced her knees to stiffen. Such lewd thoughts were bound to get a girl in trouble, especially when the two of them were alone in the isolated cottage, and—

No, better not to think of it.

Despite her good intentions, her gaze slid inexorably lower.

The shirt, as all men's shirts did, hung to mid-thigh, but in place of the usual bulky braies and laced hose, he had on some sort of tightly knit hose that looked as if they'd been painted on, so closely did they cling to those long, powerful legs.

She scarcely dwelled on the legs, however, because her attention was riveted to the commanding bulge at the top of them, which the sodden shirt did almost nothing to hide.

Not that she could really see *everything*, of course. Just a large, indistinct lump beneath the fullness of the shirt. But it didn't take much effort to sort out man from shirt, and what was left was—

Arianne forced herself to breathe.

What was left was breathtaking. Literally.

Her guest showed not the slightest embarrassment at his state of undress. In fact, he seemed to think it was no more than his due that she be tending to his wash water while he disrobed. If she didn't know better, she'd almost believe his tall tale of being the King of Avalon. Only highborn noblemen—princes and kings and the like—were so arrogantly sure of their right to be pampered at every turn.

She, on the other hand, had never once attended a man in his bath. Oh, she'd taken care of her brothers when they were little— someone had to make sure they washed behind their ears and between their toes and didn't get water all over the floor in the process—but she'd never attended a full-grown man. That sort of thing was for servants.

It wasn't proper for a princess even to see a man in this state of undress.

Granted, there was the time she'd inadvertently caught Sir Adelbert Thurgrave emerging from his bath. Sir Adelbert was sixty, short, and fat, with bowed legs, black tufts of hair growing from the tops of his toes, and a man part that dangled like an overcooked sausage.

She'd been extra cautious around the bathing room ever since.

But this . . .

If her guest noticed her perturbation, he gave no sign of it. He was frowning and fumbling at the laces of his shirt and starting to go cross-eyed with the effort to see what he was doing.

Suddenly, his fingers froze on the lacing strings, and his eyes uncrossed and focused on her, instead. The longer he watched her, the darker his dark blue eyes became.

As if that steady, assessing gaze wasn't sufficiently disconcerting, his man part started to twitch beneath the linen, threatening to stir itself to troubling proportions.

Arianne swallowed and resolutely looked away. Her hands trembled as she lifted the heavy kettle to pour hot water into the wash-basin for him.

He looked down and made one last effort to unfasten his laces, then threw up his hands in disgust. "Damn!"

The sudden exclamation made her flinch. Hot water splashed onto the rim of the basin and sprayed his legs and feet. He jumped back, cursing.

"Damn, damn, *damn!*" He swiped at his legs. "Be careful with that, will you?"

The twitching, she couldn't help noticing, had stopped.

He straightened, grimacing. "That's all I needed. A little scalding to go with the cold soaking."

She met his angry eyes with a narrow gaze of her own. It was his fault her hand had been so unsteady. Just like a man to blame her for it!

Whatever other complaints he'd been about to voice withered under her gaze and died unspoken.

"Look, I'm sorry I yelled. You caught me by surprise, and that water's hot, you know."

She shrugged, repressing her own niggling guilt at having ogled him—that he hadn't objected didn't make her behavior any less rude—and started to turn away. He put out a hand to stop her.

"It's these damn lacing strings." He tugged at one and gave her a helpless, melting smile. "They're wet and all knotted up, so I can't undo them. You wouldn't mind. Would you?"

However politely couched, it wasn't really a request. It clearly didn't occur to him that she might refuse.

He let his hand drop and tilted his chin upward, calmly waiting for her to tend to him.

Arianne turned and walked away.

His chin came down. His mouth dropped open. "Wait! Where are you going?"

She lifted the kettle, then cocked her head toward the hearth.

"But . . ."

Two more steps toward the hearth.

"Er . . . please?"

Arianne hesitated. If she didn't help him, he'd either strangle himself or end up tearing his shirt. Her thrifty soul couldn't bear the thought of ruining a good shirt.

With a sigh, she set the kettle on the floor.

He smiled, a wickedly satisfied smile, and once more dropped his hands to his sides and tilted his chin toward the ceiling, waiting.

She'd bet her best necklet he'd probably wrapped his nurse around his little finger when he was a boy. The charming ones with the angelic smiles were always the worst.

Sternly supressing the urge to mutter a few rude words under her breath, Arianne stalked to him.

She had to stand on tiptoe to reach the top set of laces. After the fifth time she had to grab a hunk of his shirt to keep from toppling over, she gave up and pulled him down to her level. He came willingly, a devilish, teasing glint in his eyes. Clearly, he'd known from the start just how difficult the task would be and how likely it was that she would have to lean on him to do it.

Yet even with his bending, she couldn't help but touch him. And beneath his shirt, he was all hard muscle. The rise and fall of his chest was mesmerizing. His skin was chilled from the wet, yet just beneath the surface she could feel the heat of him, like a banked fire waiting to roar.

Shaking away the distracting thought, Arianne forced herself to concentrate. The laces had tightened so much that she had to dig at the knot with her nails. Setting her jaw, she leaned closer, peering at the tangled strings as she tried to sort out just what went where.

That's when he lowered his head a few inches farther and kissed her, square on the mouth.

Chapter Three

So sweet. Like honey, warm and flavorful on the tongue.

The tantalizing taste and feel of her were more distracting than Richard had expected, and far more exciting. John Paul was already waking up and taking notice.

What really surprised him, however, was how eagerly she responded, and how very little she seemed to know about kissing.

He'd done it to tease her, and because he'd wanted to ever since she'd opened the door and he'd seen her standing there, bathed in the firelight, radiant as an angel. Now that he had begun, however, and she was proving such a willing accomplice, he didn't see any reason not to take things a bit more seriously. If she wanted to learn how to kiss, he was more than willing to teach her.

Gently, he nipped her lower lip, that full, sweet lip he'd been admiring from a distance. She moaned and tightened her hold on his shirt laces, pulling him closer.

Pleased, he cupped his hand against her cheek and kissed the corner of her mouth, then delicately trailed the tip of his tongue along the delicious curve of her upper lip and back again, teasing her, reveling in the sweetness of her.

By now, his heart was starting to pound, and John Paul was rapidly rising to full alert. If he'd had any idea—

The thought was cut off by a sudden shortage of air.

"What the hell—?"

He wrenched free of her vicious choke hold on his collar and backed away, astonished.

"What'd you do that for?"

Between one breath and another she'd gone from compliant to deadly, and he was damned if he knew why. It was enough to make a man turn monk, the way the creatures tempted, then turned against you without a word of warning.

She didn't look like a woman prepared to offer any explanations, either. Chin up, eyes flashing fire, she stood her ground and glared at him. Her back was so stiff and straight, he'd swear she'd gained a good three inches in height—and all because he'd kissed her, and she had kissed him back.

And she *had* kissed him back, no matter what she might say!

Sourly, he rubbed his throat. "If you didn't want to be kissed, you could have just said so, couldn't you?"

For answer, she gave him a hard, disdainful glare.

"Come to think of it . . ." He frowned, trying to remember. "You haven't said a word since you opened the door. What's the matter? Cat got your tongue?"

Her pretty mouth thinned in disgust. Without bothering to answer, she bent and picked up the kettle, then stomped back to the fireplace.

Shoeless and dressed only in his sodden shirt and hose, Richard trailed after, his washing up forgotten. "Are you a mute?"

No reply.

"I know damned well you're not deaf."

She pointedly ignored him.

"Can't even tell me to go to hell, can you?" he said, grinning now.

He hovered over her shoulder while she refilled the kettle, then hung it from a hook set in the fireplace wall.

"Is it that you *can't* talk," he persisted, "or that you *won't?*"

She threw him a scornful glance, snatched up the fireplace poker, and stabbed at the burning logs, setting sparks to flying. If looks could kill, he'd have melted into a large and very messy puddle right at her feet.

Deliberately turning her back on him, she crossed to a small cabinet on the opposite wall. While she pulled out chipped bowls and plates and mugs, Richard considered the possibilities.

A woman who couldn't speak couldn't scold or nag or chatter in his ears when he was trying to eat, as the Princess Graciella had done. She couldn't go on and on and on about how handsome and brave and bold he was when he was trying to think, as Princess Alice had.

Not that a man didn't enjoy hearing his praises sung every now and then, mind you, but Alice had become such a bore on the subject that Harry and his friends had teased him for weeks after her departure from Avalon.

If a woman couldn't speak, she couldn't titter and simper as Princess Thessia had done. Or maybe she could, though the blond beauty slamming plates and spoons and napkins down on the table hadn't shown any tendency to do either. Quite the contrary, in fact.

The more he thought about it, the more he wondered if the huge hart that had led him astray this morning hadn't been enchanted, specially sent to lead him to this little cottage and the treasure it contained—a woman who couldn't, or wouldn't, say a word. Not one single word, no matter what the provocation.

Silence. Blessed silence. Richard smiled, savoring the quiet.

What had he said to Harry this morning? Something about swearing to marry the first woman he found who didn't talk his ears off?

Mind you, that had been nothing more than talk, the sort of thing you said when you were feeling down and needed to grumble to a friend. On the other hand . . .

An idea began to take shape, fuzzy around the edges still but rather tempting in its possibilities.

Whistling in satisfaction, he strolled back to the abandoned washbasin and its rapidly cooling water.

The whistling was bad enough—the man couldn't carry a tune if you handed it to him in a bucket—but the sounds that followed were worse. Much worse.

She wouldn't think about it, Arianne told herself sternly while she stirred the soup. She just wouldn't think about it.

But it wasn't that easy. Her sense of hearing was acute—all those years of listening for signs that her brothers were up to no good, she supposed—and she could hear every soft slither and slide as he undressed. She didn't even have to turn around to know that he was stripping right down to his bare skin.

Her hand froze, spoon poised above the soup. She stopped breathing, straining to fol-

low the progress of his undressing. That snap
was his shirt lacings. He'd given up on untying
them and simply ripped the top ones out.

Just like a man, she thought in disgust, never
worrying about the cost or the extra work he
caused.

Now he was dragging the shirt over his head.
She could hear his soft grunt as he tugged at
the wet linen that insisted on sticking to his
skin. It came away with a soft slurping, sucking
noise.

She couldn't help but picture the cloth clinging to that broad back, the hollow of his spine,
his trim waist, those sculpted stomach muscles, his—

No! Don't think about *that*, she silently scolded
herself. Thinking about it wasn't right. Was, in
fact, downright indecent. Properly brought-up
princesses never thought about such things.

Well, hardly ever. But anyone, even old
Nanny, who'd always been extraordinarily
strict, would admit that the present circumstances were a little out of the ordinary.

Now he was bending, stretching his arms so
the shirt would fall forward. A little scramble
while he tugged at the cuffs—cuffs he had, of
course, forgotten to unfasten—then the soft
plop as he dropped the wet shirt on the floor.

Stupid male. As if she had nothing better to
do than pick up after him.

Didn't matter that there really wasn't any

other place he could put it except the floor. Two pennies got you ten he'd leave it where it was and forget all about it unless she made a point of reminding him.

That next rasping sound was the lacing on his pants or hose or whatever the things were.

He was having more trouble with those. She heard a little slap as the knit fabric snapped back against his skin, than a more muffled sound as he began rolling the hose down over his hips. That's right. Lower.

Judging from the sudden silence, his man parts were in the way.

She realized suddenly that she was swirling her spoon in midair, having missed the soup pot entirely. Plunking the spoon into the pot, she held her breath, straining to hear.

He cursed a little. Probably wriggling while he worked that clinging knit fabric down his legs and exposing that hard-muscled, perfectly shaped derriere—

Her lungs were burning now, hungry for air. She gasped, heart pounding, then held her breath again.

The hose hit the floor with a wet, sucking plop. He sighed as if in relief.

She bit her lower lip and managed to grab the spoon a second before it slid into the soup and disappeared. She would *not* turn around. It was unladylike. It was rude. It was . . . indecent.

She glanced over her shoulder. Her eyes

widened, and her breath caught in her chest. The only sound she could hear was the roaring in her ears.

He was completely undressed. Naked. Absolutely bare-assed starkers.

And he was glorious from top to toe, beautifully formed, sculpted to perfection. She could happily spend hours and hours just looking at him, admiring the perfection.

The only trouble was, his enormous man part was bobbing rigidly in front of him. Not dangling like an overcooked sausage like Sir Adelbert's after his bath—but *bobbing*. And growing huger by the minute.

Her gaze snapped back to the fire in front of her. Suddenly there wasn't enough air in the little cottage.

She'd known that boys grew into men, of course. They got taller, heavier, hairier. Their voices deepened, and they forgot half the manners their mothers and sisters and nurses had struggled so long to teach them, and instead of being cuddly and cute they wrestled with each other and told bawdy jokes and did silly things like see who could guzzle the most wine yet be the last to pass out under the supper table.

But she'd never realized just how much they grew down *there*.

Cheeks burning from a heat that had nothing to do with the flames in front of her, Arianne blindly stirred the soup and wondered if there was any way she could make her guest sleep in the little shed at the back of the cottage instead of in here in front of the fire. There was straw out there, and some hay, more than enough to make a bed. It would be *safer* if—

"Forgot to tell you." His deep, pleasant voice easily carried over the crackling of the fire, shattering her thoughts. "I put my horse in that shed at the back of your cottage. I hope you don't mind."

Damn! This time she almost dropped the spoon into the fire.

Not a peep out of her, but Richard could tell she was listening. She hadn't moved a muscle since he'd started undressing. If she wasn't careful, she'd go blind from staring at the flames like that.

He almost snickered in satisfaction at the thought.

Choke him, would she? And all because she'd enjoyed his kiss a whole lot more than she was willing to admit. Trust a woman to be so damned perverse! Still, there was a lot to be said in favor of a woman who couldn't interrupt when you were talking.

He glanced at her, bent over her pot of soup, still stirring.

There was no denying it—she *was* beautiful. Stunning, really despite the simple, sturdy gown she wore. Dressed in silks and satins, with pearls at her throat, she'd be absolutely breathtaking. Dressed in absolutely nothing but that incredible golden hair—

John Paul bobbed in enthusiastic agreement.

Richard grinned and forced himself to concentrate on the task at hand.

"It was rather presumptuous of me, I know," he continued, futilely trying to generate some lather from the lump of gray rock she'd given him in place of soap. "I didn't think anyone would mind, even if he does pretty much fill up the place. No other livestock around, and plenty of hay, and the poor beast was even wetter and muddier than I was. Couldn't just leave him out in the rain, you know.

"Hell of a hunt, though. And that hart! Remember I told you about him? Biggest rack I've ever seen. Thought the beast would run for hours. If all my people hadn't gotten lost like that, I know we would have brought him down eventually."

He gave up on the soap and settled instead for simply rinsing off with water. She'd forgotten to give him a cloth, but one of those rags she seemed to think qualified as towels worked just as well. A little messier, maybe, since he ended up slopping a bit of water on the floor, but good enough. A man couldn't complain over everything, and having an appreciative female audience of one—and a good-looking female audience, at that—made up for most of the deficiencies in his accommodations.

"Stupid thing, their getting lost. Never happened before that I can remember. You'd have thought a couple of 'em, at least, would have been paying attention to where we were going, wouldn't you? Isn't that what they're supposed to do? Pay attention?"

She didn't answer—by now, he didn't expect her to—so he happily answered himself.

"Of course it is! Still and all, it was a *great* hart and a good chase. Tomorrow I'll go round 'em up and see what's what."

Despite having gotten rid of those wet clothes of his, he was beginning to shiver. It was colder at this side of the cottage, and the fire looked very inviting.

"In the meantime, I'm lucky to have found you." He stood on one foot to scrub between his toes. "What with the dark and no road and all, I thought I'd end up shivering under a bush tonight. Then I saw your light, and here I am! Damned lucky, don't you think? Pity you don't have any wine, though. There's nothing like a good mulled wine to warm a man after a long, hard hunt."

All he had to do was wash his other foot and he'd be done.

Without bothering to wring out the skimpy towel, he switched to balance on his other foot and washed between his remaining toes, oblivious of the miniature lake forming on the floor around him.

There! He tossed the rag back into the basin, making the water slop over the rim and hit the floor with a splash.

The other two excuses for towels left him damp around the edges, but once finished with them, he tossed them atop the pile of his sodden clothes, grabbed the quilt, and wrapped it twice around his waist. It made a lumpy, ungainly skirt, but it was better than that sorry excuse for hose that Thurgood had foisted on him. And he didn't plan to go anywhere tonight.

Now for the fire and his supper, which his blessedly silent hostess had been pretending to stir for the past five minutes. Shame there wasn't any wine, but a man couldn't have everything, even if he was a king.

With a quick, appraising glance at the bed in the corner, he strolled back to the fireplace and the comforts that awaited him there.

The quilt was a mistake, Arianne concluded.

It might cover the glorious derriere and hobble that arrogant, masculine stride, but it left his torso dangerously, temptingly bare.

It was a magnificent torso—broad shoulders, a sculpted chest dusted with curly black hairs that invited a woman's touch, and a stomach carved of solid muscle. The breath-stealing combination tapered into a slim waist and lean-muscled hips and thighs whose outline even the double-wrapped quilt couldn't quite disguise.

She might be silent, but she wasn't blind. Seeing him like this, knowing that under that shabby quilt he was totally, distractingly naked, was a great deal more than she had bargained for.

He didn't even seem to notice, as if he was accustomed to having princesses—well, servant girls, at any rate—attend him in his bath and feed him while he lounged around half naked afterward.

He seemed to have forgotten the cut out on his forehead and the scrapes on his cheek and chin. Arianne, however, had not.

She'd thought it would be easy enough, once he was covered by the quilt, to tend to his injuries. She had, after all, had the keeping of a baker's dozen of males for the past few years, what with her father and twelve brothers and all the trouble the latter, at least, were so good at getting into.

But this big fellow—she realized with a start that she didn't even know his name, beyond his wild claim to being the King of Avalon—was neither her father nor a brother, and her reaction to him was just about as far from familial as it was possible to get.

The thought was enough to bring the heat flooding back into her cheeks.

"That fire feels good," he said, stretching his

hands to the flame. She couldn't tell if he'd deliberately chosen to stand so close to her or if he hadn't noticed. "First time I've felt really warm in hours."

If he noticed the water still dripping from his hair, he gave no sign of it.

Arianne watched one fat drop as it landed on the smooth, muscled curve at the top of his shoulder, then traced a crooked trail down his front, over the ridge of his collarbone, and into the thicket of hair on his chest. Other tiny droplets clung amidst the curls, glistening like diamonds in the firelight.

With an effort of will, she wrenched her gaze away and went to fetch the small pot of ointment and the lint she'd collected earlier. When she returned, he'd turned so his back was to the fire, his glorious big body outlined in flame-tinted gold. He'd hooked his thumbs over the wad of quilt at his waist and was watching her with the smug, unconscious satisfaction of a man who knows he has a woman's attention and is utterly convinced that he deserves it.

"Pity there's no wine."

Was it her imagination, or was there the faintest hint of lecherous intent in his voice?

"Night like this, wine's good for warming the blood, you know."

That blue-velvet gaze was more than enough to warm whatever blood hadn't already heated at the sight of him, but she wasn't about to give him the satisfaction of knowing it. Instead, she sternly pointed to the stool he'd sat on earlier.

Oblivious, he shifted position to toast his right side.

"I hope it's not much longer to supper. My belly's so empty, I swear it's starting to rub against my backbone. And with no wine to fortify my strength—"

Irritated, she tugged on his arm, trying to get him to sit.

He eyed her, then the stool, suddenly wary.

Arianne firmed her lips, set her jaw, and kicked the stool into the back of his legs, throwing him off balance so she could pull him down where she wanted him.

"Well, damn!" he said, sounding aggrieved. "All you had to do was tell me what you wanted, didn't you? I'm not accustomed to someone kicking stools at me and—"

The rest was muffled under the towel she threw over his head. Careful not to further abrade the cut on his forehead, she dried his hair as best she could, then raked her fingers through the curls, trying to persuade them into some sort of order.

If he'd been a cat, he'd have been purring by the time she tossed the towel aside and pulled the lint and ointment from her pocket. The purring stopped the instant he caught sight of the items in her hand.

"Oh, no, you don't!"

He was halfway to his feet when the quilt came undone at his waist and started to slip away. Grabbing for the ends, he tripped on the hem and sat back down with a thump.

A warning glance was enough to keep him there. Arianne leaned closer, dabbing at the cut on his forehead. The ointment, a particularly astringent goo she'd often used on her brothers' scrapes and bumps, made him wince. When he tried to peer down her bodice a second time, she pointedly shoved his nose away and smeared more ointment on an ugly scrape on his cheek.

Satisfied at last, she tossed the bit of lint she'd used into the fire and tucked the pot back into her pocket.

"Good! Now we can eat." Beaming in sudden good cheer, and with the quilt firmly clutched in both big fists, he scrambled to his feet.

For answer, she pointed toward the sodden heap of clothing and towels he'd left in the middle of the floor.

He looked at her. He looked at the clothes. And then he sighed, squared his shoulders, tightened the quilt around his middle as if he were girding his loins for battle, and hobbled across the room to reclaim his abandoned garments.

Arianne went for the bucket and mop.

For someone who'd clearly never done his own laundry, he didn't manage too badly. By the time she finished mopping up the mess, he'd wrung out his clothes and the towels, pitched the wash water out the door, and was draping the last damp item over a rope he'd strung in front of the fire.

"Looks like hell, but I guess it'll do. It'll have to," he added with a defiant glance at her, "because I'm damned if I'm doing one thing more until I've had something to eat. Go much longer and I'll die of hunger instead of cold."

Hiding her irritation under a smile—she'd mopped that floor just yesterday—she patted his shoulder and went to slice the bread and ladle out the soup. He was halfway through the first thick slice of bread before her hand stopped tingling where she'd touched him.

Facing him across the table proved harder than she'd expected. With the quilt hidden below the tabletop, there was nothing to stop her imagination from following the trail of that curly black hair down his chest to where it tapered into a neat vee just before it disappeared from sight.

If he was suffering any similar embarrassment, he gave no sign of it. "Good bread. You bake it?" he grabbed another slice without waiting for an answer.

"What's this?" He tilted the cup she'd set at his place and peered dubiously into its depths. An expression of pain crossed his face. "It's water, isn't it?"

73

She nodded, bristling a little.

He sighed and set the cup back down. "That's what I thought."

The soup got a more enthusiastic reception.

"Mmm. S'good," he said around a large spoonful. He swallowed and ladled up another big mouthful. "*Really* good."

Richard was on his fifth slice of bread and his third bowl of soup before he started slowing down. Damn, but he'd been hungry. And the food really *was* good. Simple, but good. If not for her, he'd have spent the night in the cold and the wet without so much as a crust to eat.

The mere thought made him shudder.

He glanced across the table at the girl who'd saved him from such misery. Her eyes were on her bowl, but she didn't seem to be eating much, just picking at the bread and stirring her spoon around in her soup as if she thought it hadn't quite finished cooking.

If he didn't know better, he'd have said she was shy. That would have been completely understandable, a peasant girl like her and what with him being the King of Avalon. Happened all the time.

It wasn't shyness, though. The way she'd bossed him around and poked at his scrapes and made him pick up his own wet clothes—if such thing were possible, he'd have sworn she was kin to his old nurse, and Nurse would have spit in the eye of the Devil himself if she'd ever had a chance.

Maybe the girl was just tired, though what she might be tired from he hadn't the faintest notion. She hadn't been out hunting, after all, or trying to run a kingdom. How hard could it be to live here in this little cottage and sweep the dust out now and then?

Or maybe she was just sad, thinking how lonely things would be once he was gone. Now *that* he could understand. There wasn't another cottage for miles—he'd wandered around for hours this afternoon, looking for his lost retinue, and he hadn't seen so much as a trace of smoke from a chimney. Nothing but forest whichever way you turned, thick, dark forest where the sun never shone and the trees were so tall you couldn't even see their tops, let alone the sky above them.

It couldn't be very pleasant for her, living all alone like this in the middle of such a dense forest. Nothing to do and no place to go and not a single soul to talk to. Just her, all alone, day after day after day.

The very thought made him wince.

What a waste. Downright criminal, really, a beauty like her being shut away in a place like this.

Which just went to prove that this little idea of his was the right thing, after all.

For a few minutes there, he hadn't been so sure. When she'd kicked that stool into his knees, then spread that goop on his cuts with no more thought for his comfort than if he'd been a brick, he'd started to wonder if maybe he wasn't a little dizzy from hunger to be considering it at all.

Then, on top of all that, she'd pushed his nose out of her bosom, even though all he'd wanted was a little peek, just one little peek. There wasn't a man alive who wouldn't have done the same, so why had she been so snippy about it, a peasant girl like her?

Forget about that.

Why not take her back to Avalon with him? Be the best thing for her, really. She'd live in a castle and have servants to wash and cook and clean for her instead of having to do everything herself.

And all she'd have to do was keep him company and soothe his weary brow at the end of a long day and warm his bed through the cold winter nights.

At the thought of her in his bed, John Paul stirred in sudden interest.

Yes, that would work. Definitely the best thing for her. Take her back with him, get her some nice clothes. She'd love that. There wasn't a woman born who didn't like nice clothes, and a woman like this—

76

He paused with a hunk of bread halfway to his mouth. What if—?

John Paul sank back, clearly disappointed.

No, it couldn't be. Absurd even to consider it.

Slowly, he lowered his hand and stared across the table at her. "You aren't married, are you?"

The question caught her just when she was starting to swallow a spoonful of soup. She choked but managed to clap her napkin over her mouth before she sprayed the table. Her face turned red, and her eyes started to water as she struggled to swallow.

"Have some water."

She grabbed the glass two-handedly and gulped the water down, still blinking back tears.

Richard waited until she caught her breath and set her glass back down.

"Well? Are you? Married, I mean."

For a moment, he didn't think she was going to answer. She stared at him, then chewed her lower lip, then, reluctantly, shook her head.

He grinned, relieved. "That's all right, then."

She eyed him warily, but he didn't offer an explanation, simply turned his attention back to his soup. He was halfway through the bowl when another horrible thought struck.

"Engaged?"

A moment's hesitation, then an almost imperceptible shake of her head.

"Good! Great!" said Richard, and he turned his attention back to his bowl.

He'd make sure to get her some sexy underthings, too, he decided a moment later as he swallowed another mouthful of soup. Some nice, filmy, silky things that only he would ever see.

John Paul instantly roused to show he approved of silky, see-through underthings, too.

Richard smiled.

She couldn't possibly object. None of the other women he'd invited to keep him company had ever objected, so why should she? And with her to keep him company, he wouldn't need to worry so much about finding a wife right away. He certainly hadn't had much luck so far. No telling but what it might not be *years* before the right princess came along.

Even if he did eventually find a suitable wife, he could easily find this beauty a husband among his knights. Give 'im a dukedom, say, which would make her a duchess, and everybody would be happy.

He probably wouldn't even have to go that far. There wasn't a knight in Avalon who wouldn't be more than happy to have her sitting next to him at supper or sharing a cup of wine or—

At the thought, Richard scowled.

He could already see the scramble to gain

her favor. George, who was an earl and who fancied himself a ladies' man, would be reciting poetry to her half the afternoon, and Percy, who was too damned good-looking for his own good, would be kissing her hand every chance he got and whispering sweet nothings over supper, and Harry—

At the thought of Harry and the way he'd tried to look up the Princess Graciella's skirt— twice—Richard growled and ripped off a hunk of bread with his teeth.

Better not to think about Harry, he decided, glumly chewing on the bread. Better not to think about any of 'em. One sight of her and they'd be no better than a pack of dogs after a bitch in heat, with only one thing on their minds.

Not a one of 'em would realize what a gem she was, what an absolute treasure. A woman who could tend to a man's needs the way she did, and patch up his hurts, and—

Well, all right, she'd been a little rough on the patching up, and if she'd *really* wanted to tend to his needs, she would have bathed him herself and offered him some wine, but that was maybe expecting a little too much under the circumstances, and really, she'd done her best, and probably her occasional little displays of temper were no more than a normal if incomprehensible female aversion to a bit of dirt on the floor, which any normal man would know wasn't worth worrying about. But there, that's the way women were, and no man in his right mind would waste time trying to figure it out, although in this case, with a girl like her, under the right circumstances, he might even consider—

Richard blinked.

Damned if he wasn't getting tangled in his own thoughts. The sort of thing he'd started to think about simply wasn't done. Imagine! Him! The king of Avalon, Darian, etc., etc., etc., marrying a peasant girl! Ridiculous!

Which meant he couldn't possibly have been considering what he'd almost been considering.

Could he?

Frowning, Richard refilled his soup bowl for the fourth time and forced himself to concentrate on ladling the meal down his throat as fast as he could swallow.

Chapter Four

"You can call me Richard. All my friends do."

They'd finished dinner and, after only a little grumbling on his part, done the dishes and restrung the makeshift clothesline in a less inconvenient place. Now they were comfortably settled in front of the fire, she in her chair, knitting, he on the floor, talking.

His back was propped against the trunk he'd hauled over, his rear cushioned on the limp feather pillow the trunk had contained. He was still dressed in the quilt, but so long as she kept her eyes on her work and not on him, Arianne could almost forget he was half naked.

Almost.

"Actually, my full name is James Richard Henry Michael Bledgabred Taillefer. The

81

Bledgabred was from my mother's side of the family.

"It was a very distinguished family," he added stiffly when she made a little choking noise.

Under his quelling gaze, she quieted. Only the quiver at one corner of her mouth betrayed her.

Satisfied, he continued, "On official documents, my title is King of Avalon, Darian, Longshore, and the Western Isles, Duke of Lemaire-over-the-Sea, Count of Borghame, Chosen of God and, by His Gracious Might, Anointed among Men—that's to give it the proper godly flavor, you understand," he added helpfully.

"Wouldn't want anyone to think our ancestors had gotten their lands and titles only because they could hack and bash better than their enemies. Which they could, of course, but that's simply not the sort of thing one wants to admit to in official documents, so somewhere along the line one of my forefathers decided to add the part about Chosen of God and whatnot. Been there ever since, and I have to tell you, it makes for a devil of a lot of extra effort every time I go to sign my name. Tried to add it up once, you know—the amount of time I wasted writing that damned title, I mean—but I gave it up because it was too depressing even to think about."

She nodded sympathetically. Her father had

complained of the same thing more than once. She was almost beginning to believe he really was who he said he was. If only he wasn't so good-looking!

Frowning, she cast on three stitches, then turned her knitting to start the next row.

Richard swelled with satisfaction. God! It was wonderful to be able to talk about the frustrations of his position with a woman who listened instead of chattering away like a magpie at a family reunion.

It'd be better if she'd put down whatever it was she was working on, of course—a man liked to think he had a woman's full attention when he was with her—but women seemed to enjoy having their fingers in something all the time, no matter what. Better it was knitting than his affairs, he supposed, and since it didn't seem to keep her from listening, there wasn't much sense in complaining.

"You wouldn't believe how much paperwork you have to deal with when you're a king," he assured her. "Rights for this and grants for that and proclamations about pretty much anything. These days, seems there's always someone wanting a proclamation about something or other. Damned annoying sometimes, but what can you do? Have to keep your subjects happy.

"Still, no matter how hard you work or how many proclamations you sign, people tend to forget what you did for them last week. Always demanding to know what you're going to do for them *this* week.

"Take last year, for instance. I'd just gotten home from fighting a war with the Duke of Chester, who'd been trying to steal a couple of square miles of land and a village or two on the northern border, when along comes word that there's a dragon burning the fields in the south. 'What are you going to do about it?' people demanded. 'Me?' I said. 'I just got back from fighting a war.' 'But that was in the north,' they said, 'and we're from the south, and we want to know what you're going to do for us.'"

Arianne made a little noise to show she was appropriately sympathetic and kept on knitting.

"Now, mind you, this is a *big* dragon. By the time I hear of him, he's already turned half a dozen of my knights into toast, so slaying him's obviously not going to be easy. But what can you do? Can't have a dragon going around burning up villages and eating the peasants, can you? People don't like it. Thing like that, you let it go on too long, the people start talking about not paying their taxes or finding some other king, and there you are. So off I gallop to take care of the dragon."

Arianne looked up at that. King or not, if Richard had bagged a dragon all by himself, he deserved some respect. A couple of years earlier a runty little dragon who couldn't do much more than blow smoke from his nose had caused some problems in Montavia. Her father's knights had had a devil of a time getting rid of the creature, and they hadn't even considered fighting it one-on-one.

"I'm not exaggerating when I tell you that it was a really *big* dragon," Richard assured her earnestly. "Biggest I've ever seen, and I've seen some big ones. For a while back when I was still Crown Prince, I held the record in *Ye Olde Booke of Fishe and Gayme* for biggest dragon slain. That is, I did until King Gandolf took it away from me with a huge old silver drake he bagged in the Dangerous Mountains.

"Mind you," he added, frowning, "I still think Gandolf fudged a tad on the measuring, but I could never prove it, so he got the record, and I had to make do with second-best. And then I saw *this* fellow! Took my breath away just looking at him!"

By now, he'd abandoned his languid sprawl and was sitting up, face alight with remembered excitement.

"He was big. *Big*. In his prime, not old and worn out like Gandolf's drake, and red as the fire spouting out of his nostrils. I knew if I could get him that I'd take that record back; and *then* we'd see! It'd take a hell of a dragon to beat him, let me tell you! Not to mention," he added as an afterthought, "that the villagers would be a lot happier to be rid of him.

85

"So there I was, and there was the dragon, sitting on his hill and smouldering a little . . ."

On his feet now, his body limned in gold-red fire-light, Richard recounted his battle against the dragon. He paced the hearth, swung his arms wide, crouched to illustrate the way he'd ducked the beast's flaming breath. Had he been in some castle hall, where this sort of tale was often an evening's entertainment, he would have had a hundred listeners rapt at the telling. His strong, deep voice was mesmerizing, his physical presence so overwhelming that it was impossible to look away.

Arianne's hands stilled in her lap, her knitting forgotten.

Over the years she'd heard a thousand hunting tales in her father's Great Hall—knights telling about the dragons they'd braved and the great harts that had led them for hours through haunted forests, huntsmen recounting the tricks of the wily fox, falconers rhapsodizing over the grace and strength and skill of their birds—but not once had she found herself so enthralled by the teller and not just the tale.

Watching Richard, listening to the deep, honeyed music of his voice, she felt the world and all its troubles drop away until only he remained. He seemed to fill her senses, sight and sound and smell. Touch, too. Her fingers itched to trace the glorious curve of that broad back and tingled at the remembered feel of his skin, the heat of him. She could taste him on her tongue, even now.

Was it possible that one kiss could linger for so long?

"And that," he said at last, triumphant on the hearth, "was that. I'm back on top in the record book, and the villagers are happy, and it didn't take more than a few weeks for my wounds to heal, which wasn't bad, considering."

Arianne stared at him, shaken out of the magic and back into the world. She blinked, then drew a deep breath to steady her spinning head. It was all she could do not to squirm on the chair in an effort to ease the odd, hungry ache that had grown in her while she watched him.

He took her stunned appreciation as no more than his due. His smile was radiant and very, very dangerous. Right then, if he'd pulled her into his arms for a kiss, she wouldn't have been able to resist.

Fortunately, the possibility didn't seem to occur to him. Instead, he looked around himself a little blindly, like a man surprised to find that something was missing. Then reality struck, and his shoulders drooped.

"I forgot," he said, and sighed. "Pity there's no wine."

Arianne couldn't help but blush for the deficiencies of her hospitality. In her father's Hall, as reward for his fine tale, Richard would have been given a silver cup of the finest wine and the best seat next to the hearth.

With an apologetic shrug, she picked up her knitting and started to count the stitches, then the rows, to find where she'd left off.

Richard watched her, entranced by that tiny wrinkle she always seemed to get in her forehead when she was concentrating on something.

Pity about the wine. He could have used a cup or two. Storytelling was dry work at the best of times, and he hadn't had a drink to warm him up to begin with.

At least he'd had a properly respectful audience. She'd sat quietly the whole time, her gaze fixed on him, as it should have been, her eyes alight with excitement. It made a man feel his efforts were appreciated, having her attention like that.

And not one murmur out of her the whole time! Not one question to throw him off his stride and make him forget what he was going to say next.

With a woman like that, who needed wine?

John Paul clearly agreed.

Richard licked his lips and thought of that kiss he'd stolen earlier. Sweet and hot, despite her evident lack of experience.

If a man couldn't have wine . . .

He glanced at the bed. It was a tall bed, a bit narrow for two but not impossible.

John Paul had no trouble following his train of thought.

The two of them had managed in much smaller spaces when they'd had to.

Hitching the quilt more securely about his waist, Richard picked up the stool and set it down again beside her chair.

She looked up at that, startled, eyes wide and glowing in the firelight.

He gave her his most reassuring smile, tugged up the quilt—he was getting the hang of the thing at last—and sat.

"I take it you liked my tale?"

She nodded, then pointedly turned back to her knitting.

If he didn't know better, he'd swear what she was knitting with were nettles. But who ever heard of anyone knitting with nettles?

"You know," he said, "adventures are fine, but sometimes you get a little tired of them. All that running around and fighting and trying to keep the peace. It gets awfully tiring at times, you know what I mean?"

A quick glance out of the corner of her eye, but that was it. Not even a sympathetic nod.

Richard tried again, lingering on the words to give them added meaning. "That's why I appreciate the chance to have a quiet evening like this, alone with a beautiful woman like you."

She missed a stitch, bit her lip, then backed up and tried again.

That was a little more promising. Seducing a woman intent on her knitting was proving more awkward than he'd expected.

"At Avalon there're always hundreds of people around. My knights and advisers, of course. The servants. Hundreds of servants. Visitors. Guests." Just thinking about it made him tired. "The place gets damnably crowded at times. But here . . ."

The bed was at his back, out of sight, but that didn't mean he'd forgotten it was there. He leaned toward her.

"I'm very glad you were here tonight. Very, very glad," he said, narrowing the space between them with each *very*.

"Very glad." It was little more than a whisper.

He kissed her then, a soft, quick peck on the cheek, and retreated.

She jumped, blushed, and resolutely refused to look at him.

Richard wasn't worried. Everything was proceeding according to plan, just as it always did. He'd learned the rules long ago, when he was a horny Crown Prince and there were a lot of eager young things who were more than willing to teach him everything he wanted to know about sex . . . and then some.

Seduction was rather simple, really. Flatter them. Tease them, just a little. Give them a hint of the pleasures that lie ahead. Make them want you even more than you wanted them. And never, ever let them know that they were the ones in control of the game.

Worked every time, so long as you didn't spook 'em, and he hadn't spooked one yet.

Gently, he brushed back a curl that had fallen forward across her cheek.

"You're very beautiful. Did you know that?"

John Paul was getting impatient, but Richard ignored the message. It never worked to rush this sort of thing, no matter how much he would have liked to.

"Gorgeous creature like you," he murmured, leaning closer once more. "It's a shame you're shut away here. It must get rather . . . lonely."

One fleeting kiss, just below her ear.

She hadn't touched her knitting for a long while now, and he could see the quick rise and fall of her breasts beneath her bodice.

Lovely, lovely breasts.

By now, John Paul was straining against the weight of the quilt. Richard ignored him.

He pressed another kiss to the tip of her earlobe, then flicked his tongue out and delicately traced the perfect curve above it.

"Why don't you put away the knitting for tonight?" he murmured into her ear.

Another quick, delicate flick of his tongue, then he stretched out his hand and firmly wrapped it around the knitting in her lap.

"Yeeow!"

The screech of pain came directly into Arianne's ear, jarring her out of the dangerous, sensuous daze he'd dragged her into.

She jumped, then grabbed for her knitting, but he'd already dropped it.

In fact, he'd jerked back his hand so quickly, he'd fallen right off his stool. Arianne twisted around in her chair and peered over the arm at him.

He was propped on one elbow, cradling the injured hand against his chest and glaring up at her.

"By all the saints and the seven magicians! What *are* those things?"

She sniffed, then deliberately settled back in her chair and picked up her knitting again.

"They're really nettles, aren't they?"

He didn't seem to expect an answer, which was just as well, because she had no intention of giving him one.

Still cursing and cradling his hand, he got to his knees, then to his feet. Standing, he towered over her.

"I can't believe it. Nettles! Who in the hell knits with *nettles?*"

Still muttering, he stomped across the room and plunged his injured hand into the bucket of fresh water standing near the door, ready for the morning.

The back of her neck prickled with her sharp

awareness of him, but Arianne set her lips and kept her attention focused on the work in her lap, stabbing the needle into the next stitch as if she were stabbing a knife into his heart, furious at herself and even more furious at him.

How dare he try to seduce her? How dare he!

Just because she looked like a common peasant girl at the moment didn't mean he could treat her like one! After all, she was the Princess Arianne of Montavia, and her father was a king. Even if Montavia wasn't half as big as Avalon and not a quarter as important, it was still a kingdom, and she was still a princess, and that was all there was to it.

And to think she'd let him kiss her!

How dare he even try?

Blinking back tears of rage and shame, Arianne slammed her work atop the pile of nettles in the basket beside her chair and got to her feet.

She'd had it. She was going to bed. It had been a miserable day and a miserable week, and now he'd ruined her evening, too.

Men!

The sight of her bed stopped her cold.

That's what he'd wanted. Not a few kisses, as she'd thought, but . . . *that*.

How could she have been such an innocent fool not to have realized it, right at the start?

Shooting him a glare that should have melted him in his tracks, she spun back around and snatched an extra knitting needle out of the basket.

Let him try something, she thought, shoving the needle into her deepest pocket. She'd really like to see him try.

"Shit!"

On the opposite side of the room, Richard stared at his injured hand in dismay.

Across the palm and up the length of each finger, the tiny red dots where the nettles had stung him were starting to swell. Soaking his hand in cold water hadn't done any good at all.

At this rate, he'd have a worse case of hives than that awful bout he'd had on St. Stephen's day.

So much for a carefully planned seduction.

He didn't need to look at her to know that all his efforts had gone for naught. He'd be sleeping in that bed alone tonight while his hand puffed up to three times its normal size and the itching drove him crazy.

Hell of a way to end the day. Just one hell of a way.

"I don't suppose you have anything for hives, do you?" He plunged his hand back into the water bucket, still cursing.

For a minute or two, he didn't think she'd answer. The surge of relief when he heard the sound of her footsteps coming toward him caught him by surprise. The relief died when he saw the expression on her face—it could have stopped an elephant in its tracks. If his hand didn't sting so damn bad . . .

Kneeling beside him, she gestured for him to show her his hand.

He pulled it out of the water and shoved it at her, still dripping.

"Nettles," he said on a sour, informative note, "make me itch."

She sniffed, unimpressed, but bent to inspect the damage.

"Why didn't you just poke me with one of those damned long needles? Can't be worse than hives. If I'd had any idea, even a little niggling one . . ."

Arianne's mouth thinned. To hear him whine, you'd think she'd forced his hands around the nettles.

She shoved his hand back into the bucket and went to look for the jar with a sticky unguent that might work.

"You try having hives," he called after her. "They're the very devil. Worse than a dragon burn any day of the week. You can scratch yourself raw trying to get at the itch, and all you get for your pains is more itching."

He was still grumbling when she came back. Kneeling again, she unstoppered the jar and dug out some of the unguent with a bit of the lint she'd gathered earlier. The smell, she was glad to note, was atrocious.

"What the hell is that?" His nose wrinkled with disgust. "Phew! I've smelled cess pits that didn't stink that bad."

Despite the stench, and with only a little muttering, he held out his hand for doctoring.

Arianne stared, horrified. In the few minutes it had taken her to find the unguent and the lint, the red bumps had turned a virulent purple and swelled to twice their size.

"Told you," he said, looking grimly satisfied. "They're bloody damned hell, hives are, and no mistake. If I'd had any idea you were knitting nettles . . ."

I'd be kissing you till my head spun right off my shoulders. Or worse, Arianne thought involuntarily.

She firmly squelched the notion and turned her attention to the task at hand. So to speak.

Unfortunately, that wasn't much better at getting her thoughts off dangerous things. Despite the discoloration and swelling, he had a beautiful hand—large, well-shaped, with long, sensitive fingers. The calluses natural to a man of the sword only emphasized its power.

The Mound of Venus, she couldn't help noting, was especially pronounced. It didn't take much imagination to picture those fingers trailing across her skin, that hand open upon her breast—

The thought brought heat rushing to her face in a dangerous, revealing flood.

To her relief, his attention was on his hand and not on her. And, just like a man, he was an extremely fidgety patient.

"Can't you work a little faster?" he grouched. "You missed that spot. And that one. Put a little more there. I'm telling you, it itches like a dozen demons. And don't forget between the fingers."

He spread his fingers to show what he meant. She couldn't help wincing. If they swelled much more, they'd look like sausages about to burst from their casings.

"Had to be my sword hand, of course," he muttered, turning it so she could tend to the blessedly few pricks on the back. "That stuff feels like I don't know what, and the smell's enough to turn your stomach inside out, but whatever it is, thank God, it's helping."

Despite his protests, she bound his hand in lint, wrapping it around and around until it looked like a ball at the end of his arm. To keep him from scratching, she would have said if she could speak, but that was just an excuse.

The way she figured it, he'd be less likely to get into trouble if he was one hand short of a pair. He couldn't even try to slip into her bed— she'd smell him coming from halfway across the room, even in her sleep. That stuff was foul enough to rouse the dead.

Besides, this way he wouldn't get any of that unguent on her quilt. She didn't have time to wash the thing a second time.

And thinking of quilts and beds . . .

She yawned—she couldn't help herself—and started gathering up the scraps of lint. By the time she'd finished putting it all away and washed her face and hands for bed, he was looking a little cheerier but not the tiniest bit repentant.

"Still beats me why you'd be knitting with nettles," he said. He was hunched in the chair, nursing his swaddled hand and watching while she banked the fire. "At least that godawful goo seems to work. My hand feels better, despite the stink. I'll have to tell Dr. Arbustis about it when we get back to Avalon. No, better yet, you can show him how to make it up. Doesn't hurt to have a good supply on hand. You never know when you'll need it."

She nodded, too tired to pay much attention, and bent to fluff up the sorry excuse for a pillow that he'd been sitting on before he got bigger ideas. He wouldn't be comfortable, lying on the floor with nothing but the pillow and that quilt around him, but at least he'd be warm. The embers would burn for hours.

When she straightened, he stood up, too. His yawn gave her a great view of an excellent set of teeth. He stretched, yawned again, then sleepily scratched his belly.

She had to force herself to look away so she wouldn't be tempted to watch the lazy play of those long fingers over that gorgeous stomach.

Evidently she wasn't as discreet as she'd thought, for he stopped abruptly, a dangerous gleam in his eye, and gave her a lazy, knowing grin.

"If you're wondering whether we'll both fit in the bed, you should know that I sleep on my side. And I'm *very* good at cuddling."

The sensuous promise in his voice sent an involuntary shiver down her spine.

Then Arianne stiffened, indignant. Presumptuous beast! Oh, if only she could speak! She'd give him such an earful that his head would be ringing for a week.

Failing words, she settled for kicking his pillow across the floor. It landed at his feet with a dull thump and a sigh of escaping air and feathers.

He frowned at the pillow, then at her. "What the—?"

Chin up and hands on her hips, she eyed him coldly.

Comprehension dawned. "No! Absolutely not! I'm a king. I do *not* sleep on the floor!"

She snorted.

"I don't! And anyway," he added balefully, "what would you know about kings?"

They're generally old and bald, and the ones that aren't fat are skinny and stoop-shouldered and half blind.

And not one of them looks like you.

That's what she wanted to say. Instead, she bit her tongue and glared at him. He glared right back. And then he leaned toward her, brow furrowed, eyes pinched into threatening slits.

"I am *not* sleeping on the floor."

She shrugged, deliberately provoking, and nudged her chair to show that he could sleep there if he didn't like the floor. And there was always the shed out back if that didn't suit. His horse might like the company.

For all she cared, he could sleep in the forest, but he was *not* sleeping in her bed.

He came a step closer. "I absolutely"— another step—"am *not*"—and another—"sleeping on the floor."

By this time he was looming over her. She had to tilt her head back to meet his angry gaze, but she hadn't budged an inch.

He took a deep breath, then slowly let it out, clearly fighting for control.

"Now, mind you," he said in what he probably thought was a reasonable tone, "I don't mind sharing. I'm perfectly happy to do it, no matter how small the bed. But I am *not*—"

He never finished the thought. He'd taken one more step, and that was one step too many as far as Arianne was concerned.

Mouth open, he looked down to where the point of her knitting needle pressed against his stomach.

She poked a little harder. As a weapon, it wasn't much, but at least he got the point. So to speak.

He protested nonetheless.

"Now, look here—"

She took a step forward; he took one back.

"Can't we talk this over?"

Another step forward, another one back.

"Really, it's such a silly thing to be quarreling over. If you'd just—"

He grabbed for the needle, but she was quicker. She spun away from him, snatched the pillow off the floor, and flung it at his chest. He caught it with both hands, then winced and shook his bandaged appendage.

She didn't bother to offer any sympathy, just shoved past him and crossed to her bed. The bed she would be sleeping in alone, thank you very much!

Behind her, she could hear him take a step toward her. Without glancing back, she waved the needle in warning. He froze where he was.

"Well, damn!"

Her sentiments exactly.

Still clutching the pillow, Richard watched in

stunned disbelief as she turned down the quilt on the bed.

Sleep on the floor? She was making him sleep on the *floor?*

The question was purely rhetorical. He already knew the answer.

All right, then, he'd annoy the hell out of her by watching her undress.

She outmaneuvered him there, too. With a last defiant glance over her shoulder, she pulled off her shoes, then climbed into bed still fully dressed and pulled the quilt up to her chin.

With no light except that cast by the dying fire, she virtually disappeared in the shadows so that all he could see was a lump. A lump in a bed that he, it was clear, would not be sharing with her.

Damn!

Richard turned back to the fire, then, deprived of any other release for his feelings, slammed the pillow to the floor.

The dust and feathers that billowed out of it made him sneeze.

Damn, damn, *damn!*

He glared at the thing. It lay there, mocking him.

All he had to do was climb into that bed with her. Forget the knitting needle. As a weapon, it was laughable. If she hadn't been so quick, he'd have easily taken it from her.

What could she do to stop him? He was bigger than she was. Stronger and tougher and trained in unarmed combat.

The trouble was, it galled his pride to think that it should come to that. He'd never approved of forcing a woman, had, in fact, severely punished any of his men who'd tried. On the other hand, he'd personally never run into the problem before. Not once had a female turned him down. Not once! Yet here he was, and there *she* was, and what in the hell was he going to do?

He eyed the pillow grimly, then cursed and gave in to the inevitable.

Unwrapping the quilt from around his waist, he gave it one good shake, then spread it out on the floor in front of the fire. The floor, he discovered, was just as hard as it looked.

Punching the pillow a couple of times produced no improvement in its shape or softness but did relieve a little of his frustration. Not much, but a little.

Grumpily, he rolled himself up in the quilt, shut his eyes, and tried to summon sleep.

His people were bound to find him tomorrow. A couple days' ride—with no stopping for a hunt, no matter how big the hart!—and he'd be home again, with hot baths and wine and his own bed. And women who knew when to count themselves lucky.

Maybe, he thought as he drifted into sleep despite the hardness of his accommodations, maybe he'd leave her here after all. That would show her.

Chapter Five

Arianne was never at her best in the morning. Which was a nice way of saying that she was clumsy, taciturn, and grumpy. And that was on a good day.

Today was not a good day.

She hadn't slept well, and the reason for it wasn't hard to find—he was lying on the floor in front of the hearth, head pillowed on one arm, sound asleep. All she could see of him was a spiky shock of black hair sticking out one end of the shabby quilt and a bare, oversized foot sticking out the other. The rest of him was nothing but one massive, masculine lump.

Arianne watched without breathing, eager yet also reluctant for him to wake. She'd had her doubts a moment ago, but with a slight motion the blanket had tautened over his hips and thighs in a way that dispelled every one of them—beneath the lumpy quilt, the man was still stark naked.

She did not want to deal with a naked man first thing in the morning. In fact, she didn't want to deal with a naked man at any time of the day. The only reason she was staring, she told herself, was so she'd be warned to look away if he happened to throw off his blanket before he remembered she was there.

The very thought made her heart skip a beat.

Maybe she could bury her head under the covers until he went away. She hadn't slept well last night. She could use a little extra rest. The temptation was almost overwhelming, but rather than give in, she threw back the covers and swung her feet to the floor.

The lump on the floor stirred, drawing the quilt more tightly around him.

When he showed no additional signs of rousing, she let out her breath and tried not to feel disappointed.

Watching for any sign of movement in front of the hearth, she went about her morning chores, scowling at him so fiercely that he probably felt it even in his sleep.

Her gaze traced every inch of him, from the spiky hair that made her fingers itch to smooth it into reasonable order, over the high mound of shoulder, and down his side. She lingered on the faint, firm curve of his buttocks under the blanket and the even fainter curves marking the solid muscle of his thighs before sliding down to that one bare foot.

The foot twitched.

Arianne blushed and hastily looked away. She was as bad as Drucilla, Sir William Montgomery's eldest daughter, who was forever ogling the knights. And any other eligible male under the age of fifty, if it came to that.

She, however, had never ogled the knights. Or anyone else, really. Really.

Well, not often, anyway. And never, ever when she thought someone else would see.

Blame her current indiscretion, then, on the dreams that had teased and tormented her all night long. Lustful, heated dreams unlike any she'd ever had before.

Just thinking about the dreams made her blush.

It was his fault, of course. If he hadn't kissed her, hadn't made her think the unthinkable, this never would have happened.

Well, it wouldn't happen again. She'd feed him breakfast, then kick him out to find his way home as best he could. For herself, she had work to do. She didn't want her brothers to be swans forever, and all because she'd wasted time on a stranger. As it was, she'd have double duty today because she was almost out of bread and soup—Richard had eaten enough last night to keep her fed for days—and she'd have to bake and cook some more, as well as catch up on the on the knitting she hadn't done last night.

Not to mention the state of her floor.

Sighing at the thought, she picked up the bucket by the door, pitched the water he'd soaked his hand in outside, and went to fetch more.

It was a beautiful day, at least. The ground was still so wet that it squished beneath her feet, but the sky—what little she could see of it through the tall, dense trees—was a brilliant blue, and the breeze was sweet and mild. Everything looked newly washed and fresh, full of sparkle and promise. The sound of a lark somewhere nearby made her smile in spite of her woes.

As soon as he was gone, she told herself, she'd set about repairing the damage to her larder and her floors; then she'd take her chair and her knitting and move outdoors for the rest of the day. She would finish Rheidwn's shirt and get a good start on the next. If she really concentrated, and no one else decided to drop in uninvited, she ought to be able to knit two shirts a week. And it would go faster as she went down the line, of course, because the shirts wouldn't have to be so big.

Twelve shirts, two a week. Her shoulders

drooped. Even working her hardest, she'd need six weeks to finish.

Six weeks without so much as a soul to talk to. Her father must be mad with worrying, but what could she do? Rheidwn had said she couldn't go home till they were free of the spell that entrapped them, and they couldn't be free until she'd knitted enough shirts for all of them.

And then there was the problem of food. The cottage's former occupant had left little in the cupboards, and if Arianne was going to make the supplies stretch the full six weeks, she was going to have to be very, very careful about what she ate.

It didn't bear thinking about.

All right, then, she told herself firmly, she wouldn't think about it. Crying had never yet put spilt milk back in the bucket. She'd learned that lesson when her mother died all those years ago; it wouldn't do for her to forget it now.

Resolutely squaring her shoulders, she filled her bucket at the well, then headed back for the cottage. She hadn't gone a dozen steps when she stopped abruptly in her tracks.

He was up.

Dressed in hose and torn shirt—both dry, she was relieved to note, and therefore *not* clinging to his body—he was standing in the open doorway, yawning and stretching and scratching his ribs one-handedly. His hair was still rumpled, there was a pillow crease on his cheek, his jaw was dark with a day's worth of beard, and he looked . . .

She sucked in air, fighting to breathe.

He looked absolutely marvelous.

He did not, however, look happy to see her.

At the sight of her, his perfect mouth turned down in an aggrieved scowl.

"Well?" he said, in a sexy, raspy, early-morning sort of voice. "Aren't you going to ask me how I slept?"

Arianne shifted her grip on the bucket handle and wondered whether it would be smarter to fling its contents at him and run, or if the sight of him in newly soaked undergarments wouldn't just make things that much worse.

"No?" he said when she made no effort to answer. "You aren't going to ask? Well, let me tell you anyway. I didn't. Sleep, that is. I tossed and I turned and I swear I bruised every bone in my body, but I did *not* sleep. It's a wonder I can even stand, as stiff as I am right now. In fact, I wouldn't be surprised if I were crippled for life, and it will be all your fault if I am."

And she'd thought *she* was grumpy before breakfast!

Head high, Arianne pushed past him into the cottage. He turned to follow, clearly determined to have his say whether she wanted to listen or not.

"Your floor is the most damnably uncomfortable thing I've slept on in my life, and let me tell you, I've had more than my fair share of uncomfortable beds!"

Stirring the embers in the fireplace into life, she tossed on some kindling, then swung the kettle over the flames to get the water boiling.

Richard hovered behind her, clearly perturbed.

"I've slept on campaign cots and grass and pine needles and bare ground as often as not when I'm off fighting wars and dragons and whatnot. But not once have I been as miserable as I was last night. Not once!"

Assured that the fire was going well, she turned her attention to breakfast. Not that there was much choice—bread and porridge, and lucky to have that, if you asked her, though *he* wouldn't think so, guaranteed.

He trailed across the room after her.

"And that pillow! Though how you have the nerve to call it a pillow beats me. Three feathers and a sack, *I* call it, and that's being generous. I'd have done better to sleep in the straw with my horse."

If she'd known he would complain *this* much, she would have brought the horse indoors and let *him* have the straw.

Fortunately, his grumbling complaints were

growing weaker, whether because they'd produced no results or he lacked the energy to keep at them, she didn't know. And didn't care, come to that.

Pulling out a small canister from the cupboard, she set about making the one thing that was likely to turn him human again.

Richard scratched his chin and glared at her back.

How the devil did she manage to look so spruce and chipper at such an ungodly hour of the morning? It wasn't right. It wasn't decent. It wasn't *normal*.

He'd heard her get up, of course—he hadn't been lying when he'd said he hadn't slept well, though his complaints about the floor were a bit exaggerated—but he'd forced himself to lie as still as he could, feigning the sleep that had eluded him most of the night.

It was all her fault, of course. It wasn't the floor but thoughts of her that had kept him awake—thoughts how of she'd tasted when he'd kissed her, the way she moved, and the fire in her eyes when she was angry. Not content to plague him when he was awake, she'd had the nerve to haunt his dreams, as well.

They'd been fantastic dreams, hot and lusty and maybe just a tad depraved, but they hadn't been very restful. Twice he'd awakened in the middle of one, as hard and aching as if she'd been lying there right beside him.

He hadn't had those kinds of dreams for years, not since he was a boy and his voice was beginning to break and his beard beginning to grow.

Frowning at the thought, and with nothing else to do for the moment—God knew how long it would take Harry and the rest to find themselves and catch up with him—he slumped down at the table and glumly watched her work.

Five minutes later, still frowning, he took the steaming mug she shoved under his nose without a word of warning.

"What's this?" He sniffed the contents, then, suddenly hopeful, sat up straighter. "Coffee?"

She nodded.

"Mmm." His frown melted into a look of satisfaction. He took a cautious sip, held it on his tongue a moment, then happily swallowed it. "I usually have ale."

As far as Arianne could tell, the complaint was more for form's sake than for any real objection to the beverage, because he didn't pursue the matter, just took another couple of healthy swallows, then got up and ambled to the open door to squint out at the morning.

"Going to be a good day, looks like," he informed her, just as if she hadn't been out to see it before. "It'll take hours for the ground to dry, but at least the rain has stopped and the sun's come out. That's something, anyway."

Sipping her own coffee appreciatively, Ari-

113

anne studied the man who'd played such a vivid role in her dreams last night.

King or not, he was an impressive creature. She'd even forgive him his morning's grumpiness. She wasn't particularly sweet-tempered first thing, either. Even her father, who was the sweetest of men, was cross as a bear before breakfast.

Whatever he was, Richard wasn't sweet. But he *was* desirable. Arrogant, presumptuous, and infinitely desirable.

Last night he'd infuriated her, but this morning, in the bright light of day, she was willing to admit that some of her fury, at least, had been directed at herself and her reactions to him.

Heaven knew, she'd indulged in a little flirtation on occasion, too. Nothing serious, not like what he'd been thinking of last night, but not totally innocent, either. Until last night, she'd never realized just how easily things could get out of hand, or how much she might want them to. The solitude of this cottage in the woods had something to do with it, no doubt. In her father's court, she was never left alone with a male above the age of ten or so. Except for her brothers, and they didn't count.

But last night . . .

No, it was only fair that she shoulder some of the blame for what had almost happened between them last night. Not all of it, since he'd been the one to get things started, but some of it. Enough so that, while she didn't intend to forgive Richard for his presumption, she wasn't going to belabor it, either.

It was unsettling, this intense awareness of someone else. It was also rather . . . intriguing. Tempting, even.

The trouble was, she didn't have time for intriguing or tempting.

And she shouldn't waste time in daydreams, either.

Enough, she told herself. Get breakfast, then get to work.

But before she could follow through on those good intentions, he turned and looked at her across the room.

Her breath caught. She'd swear her heart skipped a beat.

He looked like a pirate, wild and dangerous, a man who had no place in her ordinary life. And she wanted him, suddenly. Really *wanted* him, as a woman wants a man, and as she had never wanted anyone else before.

"I'm going to get dressed," he informed her, as casually as if she saw him in this disgraceful state of undress every morning. "Then I have to feed and water my horse. Will breakfast be ready when I get back?"

She nodded and clasped her hands in front of her to stop their sudden trembling.

There was that smile again. The lopsided, appealing one that showed the dimple in his

cheek and made her heart start tripping dou-
ble-time.

A little ball of heat settled in her stomach

He really was an extraordinarily good-looking man.

And she was a fool to notice.

Fortified with a second cup of coffee each and
cheered by finding, after she'd carefully
unwound the bandages, that his hand had
returned to normal, they managed to make it
through breakfast on reasonably courteous
terms. He'd wrinkled up his nose at the bowl
of porridge she'd set in front of him, and for
an instant she'd been tempted to toss it into
his lap. Considering some of their previous
exchanges, however, that little disagreement
wasn't even worth remembering.

It helped that she'd kept her attention glued
to her bowl and tried hard not to think about
him, sitting there on the other side of the table,
close enough that she could have reached
across and touched him, if she'd dared. She
hadn't dared.

Despite his lack of enthusiasm for the breakfast selection, he finished quickly, then thanked
her with exquisite courtesy. So courteously, in
fact, that she looked up quickly to see if he was
suffering a sudden fever.

"I'm going to shave and wash," he informed

her, shoving back from the table. "I hope you won't mind if I claim some of your hot water?"

She shook her head.

He retrieved the washbasin himself, poured the water, even grabbed a towel from the rope he'd strung last night rather than waiting for her to do it for him.

Much more of this and she'd get suspicious, which is what came of having twelve brothers, all of them capable of the most angelic behavior while privately contemplating the most outrageous crimes.

Arianne shook off her doubts. She was being foolish. Next thing you knew, she'd be accusing him of plotting to abduct her.

With an excess of clatter and bustle, she gathered up the breakfast dishes and dumped them in the bucket she used for washing up. Out of the corner of her eye, she saw him pull one arm out of his tunic sleeve, then the other, then do the same with his shirt. The garments bunched at the top of his belt, empty sleeves hanging down untidily.

Since he had to leave soon, Arianne decided, it was nice to have one last good look at that broad, bare chest of his.

The thought drove her back to her dishes, flushing in embarrassment. Despite the sound of splashing, followed by the steady *scrape-scrape* as he shaved off his beard with his knife,

Arianne resolutely kept her head down and her attention on the dishes. If she was lucky, he'd never notice that it was taking her three times longer to do them than it ought.

A sudden loud shout from outside shattered the quiet.

"Ho, there! Anybody home?"

Startled, Arianne dropped the empty porridge pot. What in the world . . . ? A whole week without anyone passing through, and suddenly the cottage might as well have been in the center of town.

She started for the door, but the sight of Richard, naked to the waist, distracted her.

He raised his head from the washbasin. Water dripped from his chin to snag on the curling hair on his chest, glistening in the bright morning light streaming through the cottage windows.

For a moment he stood there, head cocked, calmly listening to the ruckus without. Then he glanced at her, and his mouth curved in a faint, rather smug little smile. He didn't bother to explain, however, just calmly kept on shaving.

Arianne wrenched her gaze away and went to open the door.

For a moment, she wondered if she was dreaming. Half a hundred mounted men filled the small clearing in front of the cottage, and all of them were staring straight at her.

She blinked, rubbed her eyes, and looked again.

They were still there. Every single one of them.

They didn't have to say a word—she already knew what it was they wanted. Only a king would have such a large and anxious retinue out looking for him.

Richard, it seemed, had been telling the truth after all.

As she scanned the crowd, she couldn't help noting how well-dressed and well-armed they all were, or how fine their horses were and how rich the animals' caparisons.

Montavia couldn't mount such an impressive display if it tried. Nor could Batch or Dain or Millersville-on-the-Marsh or anyone else she knew of. Not without bankrupting the treasury, anyway.

No kingdom could. Except Avalon. Only it, of all the monarchies in all the land, was rich enough and powerful enough to send out such a force for a mere day's hunting.

And she'd made their king sleep on the floor last night.

Thank heavens she couldn't say a word. She'd have hated to have to apologize for having doubted him.

Gathering her dignity about her, Arianne stepped out onto the cottage's low stone step.

At she did so, the tall, good-looking fellow at the front of the crowd swung down from his saddle and swept her an elegant bow.

119

"Madame, your pardon for the disturbance. We wondered—that is—" He cleared his throat and tried again. "You haven't by any chance seen a man wandering around loose, have you?

"Tall fellow," he added helpfully when she remained silent. "About this high. Black hair, blue eyes. Good-looking, too, though I'd appreciate it if you didn't repeat that in his hearing. Walks with a bit of a swagger."

Arianne glanced behind her helplessly. With the sharp contrast between the sunlit clearing and the shadowed interior of the cottage, she couldn't see a thing beyond the open door.

The blond knight came nearer. This close, she could see the lines of worry in his face and at the corners of his eyes.

"Please tell me you've seen him," he pleaded. "We've misplaced him, I'm afraid, and we'd rather like him back."

As if conjured by a genie, Richard stepped through the door and into the sunlight, calmly drying his face on a towel. He hadn't bothered to dress.

At the sight of him, a great roar of relief went up from the throng. "The king! The king is here!" they cried. "Long live King Jim!"

The golden-haired knight stopped dead in his tracks. "Damn you, Richard!"

Unperturbed by the commotion, Richard swiped the last of the water from the corner of his jaw, tossed the towel over his shoulder, and casually leaned against the door frame.

"Hullo, Harry."

Harry did not look pleased. In fact, now that he'd found his friend in one piece, he looked downright annoyed.

"Damn me for a fool! Should've known you'd find a dry roof and a comfortable bed while I spent the night slogging through this damned soggy forest looking for you."

"Of course you should've," said Richard amiably. "That's what you get for getting lost like that. Next time, maybe you'll pay attention to where you're going and whom you're supposed to be with."

"Me! Lost!" Harry exclaimed, indignant. "*You're* the one who got lost! What in the devil possessed you, wandering off like that?"

"Your Majesty!" exclaimed one elegantly garbed but muddy courtier, rushing forward and falling to his knees. "Forgive us! We did not mean to abandon you!"

"To our shame, Sire!" added another, equally distraught. "Each of us thought you were with another. We wouldn't have followed that hart had we known you were lost. Truly we would not!"

"Er, yes, quite," said His Majesty, looking embarrassed.

Arianne ducked her head to hide her smile. At least the truth was safe with her; she *couldn't* tell his men that he'd fallen off his horse and gotten left behind like some silly page just learning to ride.

"But, Sire! How can you forgive us? Riding away like that and leaving you to the mercy of the wolves and the witches and . . . and what-not."

"You're not injured, are you? You didn't suffer any harm?"

"No, no harm," His Majesty assured them, reluctantly straightening.

"You're not cold?"

"Or fevered?"

"No inflammation of the chest?"

"You haven't—"

"*I'm perfectly all right!*" roared His Majesty.

A sudden nervous hush fell over the crowd. Half a hundred pairs of eyes suddenly grew round and stared at him.

"Really," said His Majesty, a little more calmly this time. "I'm fine."

The crowd went wild.

They cheered and shouted and sent up another enthusiastic round or two of "Long Live the King!" Eventually the echoes began having echoes.

Arianne, mindful of her dignity, barely stopped herself from clapping her hands over her ears to shut out the noise.

"Can't say I'm surprised," said Harry. "If you spent the night with this prize little piece"—he flashed her a wickedly brilliant smile— "you had a much more enjoyable time than the rest of us, I promise you that!"

"I di—"

Richard caught her warning glare before he could finish. His mouth worked as if he'd taken a bite of something vile, then he coughed, cleared his throat, and said, rather sharply, "Mind your manners, Harry."

He deliberately avoided looking at her when he said it.

As if to cover his near fumble, he turned to the muddy-kneed courtiers, who were watching him with the ecstatic look of hounds who'd just found a master they'd thought lost forever.

"I'm damned glad to see you all, and I'm grateful you took the trouble to find me, but if you wouldn't mind . . ."

"Anything, Sire!"

"Anything!"

"My horse is in a shed around back. I'd appreciate it if—"

They didn't give him a chance to finish before they were off, each one more eager to do his bidding than the next.

He'd *appreciate* it! Arianne thought, disgusted. A little courtesy was all to the good, but where had it been when he'd demanded to be let in last night? Demanded comfort and bedcovers and whatnot.

She was starting to feel better about making him sleep on the floor.

"So, what in the hell happened to you?" Harry demanded.

"What—"

Richard held up a hand. "Why don't we go inside first? It's a little, uh, quieter there."

Private, he meant. As in, no one else would hear his confession about having fallen off his horse and gotten lost in the woods. Arianne could spot a defensive maneuver when she saw one, and there was no one more defensive than a male out to protect his masculine pride.

He gestured to the assembled multitude to indicate they could take a break, then, without so much as a glance in her direction, stepped back into the cottage.

Just as if he owned the place, she thought sourly, right before she remembered that she didn't own it, either.

Still frowning, she started to follow and almost found herself jammed in the doorway, shoulder-to-shoulder with Harry.

He glanced at her, clearly as surprised as she was, then, belatedly remembering his manners, stepped back and gestured for her to enter. "Please. After you."

Head high, back stiff as a poker, Arianne stepped into the cottage with Harry right behind.

She immediately wished she hadn't.

She'd forgotten about the unmade bed with its tumbled covers and the sheets she'd pulled out at the corners with all her tossing and turning. She'd also forgotten that Richard had already put away the pillow he'd used and uncharacteristically folded up the quilt and set it neatly atop the trunk at the foot of her bed, leaving absolutely nothing to indicate where he had spent the night.

"Nice bed," said Harry.

Arianne was mortified.

Harry was oblivious. "Damn you, Richard!" he said, turning on his friend. "I should have known. I'm out all night in that bloody storm, looking for your dead body, while *you*—"

Richard grinned. "My dead body?"

"That's right. I told the others you'd probably found a nice, cozy tavern with a wench or two to warm your bed, but Thurgood was convinced you were dead, and you know how he fusses. Worse than an old hen with her chicks, that one. So there was nothing for it but we all had to go out looking for you instead of staying put in camp and letting you come looking for us." He 'shook his head, disgusted. "I really should have known."

"Speaking of Thurgood . . ."

"He's back at camp." Without so much as a by-your-leave, Harry dragged Arianne's only chair up to the table. "I tied him to a tent pole before we started out this morning."

"You what?"

Harry shrugged. "No help for it. Another few hours of listening to him fret, and I'd have strangled him for sure."

As if to underline his lack of concern for the poor fellow named Thurgood, Harry sank down in the chair and propped his feet on the table, then smiled at Arianne with the cocky confidence of a man who knew where he stood with women.

"How about taking pity on a fellow, luv, and giving us some wine?"

For answer, Arianne walked over and, with the tips of her thumb and forefinger, grabbed hold of the toe of his boot, swung his foot out over the empty air, and pointedly let it go.

"Hey! What—?"

One look at her face and Harry rapidly removed the other foot from the tabletop and sat up straight in the chair. She brushed the bits of mud he'd left into his lap.

Harry stared at the mud in his lap. Then he looked up, mouth agape, and stared at her.

"She hasn't got any wine," Richard informed him helpfully.

Harry turned a horrified stare on his king. "No wine?"

"No. And no ale, either."

"Damn," said Harry with feeling. He swallowed hard, digesting the bad news, then turned back and stared at her some more.

The more he stared, the more Arianne's fury grew. He let his gaze slide down her body, then slowly dragged it up again. A wide smile lit his face as he met her furious gaze.

He cocked a knowing eyebrow at Richard. "As I said, I should've known."

Suddenly, the king was not amused. "Your trouble, Harry," he said coldly, "is that you don't know half as much as you think you do."

Arianne glared at both of them.

Harry frowned. "What's the matter? Cat got her tongue?"

Just as if she was deaf *and* an idiot, thought Arianne, indignant. She glared at him some more as he looked at her breasts.

"She doesn't talk," said Richard.

"What? Never?"

"No, never says a word."

Harry opened his mouth, closed it, and stared at her. Then he turned and stared at Richard.

"You're not— That is— You wouldn't, would you? Really?"

"Wouldn't what?" said Richard, confused.

"Marry her?"

"*What?*"

Arianne gasped.

"Yesterday. Remember?" Harry was starting to look worried. "You swore you'd marry the first woman you found who didn't talk your ears off. On your honor, you said."

"Oh." Richard looked distinctly uncomfortable all of a sudden. "Well, uh, that was just a figure of speech. You know how it is."

Arianne relaxed again.

"But—"

"That isn't, uh, exactly what I had in mind."

"Oh?" said Harry, looking blank.

Richard rolled his eyes.

"*Oh!*" said Harry, and abruptly he looked a good deal cheerier. "Well, that's all right then, isn't it?"

Arianne looked from one to the other, then back again. Somewhere along the line, she'd missed something. Something important.

Trouble was, she hadn't the slightest idea what.

Chapter Six

In the end, Arianne served them tea and the last of her bread, much as it annoyed her to do it. While the two of them sat there laughing over Harry's mishaps of the night before, she knitted furiously.

Why didn't Richard go? His men were out there waiting for him. Why didn't he just *leave?*

And when he did, what then?

She'd be alone again, with at least six more weeks of work ahead of her. She wouldn't mind so much if she could send her father a message. Richard could arrange to have it delivered—he owed her that much, at least—but was it safe to write?

Not one word, her brothers had warned her. No talking. No singing. They hadn't mentioned writing, but what if she wasn't supposed to write, either?

She'd couldn't risk it.

And then there was the matter of food.

Between them, Richard and Harry had finished off a week's worth of bread. She wasn't sure she had enough flour left to cover six more weeks of baking, even if only for herself. What if she ran out too soon? And what about the few shriveled carrots and onions and turnips she'd found in the shed? She could always scrounge for roots and berries in the woods, but that would take precious time from her knitting. And what if she couldn't find enough?

Her thoughts spun around, keeping time with the rapid clicking of her needles, and led her absolutely nowhere.

It was Richard's hand upon her arm that brought her back to the present. Harry, she saw, was already gone.

Reluctantly, she put her knitting aside and got to her feet.

"We have to leave now," Richard said.

She nodded. Of course he did. She ought to be grateful he hadn't stayed longer than one night.

Why, then, did she suddenly feel so desolate?

"Have to get back to pack up camp then get on the road." He gave an embarrassed grin. "I imagine Thurgood's a bit impatient by now."

She nodded again. Poor Thurgood.

"Harry thinks if we hurry we might be out of the woods before dark."

This time she didn't bother to nod. It would be nice to be out of the woods, she thought wistfully.

"You're coming with us, of course."

He said it just the way he might have said "nice day" or "the pot roast's really tasty." As if he expected her and everyone else to agree with him automatically.

"Just point out what you want to take, and I'll have my men pack it up."

He frowned at the unmade bed. "Except for the furniture. It's too heavy, and you won't need it anyway. Actually, you don't need anything except what you're wearing. Clothes, shoes, ladies' whatnots—we have all that. And the castle's already fully furnished."

Go with him? To Avalon? Forget about the shortage of flour and carrots and turnips? Stop worrying about what lurked in the forest, waiting to pounce? Be free to spend her time working on her brothers' shirts instead of everything else?

"You'll like Avalon," he assured her cheerfully. "There's plenty of room in the castle and all the food you can eat. You won't have to bake or cook or sweep or . . . or make the bed or anything if you don't want to. *Much* better than staying here by yourself."

Arianne's stomach churned. She wanted to go. Oh, how much she wanted to go! But what about her brothers? How would they know where to look for her if she left?

"I'll get you a maid. Two, if you like, and all the pretty gowns you want. You'll love the gardens. There're dozens and dozens of 'em, and I hear they're at their best this time of year. Besides— What? Why are you shaking your head like that? What's the matter? Don't you *want* to go?"

She couldn't quite bring herself to lie, so she stopped shaking her head and stared at him instead.

"You're not worried about what folks might think, are you? Because if you are . . ."

That was safe. She shook her head.

"Good, good. Trust me. There's no reason to be worried."

He thought about it for a minute, clearly at a loss.

"If you don't mind going, and you're not afraid of what people think, what's the problem?"

Arianne barely kept from stamping her foot in frustration. Why did he have to make this so hard? Why couldn't he just accept a simple *no?*

"Is it Harry? No? No. Hmm."

His noble brow furrowed as he struggled to grasp the workings of the female mind.

"Is it . . . me?"

Shivers ran down her spine from just thinking of his kiss. She didn't dare dwell on what he'd done in her dreams.

"Well? Is it?"

Arianne shook her head. It *definitely* wasn't him.

Or maybe it was, a little. A man like him—

No, don't think about that, either. Think about her brothers. They were what mattered right now.

"Don't be a fool! You can't stay here like this, all alone in this damned, dark forest. It isn't safe, not without someone to protect you. Besides, I don't want you to stay. I— You— Damn it, you just can't!"

For answer, she set her jaw, crossed her arms in front of her, and glared right back.

"I see," he said stiffly, offended. "That's your choice, of course."

It seemed to cost him dearly to say it.

"That's it, then."

But he didn't move.

Reluctantly, fighting the urge to throw herself into his arms and beg him not to leave her, she extended her hand to shake.

He pointedly ignored it.

Oh, well, she thought, and swallowed down the sudden ache in her throat.

He didn't look back when he walked out the door.

Immediately upon his leaving, the cottage seemed twice as big and three times as empty as it had before he'd come. Standing there, listening to the silence, Arianne thought her heart would explode, it was pounding so hard.

Outside she heard an eager stir of men and horses. The sound of it was like an arrow piercing her breast, sharp and final.

She blinked back tears and glanced at the open door. At least she could wave good-bye.

He must have been watching for her, because the instant she appeared he called a halt and pulled his horse around to face her.

Half a hundred men fell silent, waiting. Arianne had eyes for only one.

Their gazes locked across the muddy clearing.

So many questions, but where, she wondered desperately, was the right answer to them?

Suddenly a shadow swooped across the clearing, and then another and another. Shading her eyes against the sunlight, Arianne looked up and saw a dozen wild swans filling the air above her.

The largest one dipped low—she could feel the brush of air from his wings as he flew past—then swooped up to join the others. Twice they circled the cottage, then climbed higher and, assembling themselves into an arrow formation, flew off in the direction in which Richard had been heading.

Arianne watched until the last little swan was out of sight, and then she looked at Richard and laughed.

The grim look on his face vanished beneath a wide, triumphant grin.

"Someone bring me a horse!" he yelled. "The lady is coming with us."

* * *

She insisted on bringing the baskets of nettles, of course. Four of Richard's men gingerly carried them out, then even more gingerly covered them and tied them on behind their horses. Judging from their expressions, they'd rather have brought the pots and pans.

Rheidwn's shirt she bundled into her apron, then watched while it was stuffed into a bag and tied on the front of her saddle.

Over Richard's objections, she straightened the bed and swept out the worst of the mud that had been tracked across the floor, then made him smile by handing him the jar of unguent that had proved so effective against his hives.

As she pulled the cottage door closed behind her, she felt as if a weight had suddenly been lifted from her shoulders. Her brothers were still swans, and she still had eleven shirts to go, but somehow everything didn't seem quite so impossible as it had a day before.

Richard was standing on the stoop, waiting for her and looking smug and impatient, both. "That's it? That's everything?"

She nodded.

"You're sure?"

"Don't badger the girl," Harry said, strolling up. "A gem like her wants careful handling and a bit more respect. Don't you, luv?" he added, grinning and chucking her under the chin.

135

Her eyes narrowed, but he was impervious to subtle threats.

"Since we're going to be traveling together," he added, a teasing glint in his eyes, "it occurs to me that it might help to know your name."

Arianne stared at him, nonplused. Judging from his expression, the problem hadn't occurred to Richard, either.

"I'm Harry, of course. Actually, I'm Harold David Jellison Smith, Earl of Sunnyvale, Viscount Wiggins. At your service." He swept her an exaggerated bow. "And you are . . . ?"

Bristling like a dog guarding its bone, Richard deliberately stepped between them. "I told you, Harry," he said through gritted teeth, "she doesn't speak. Ever. Not a word."

"So you don't know her name."

"I didn't say that." Richard glanced at her, a look of panic in his eyes.

Her eyebrows arched. This ought to be interesting.

"It's uh . . . it's Goldie." He turned back to Harry. "Her name's Goldie."

"Goldie?" said Harry doubtfully.

Arianne rolled her eyes.

"That's right. What's the matter? Don't you like it?"

"Oh, no! Not at all. Fine name, Goldie. Really." Harry's mustache twitched with the effort to keep from laughing. "Uh . . . that's it? She doesn't have another?"

"No," Richard assured him. "No, that's it. Just . . . Goldie."

He didn't look at her when he said it.

It wasn't hard finding the way out of the wood—they simply followed the trail they'd made coming in—but that didn't mean the going was easy.

Last night's storm had made pudding out of the ground, and fifty shod horses had turned the pudding to a slippery soup. The huge old trees above them blocked out much of the light and grew so close together that it was impossible to see far ahead or to ride abreast to carry on a conversation.

Arianne didn't mind. The Dark Woods didn't seem nearly so menacing when she was surrounded by fifty armed men.

Still, it wasn't long before she started to worry. About her brothers. About whether she'd gathered enough nettles, and if she was making Rheidwn's shirt big enough, and how you put a nettle shirt on a swan, anyway.

Most of all, she worried about Richard and what would happen once they arrived in Avalon. With a few notable exceptions, she'd managed to keep him at a safe distance within the small cottage. She wasn't sure it would be so easy once he was on his own turf.

On the other hand, she was probably making monsters out of mush. A man like Richard must be used to the flattering attentions of any number of beautiful women. With other, more promising flirtations available, he wouldn't waste time on a very ordinary princess from one of the least important and out-of-the-way kingdoms in the land.

Besides, he had his own kingdom to run and no time for princesses, no matter where they came from. He'd probably make sure his housekeeper found her a comfortable guest room and a change of clothes, and that would be the end of that.

A most convenient arrangement, really, when you thought of all the knitting she had to do. So why did it sound so grim?

From the look of him, Richard must have been mulling over equally troublesome thoughts, for he was frowning at the trail in front of him, oblivious to the woods around him. Affairs of state, no doubt, or questions of the treasury.

When a chance thinning of the trees brought her up on his right side and Harry on the left, he blinked like a man suddenly brought back to awareness of his surroundings, then straightened in the saddle.

"Say, Harry?"

Arianne, always fascinated with the workings of a kingdom, leaned closer so she wouldn't miss a word.

"Yeah?"

"I forgot to ask. Did anyone catch that hart?"

* * *

Thurgood, freed from his temporary confinement, was waiting when Richard rode into camp with the others later that afternoon.

Richard evinced hearty cheerfulness. "Thurgood!"

"Your Majesty," said Thurgood reproachfully.

It would have been better, Richard reflected, if he'd come back broken and bleeding. As it was, a quick glance was all Thurgood needed to know that His Majesty had survived but the knit hose had not.

Richard sighed and dismounted.

"I should not have been kept in camp. You might have *needed* me." Thurgood at his most reproachful had eyes as sad as a whipped hound's. "Those cuts, that tear in your clothing. Heaven knows what might have happened, and me not there to help. I'd never have forgiven myself—I'd never have forgiven Master Harry—if I hadn't been there at your time of need."

His canines showed when he said *Harry*.

"I'm sorry for the confusion," Richard said soothingly. "I'm sure I would have been much more comfortable if you'd been there to tend me, but these things happen. You've been tending to me since I was out of the nursery, so you know they do."

He clapped an arm around the old man's shoulder. "I want to introduce you to someone, Thurgood. The lady whose cottage I took

139

shelter in last night is coming back to Avalon with us."

He wouldn't, he decided, say anything about having had to sleep on the floor.

"A lady? With a cottage?" Thurgood gave a disdainful sniff. "Ladies don't live in cottages."

Richard stifled a sigh. There was no one more protective of His Majesty's dignity than Thurgood, or more disapproving of his favorite pleasures.

"A gentle creature, Thurgood, with an extraordinarily kind heart." That was a wild exaggeration but made in a good cause. "If not for her I'd have spent the night out in the cold and the rain and the mud."

Thurgood's jowls quivered. "Where is she?"

A peasant could be forgiven her lowly state if she'd kept His Majesty's precious hide out of the mud.

They found Goldie still on horseback at the edge of the camp, safely out of the path of the men scurrying to take down the tents they'd put up in such a rush the night before.

"Goldie!" Richard strode toward her, Thurgood trailing after him. "I've brought someone I'd like you to meet."

She came down from the saddle gracefully. Her hair was a tangle, her skirts splattered with mud kicked up by the horses' hooves . . . and she looked good enough to send a dozen knights out to do battle for her favors.

Thurgood jarred Richard out of his fascinated perusal by clearing his throat.

Richard sighed. Thurgood was Not Pleased.

The old man wouldn't object to the mud or the tangled locks, but great beauty garbed in a peasant's dress was trouble with a capital *T* in Thurgood's book, and he made sure his master knew it.

"Goldie, meet my manservant, Thurgood. Thurgood, this is Goldie."

"Madame," said Thurgood with awful formality.

Richard had seen duchesses check to see if their petticoats were showing when Thurgood took that frosty tone. Lesser women turned pale and tried to slide out of sight under the table, while chambermaids had been known to take to their beds and not emerge for days. His bow would have made a broomstick look limp.

Goldie merely smiled and graciously extended her hand like a great lady acknowledging an old and trusted servant.

Thurgood blinked, then gingerly took her hand and bowed again, a fraction of an inch lower this time.

The thaw didn't last long. When Thurgood straightened, he was still facing a beauty in bad shoes, and his demeanor showed it even if his face did not.

Harry saved them by strolling up with a wineskin in his hands. "Are you going to stand out here forever, or do you want something to eat?" He grinned and raised the skin. "And drink."

Thurgood, it seemed, on learning the king was approaching, had saved the royal tent from being packed and ordered a meal set out for his return. The big tent stood in the center of the confusion like an island of calm in the midst of a restless sea.

To Arianne, it looked like heaven. After a sleepless night and hours in the saddle, she would have been glad of a tree stump to sit on and a glass of water to drink. To find herself seated in a cushioned camp chair with servants to wait on her and a meal literally fit for a king on the table before her was far more than she had bargained for.

Evidently unharmed by his stint at helping hold up a tent pole, Thurgood insisted on serving them himself. Once the platters of food and bowls of fruit were laid out, he hustled the other servants out of the tent and officiously poured the wine.

Arianne had to struggle to keep from laughing at his punctilious formality. She'd had too much experience with old, loyal servants who had known one from the cradle not to recognize that Thurgood did not approve of her. Nameless strangers in plain gowns should not dine with the king, and that was that. Richard and Harry might lower their standards, but

Thurgood would not. She'd have to do more than show she didn't eat her meal with her knife before Richard's manservant would unbend by so much as an inch.

Not that it mattered. Once at Avalon, she'd probably never see him again.

To Richard's credit, he gave orders for everyone else in the retinue to be fed before he himself settled into the chair that Thurgood held for him.

He rubbed his hands together in satisfaction. "Thurgood, you've outdone yourself."

Harry would have started eating immediately, but Richard held him back. "First, a toast. To Mistress Goldie for her . . . generous hospitality." His eyes teased, daring her to object.

"Hear, hear!" said Harry.

"And," Richard continued, making Harry's hand freeze inches from his lips, "to her soup. Excellent stuff, that soup."

The force of his smile shot straight through her, tingling all the way to her toes.

Thurgood's face turned even more inhumanly expressionless.

Richard set down his goblet and stretched out a hand to lightly touch hers where it rested on the edge of the table.

"I was grateful, you know," he said, "no matter what I might have said at the time."

Arianne ducked her head to hide her reaction to his touch. When he took his hand away she had to fight to keep from rubbing the spot.

143

Conversation lagged while they hungrily worked their way through several kinds of cheeses and dried meats. When they reached the fruit, Richard dismissed Thurgood.

The servant threw a disapproving glance at her but without a word dutifully refilled their goblets and left the tent. Arianne wasn't sorry to see him go.

Harry settled back in his chair, goblet cradled in his hand. "Y'know, Richard, I can't help wondering how you managed to get lost yesterday. I've never known you to get lost before."

Richard's eyebrows drew together. "I wasn't lost. I was simply . . . uh . . . diverted."

Harry grinned. "Me, I'd say the diversion came afterward. But that's not the question," he hastily added. "What I want to know is, how'd you come to be separated from the rest of us? You say you were chasing that hart, and I say *I* was chasing him. Since we ended up going in opposite directions, one of us must have been mistaken. I have fifty other hunters to back me up. What's your excuse?"

The answer came so promptly that Arianne suspected Richard had been asking himself the same question.

"The beast was enchanted."

Slowly, she put down the apple she'd been slicing. *Enchanted?*

"Had to be." Richard thumped the table to emphasize the point. "I *never* get lost, and I *was* chasing that hart. The biggest damned hart I've ever seen in my life. And where does it lead me? Into the Dark Woods. And what did I find there?"

This time he paused and looked around the table, waiting for them to answer. When no one did, he answered himself. "I find a cozy cottage with an incredibly beautiful woman—"

Arianne hastily turned her attention back to the apple, caught between a laugh and a blush at his teasing.

"—who takes me in and patches my wounds," Richard continued: "and feeds and shelters me for the night, then gives me the honor of her company the day after. Now, that had to be magic. Right? *Had* to be."

He settled back in his chair and picked up his goblet. For an instant his gaze met hers, and suddenly his teasing didn't seem to be teasing at all, but something far more dangerous.

Fortunately, Harry chose to take Richard's remarks as a joke. He laughed and leaned over to slap his friend on the arm, and she was able to hide her sudden worry by feigning an intense interest in her apple.

From outside came the restless neighing of a horse.

Harry set down his goblet. "Well, can't leave old Archie to run Avalon forever, I suppose. We'd best get going. Leave it too late, and we won't have any place to sleep tonight either."

"I suppose," Richard said. He didn't look in any hurry to move.

Arianne raised her eyebrows in a silent query.

"Hmm?"

She walked the first two fingers of her right hand across the table toward him.

"How far? How far are we going?" He shrugged. "Don't know. However far we get before it's too dark to go farther, I suppose. Two, three hours' ride, I'd guess."

Her shoulders slumped wearily. She couldn't help it.

His gaze sharpened. "Tired?" At her quick negation, his lips quirked, showing the dimple. "Liar."

For a moment his gaze lingered on her face as though he was trying to hear the words she couldn't say. Then he stood abruptly and threw back the tent flap.

The clearing beyond was nothing but an empty sweep of trampled grass. Everyone was assembled at the far edge, sitting or standing by their mounts, the dozens of packhorses loaded with the dismantled tents, waiting to go. At the king's appearance, there was a sudden stir as a hundred men got ready to ride.

Richard raised a hand, palm out. "Set up the tents again," he shouted. "We're staying here for the night."

That was all. Then he dropped the tent flap

and strolled back to the table and picked up the flagon of wine.

"More wine, Goldie? Harry?" With a contented sigh, he plopped down in his chair and picked up his goblet. "It really is excellent. I'll have to ask Thurgood to make sure the butler gets some more of it."

Beyond the tent, Arianne could hear the sound of tents once again going up on the greensward.

This was the way things ought to be managed, Richard thought, contentedly sipping his wine. A nice dry tent at the end of a long day, with carpets on the ground and a comfortable featherbed awaiting him. A fire in the brazier to keep away the cold. A good meal and good wine. And a beautiful woman to make it all worthwhile.

He'd dined alone with Goldie. Harry had chosen to have his meal with some knights who'd taken advantage of their early stop to get a card game going.

Over dinner, Richard had regaled Goldie with tales of his adventures, and occasional misadventures, making her laugh and her eyes glow in the candlelight.

God, but she was a restful woman to be with. Never a word to interrupt him, not even one slid in edgewise. She listened—really *listened*—and nodded or shook her head in all the right places. Before he knew it, he'd found himself

talking about some of the more vexing problems facing Avalon—that ongoing disagreement with the king of Thrax, the question of
tariffs on the import of spirituous liquors from
those crazy Celts. Every now and then she'd
raised an eyebrow or pursed her lips or given
some sigh that had made him go back and
reconsider what he'd just said. If he didn't
know better, he'd swear she'd spent her life
dealing with the ins and outs of diplomacy and
the management of a royal treasury.

Afterward, while he reviewed the pouch of
dispatches that had come by courier from
Avalon and would go back tomorrow the same
way, she'd sat contentedly by the fire and knitted. He wouldn't have thought it, but the sound
of clicking needles was oddly relaxing.

Now the dispatches were answered, his supper was digesting nicely, and they were alone
with the night stretching ahead of them.
Through the half-parted curtain at the far end
of the tent he could see the camp bed Thurgood had set up for him with its fat feather
mattress and fat feather pillows. Beneath the
soft, thick wool blankets, he knew, would be
fine linen sheets. Thurgood would have
insisted on their being packed even if the
troops were going to war against the trolls in
the Dangerous Mountains.

It was a very comfortable bed, and it was big
enough for two, if you cuddled.

To hell with his standing rule of no seduction while in camp. It was five days' ride to Avalon unless he pushed it, and he didn't want to wait that long for Goldie. So she'd put him off last night. Been downright prickly about it, in fact. So what? That was last night. And this . . .

Richard smiled and leisurely got to his feet.

This was tonight, and he was alone in his tent with the most beautiful woman he'd ever known.

Richard fairly purred. Goldie's sudden flush told him all he needed to know about her thoughts. Despite her seeming fascination with those nettles, she'd been as aware of him as he was of her.

Tonight he wouldn't make any mistakes. He wasn't wet, hungry, or cold. A few pretty words, a little flattery, a little wine, and all would be well.

His gaze slid from her face down that lovely, lovely bosom to the knitting that lay forgotten in her lap.

Those damned nettles.

With one foot he reached out, hooked a stool, and drew it up beside her chair. It didn't escape his notice that her breathing quickened ever so slightly.

Deliberately avoiding her eyes, he settled on the stool and leaned closer, as if studying the knitting.

"I wish I knew why you're so attached to those damn nettles. A woman like you, with beautiful hands like these . . ."

Careful to avoid the nettles, he gently claimed her hand.

"Such a beautiful hand," he murmured, cradling it in his. He didn't miss the almost imperceptible tremor that rippled through her at his touch.

Lightly, he trailed one finger across the center of her palm. Her breath caught.

He ducked his head to hide his smile of satisfaction. This sort of thing got 'em every time, guaranteed.

He trailed the tips of two fingers down her wrist and up the inside of her arm as far as her sleeve would let him, then slowly glided back down and around that palm again.

She stopped breathing.

"Why don't you put that knitting aside?" Not quite a whisper, but low enough not to break the mood.

Goldie, dazed, obediently dumped her knitting into the basket beside her.

When he stood and, with a gentle tug on her hand, urged her to her feet, she came willingly. He drew her to him.

John Paul was starting to complain about wasting time, but in matters like this, one had to be stern. Seducing women, he'd found, was like breaking in a green colt. Do it right the first time, and things went a hell of a lot more smoothly from then on.

Still, knowing all that didn't appease John Paul or dampen the fire spreading outward from that demanding member. Richard ignored the growing tightness in his chest as he raised a hand to brush a wanton curl back from her brow. This close, he could see the fine blue veins beneath the pearl-pink skin at her temple.

Her head tilted back, and her lashes lowered, hiding her eyes. Her lips parted.

Richard knew an invitation when he saw one.

A light brush of mouths first, scarcely grazing that full, tempting lower lip.

She sighed.

With John Paul signaling his approval, Richard claimed another kiss, a longer, stronger one this time.

When he slid an arm around her back and pulled her closer, she swayed, letting her hand move up his biceps. He wasn't sure she even realized that she'd done it.

Doing good, old king, old boy. Yes, sir, doing just fine.

Little hard to think, though. The taste of her, sweet and dark as wine, made him dizzy. Or maybe it was the sudden, inexplicable shortage of air that was to blame. Not to mention the way his arm brushed against the side of her breast, or the pliant arch of her body against his, or—

Holy Joseph and Mary! Had she deliberately pressed against John Paul like that?

Richard grabbed for air, panting just a little, then shifted to take better advantage of the angle and thrust his tongue into her mouth, driving deep. John Paul was rising to the occasion, too, despite the tight location.

A deeper tongue thrust, then retreat, nipping at her lip. He dragged one hand down her spine, low enough so he could pull her even harder against him.

She moaned. The fleeting brush of warm air across his lips shot fire right through his center.

Surely she could feel what she was doing to him? What she was doing to both him and John Paul?

Judging from the way her slender frame was melting into him, he wasn't doing too badly, either.

To hell with a gentle breaking in. She wanted him as much as he wanted her. And he was more than happy to let her have him.

He slid his right hand down her arm, then slipped to the delicious curve of her waist, then back up along the arch of her ribs until he cupped the curve of her breast.

She sucked in air.

Good! A little squeeze, slip his fingers down there, then snag the laces, and—

Her sudden jerk away from him caught him by surprise.

Before he could pull her back to him, the palm of her hand connected with his cheek.

Hard.

Really hard.

Richard's head snapped to the side.

By the time he brought it around again, she was three feet away and armed.

"What the hell? Nettles? Jeeze! Look—"

Silently she advanced on him, a clump of nettles brandished like a sword in front of her. When he made a move to grab her wrist, she swung at him.

"Hey!" He jumped back, hands out to fend her off. "No. Hey, really. I didn't—What the hell? *Cut it out!*"

The last was a roar as he dodged another ferocious swing.

"Stop that, damn it!"

Desperate, he grabbed one of the camp chairs and brought it up as a shield. A fraction of a second later the nettles scraped the chair leg where his hand had been.

"Shit!"

He could see the soft inner curve of her left breast where he'd loosened the laces of her bodice. Just a glimpse and then she was turning, trying to get under his guard.

"No! Stop! Hell!"

At the last second he spotted the stool in his way and managed to dodge, then kick it into her path. It distracted her long enough for him to shift the chair to his left hand and grab for his sword. With one smooth sweep he pulled the weapon free of its sheath and swung around.

She stopped, the deadly tip only inches from the breast that had started it all. Her bosom rose and fell in quick, angry gasps. Her eyes flashed blue fire, and her mouth—those sweet, perfect lips he'd been kissing just a few moments earlier—was twisted into a pinched, scornful slash.

He moved the tip of the sword a fraction to the right to show his good intentions.

When she'd slapped him, it had been on the left side, the one with all the scrapes, and it stung like the devil.

"Grabbing those nettles was a damned dirty, sneaky thing to do, you know."

Her nose wrinkled in disgust. She eyed him, then his sword. Then she deliberately shoved aside the point.

He lowered the sword, but he wasn't ready to let go of the chair. Not yet. Not while she still held those nettles.

"Put 'em away." He indicated the nettles with his chin. "I'm not going to touch you, if that's what you're wondering."

She gave a snort of contempt and tossed the nettles aside. They fell short of the basket, but she didn't bother to pick them up. Instead, she relaced her bodice, jerking on the laces so hard that the fabric pulled too tightly across her chest.

He didn't bother to tell her that.

Disgusted, he set the chair down, then slammed his sword back into its sheath. John Paul had retreated long since in a sulk.

"*You're* the one who agreed to come. You could have said no. Hell, you *did* say no. Then, just like a woman, you changed your mind and damned near begged me to bring you along. And now . . . this!"

He threw up his hands, feeling aggrieved. Women!

"Why'd you come if you didn't—"

Her chin came up to a dangerous angle.

To Richard's chagrin, John Paul showed signs of interest in spite of everything.

"I'll tell you one thing," he said bitterly. "You can forget the pretty clothes and the nice shoes and . . . and whatnot. If you think—"

The contempt in her gaze wilted both of them.

He sighed. "No, I didn't mean that. I meant— That is . . ."

He couldn't help himself. His gaze slid down her body, then slowly rose again.

Damn. Damn damn damn damn *damn!*

Head defiantly high, she tossed her tumbled hair back over her shoulder, exposing the graceful curve of jaw and throat, the smooth slope of shoulder under her gown.

Richard shut his eyes against the sight.

Then—damn again—he looked because he couldn't help it.

Proud, indignant, and flushed with anger, she was even more desirable than when she was being sweet and shy and beguiling, and she could tie him into knots without even trying when she was being sweet, shy, etc.

Even more crazily, he was beginning to suspect she had no idea she could do it.

"Well, shi—"

Her eyes narrowed dangerously.

"I'm going to bed. You want to join me, go right ahead. *I* don't hold grudges."

There was a flicker of something deep in her eyes, but it was gone too quickly for him to be sure.

"If you don't want to join me . . ." He waved to indicate the rugs spread on the tent floor. "There's plenty of room. In case you're wondering," he added sarcastically, "a rug laid on grass is a hell of a lot more comfortable than a wooden floor or a stone hearth."

She didn't look impressed.

"Or you can stay up all night and knit. That is, you can if you can do it in the dark. Take your pick."

It was a challenge.

But instead of backing down and turning away in a sulk, which he'd half expected, she moved to the curtain that divided off the sleeping area, set her feet apart, crossed her arms over her chest, and glared at him.

There was no mistaking her meaning.

"I'm the king, and this is *my* tent, damn it! I'm sleeping here, and I'll sleep in *my* bed!"

She lifted her chin defiantly.

Richard eyed her from under a darkling brow. It was a look he'd used to good effect against murderous enemies and obstreperous squires. It even worked on Thurgood now and again.

It didn't work on Goldie. She merely glared back, unimpressed.

That didn't leave him many options. He could grab her before she had a chance to grab the nettles, then take her off to bed with him whether she wanted to go or not. He could shove her aside, then dive for the curtained-off bed and hope she didn't seize the nettles and come after him. Or he could admit defeat and find someplace else to sleep.

He threw up his hands, disgusted.

"All right! Hell! *Have* the place. I'll go sleep with Harry."

He'd actually expected her to give in. Instead, she kept her arms crossed in front of her and simply stood there, waiting for him to leave. He'd known queens who didn't look as regal.

Defeated, Richard flung aside the tent flap and stepped out into the night. Behind him, Goldie yanked the flap back into place. He had no doubt she'd tie the flap strings in double knots, just to

157

make things difficult if he tried to come back.

"Your Majesty?" said the startled guard.

Richard glared at him. The fellow shrank back, eyes wide.

"Where the hell's the Earl of Sunnyvale's tent?" growled His Majesty.

"Sire?"

"Aarrgh!" said His Majesty and stomped away without waiting for an answer.

Chapter Seven

They reached Avalon on the afternoon of the third day. His Majesty had junked the five-days-to-Avalon plan. Three days, he'd said, and the hardness to his jaw had stifled all argument before it started.

Well, almost all.

"Three days?" Harry had said over breakfast that first morning. His mustache twitched so hard from outrage that he shook out the bread crumbs caught in it. "Are you out of your bloody mind? You aren't expected back for another week, at least, and there's nothing going on that you have to worry about sooner. No wars. No dragons. No trolls stealing virgins. Nothing! And you want us to get back to Avalon in *three days?*"

Richard stabbed a bit of bacon as if he wanted to make sure it was really dead, but he didn't say a word.

Arianne calmly kept on buttering her roll. His Majesty's bed had been wonderfully comfortable. She hadn't had such a good night's sleep in ages.

Harry looked at Richard. Then he looked at her. Then he frowned at them both.

"I can guess what went on between you two last night, and your little disagreements are your own business," he said, waggling his breakfast knife in Richard's face to emphasize his point. "But when you make all the rest of us suffer, too—"

Richard snatched the implement out of Harry's hand, then plunged it into the table with so much force that the tip sank more than an inch into the wood.

Arianne eyed the knife with disapproval—though it wasn't her problem, that hole in the tablecloth would be a real nuisance to mend—then deliberately popped a bit of the roll into her mouth and chewed. Harry glanced at Richard in disgust, cursed under his breath, and turned his attention back to the job of polishing off everything on his plate.

Richard glared at them with an expression that would have given thunderclouds a bad name. Neither of them paid him any heed. He kicked back his chair and stalked out of the tent without a word.

Arianne hadn't had so much as a good "Damnation!" out of him since.

Each day he'd ridden at the head of the cavalcade, and each day she'd ridden at the back, where she had a great view of a lot of horses' rear ends and all the dust she could eat.

Each night he'd dined in royal but silent state with her and Harry, then spent a couple of hours afterward wordlessly sitting by the brazier, working on dispatches or sipping his wine while she'd doggedly kept on knitting.

The first night, Harry had said some rather pointed things about damn fools before he left to find more entertaining company. He hadn't wasted his breath on arguing since.

To Arianne's relief, Richard hadn't tried to reclaim his bed, with or without her in it. As for the nebulous, yearning ache that plagued her whenever he was around, she told herself that that was indigestion, nothing more.

Riding at the end of the cavalcade had been her idea, not his. Determined not to waste a minute, she'd worked at her knitting whenever Richard slowed their pace to a walk to give the horses a rest. Trying to ride and knit at the same time made her eyes cross and her head spin. Her hands ached from cramp, and the tips of her fingers developed some unattractive calluses, but she'd kept at it.

She'd finished Rheidwn's shirt yesterday and cast off the last stitch on the back of William's garment not a quarter of an hour ago. Tonight she'd start on William's sleeves, but *not* until after she'd had a bath and a change of clothes.

As far as she was concerned, they couldn't get to Avalon too soon. Her backside was numb from so many hours in the saddle, and she'd swear her legs were starting to bow.

"Not long now, miss," said a gap-toothed old servant riding beside her. "We gets out o' this wood here, and you'll see."

She saw.

They'd been following a broad, well-tended road through forestland for some miles, but the wood ended abruptly at the top of a hill, providing a panoramic view of the broad plain below.

Arianne gasped and drew her horse aside, out of the way of the other riders.

The plain swept clear to the horizon, its rich green expanse broken here and there by a multicolored patchwork of cultivated fields with neat little villages at their heart. At least two rivers cut sinuous paths across the green, and Arianne could see a number of smaller streams as well.

Yet all that magnificence paled beside that of

the great castle that stood in a bend of the nearest river, right at the heart of Avalon.

It was a spectacular place, more than five times the size of her father's castle and perched atop a rocky hill that made it seem even bigger. Its high walls and soaring towers gleamed so white in the sun, it was hard to look too long for fear of going blind. Flags in a hundred different colors flew from the battlements, snapping and flashing in the afternoon breeze, echoing the trumpet fanfares announcing the king's return.

Arianne stared, awestruck. She had heard of the glories of Avalon, but even the wildest tales paled beside the reality of the place.

And she had made the king of all this splendor sleep on her cottage floor.

The thought made her laugh and glance about her for the king in question.

Too eager to be home again to worry about a straggler, the soldiers and the servants in charge of the baggage animals had already ridden past her down the hill. Richard and Harry and all the other important folk were a good half mile away, their horses kicked into a canter, the king's great banner of blue and white and gold streaming above them.

Also suddenly eager to see the wonders that awaited her, Arianne set off down the hill after them at a gallop.

* * *

"See?" said Harry as they rode across the great drawbridge. "What'd I tell you? Nothing going on here. Except for old Archie, all's right with Avalon, and there was never any need to rush."

Richard pretended to ignore him. Harry was right, of course. There hadn't been any need to push the men and horses as he had. But he was the king, and they did as he said, and that, Richard thought, ought to be that.

If only things were so simple with one independent-minded female of his acquaintance.

Damned if he knew why he hadn't booted Goldie out of his tent that first night. He'd been more than angry enough to do it. But something about her, something about the way she'd faced him down, had made him surrender before the battle had really commenced.

The way she acted, you'd think she'd been raised to be a queen.

A queen? Hah!

Iron-shod hooves rang on the bridge while trumpets blared from the parapet. The roar of the eager crowd come to welcome them home was deafening.

Richard scarcely noticed. If word came now of an invader on his borders, he'd gladly turn his horse around and head off to battle. Better that, he thought sourly, than to have to deal with Goldie.

Far better that than to have to deal with an

unctuous, self-satisfied prelate, he silently added as he caught sight of His Grace the Archbishop of Avalon standing at the top of the steps leading into the Great Hall.

With Harry at his side, Richard rode forward through the crowd and drew rein at the base of the stairs.

"The old fart looks like he had a good time playing king while you were gone," Harry grumbled.

The archbishop lingered at the top of the steps just long enough to be insulting but not quite long enough to make the insult obvious, then slowly descended. His thin yet ungainly figure, garbed in the heavy robes of his office, made him look like a praying mantis creeping toward its prey. He stopped at the third step up so his head was on a level with Richard's. "Your Majesty, welcome home."

Richard forced himself to nod in recognition. "Your Grace."

Archibald smiled. He had sharp white teeth.

"Your people rejoice at your safe return, Sire. We only regret," he added with mock concern, "that you bring us no promise yet of a queen."

"Saw a couple of pretty boys you'd have liked, though, you old buggerer," Harry muttered too low for anyone but Richard to hear.

"Mmrph," said Richard, dismounting. Suddenly he felt very, very tired.

Together, the three of them mounted the

stairs. At the top he turned to acknowledge his people's acclaim, but there was only one face he sought in the crowd.

He found her at the far edge of the throng, still mounted, a stranger no one else seemed to see, let alone care about. She kept her back straight, her expression impassive, yet he could see the weariness in her even at this distance.

More guilt stabbed through him. He shouldn't have pushed everyone so hard. He'd thought only of his need to be out of camp and back in Avalon, not of what such a hard ride might mean for Goldie.

He took a step back down the stairs, then another.

Harry froze, surprised. "Richard?"

Archibald halted. "Your Majesty?"

Richard stopped, cursing under his breath. The king couldn't go to a peasant woman. Not in a public gathering like this.

Besides, what would he say to her if he did?

After a moment's hesitation, he waved for a page. "Find Thurgood. Tell him he's to see to Goldie, that he's to take care of her as she deserves. Got that? He'll know what to do."

The boy nodded and dashed off.

"*Goldie*, your Majesty?"

With a last glance across the bailey, Richard turned back to the archbishop.

"A guest, Archibald. Simply a guest."

"Of course, your Majesty," Archibald said.

But his eyes narrowed as he looked out over the crowd.

"The chamber is yours alone. I think it should serve." Thurgood gestured the two menials who carried Arianne's baskets of nettles to set their burdens in the corner.

Arianne stared around her, too shocked and angry to try to stop them.

The room was cramped and cold and dark. Its one narrow window grudgingly showed a bit of sky but didn't do much to relieve the gloom. A stool, a bucket, and a narrow bed were shoved against the far wall. The bed held a mattress too thin even to qualify as lumpy, a coarse wool blanket, and no pillow.

That was all. There weren't even any rushes on the floor and not so much as a stub of a candle.

"You may take your meals in the kitchen," Thurgood informed her. "I've sent word to the cook to save a bit for you. There's somebody who can't finish everything on his plate, you know," he continued. "The garderobe's down the hall, there," he added, pointing. He smiled with malice even a blind woman could see. "You should find it eventually."

The menials silently scuttled out the door, and Thurgood's smile vanished. No loss, really, but the pinched look that replaced it wasn't any improvement. A man must have to eat a lot of lemons to drum up an expression like that.

"His Majesty is brave and strong and wise," Thurgood said, "and he should not be diverted from his work by a scheming chit of a peasant like you. Patched up his wounds, indeed!"

He sniffed like a man who knew there was a skunk around, gave one last satisfied glance at the chamber he'd found her, then left, slamming the door behind him.

Arianne stared at the door, her fury growing by the second. Now might be a good time to scream. Screaming could be wonderfully cathartic.

She settled for drop-kicking her bundle of knitting across the miserable chamber.

"What'dja do with Goldie?" Harry inquired a couple of hours later around a mouthful of roast pork. "Haven't seen her since we arrived this morning."

The castle staff, informed by messengers of His Majesty's impending return, had prepared a feast to welcome him home. Richard would just as soon have had a quiet meal in his quarters—preferably with Goldie—but the cooks and serving staff had gone to a great deal of trouble, and he didn't want to appear ungrateful.

Richard poked at a bit of something or other his squire had dumped on his plate. "Thurgood's taking care of her."

The Wild Swans

Where had Thurgood put her? he wondered. The blue guest chamber? Or maybe the red? There was that great big suite with the view out over the valley, but that was too damned far from the royal apartments. Surely Thurgood wouldn't have put her there.

"Goldie?" Archibald's thin eyebrows arched. "Ah, yes. A guest, I think you said?"

If he'd had antennae, they'd have been waving over his head, nervously searching for bits of information he might use to his advantage.

It would, Richard thought sourly, have been a lot easier to look grateful for the feast if the archbishop hadn't been seated beside him.

"Goldie's a peasant girl who gave me shelter and care when I was stranded in the woods a few days ago. She'd been cooped up in a dark cottage, and I thought she might like to see Avalon." He shrugged. "A little reward for her efforts."

He tried his best to sound offhand, as if peasant girls sheltered the king every day of the week and twice on Sundays. He didn't need Harry warning him about the Archbishop of Avalon, Archibald had been his father's enemy long before Richard had inherited him. No need to tip one's hand to such as Archie.

"Ah," said Archibald, his thin lips stretched in a knowing smile. "I take it she's very beautiful, then?"

"Not bad," said Richard.

More like knock-your-hose-off gorgeous.

Frustrated, he speared a piece of pork from the platter in front of him and dumped it onto his plate.

"She's stunning," said Harry. "Absolutely gorgeous, in fact. Got golden hair down to here and eyes blue as a robin's egg and bre—" His hands froze in midair, cupped palms just below his own broad chest. "Uh . . ." He grabbed for the basket in front of him. "She bakes great bread," he said from around a mouthful of light rye.

Richard did *not* want to think about Goldie's breasts.

John Paul, however, didn't see anything wrong with it. Richard's fingers twitched with the remembered feel of skin as soft as silk.

"She bakes bread?" said Archibald. "How . . . interesting."

Richard pushed the chunk of pork around on his plate, tried a bite, and grimaced. Too dry. He heaped some grated horseradish on it.

He didn't want to think about Goldie, but even less did he want Archibald thinking about her. You could never be sure what Archie would do with the bits and pieces of information he collected, but you could be very sure that whatever it was, you weren't going to like it.

"And this paragon is a peasant. Imagine that. Your Majesty has the most . . . mmm . . . *diverting* affinity for the common classes." Archibald looked positively feral when he smiled. "I imagine it's one of the reasons you're so popular among them."

Richard tried another bite. The horseradish helped, but there was still something missing.

Breasts, said John Paul.

"He's popular because he's a damned good king." Harry wasn't quite growling but close to it.

"But of course," said the archbishop in his oily voice. "I wouldn't dream of suggesting otherwise."

Maybe a little salt to go with the horseradish?

He wasn't thinking about Goldie.

A little pepper probably wouldn't hurt.

He wasn't worrying about Goldie. Thurgood would take care of her. He didn't have to.

Maybe some mint jelly? Or was that lamb that went with mint?

He was *not* going to ask Thurgood which room she was in. That was Thurgood's province. Didn't have anything to do with him.

Oh, yeah? said John Paul. *Just try roaming the halls with nothing but a hard-on to guide you.*

Desperate, Richard reached for the pepper sauce. Maybe it would help if he made it really *hot.* Sweating usually cooled the blood, didn't it?

"Uh . . . Richard?" said Harry, watching him douse his meat. "You sure you want to do that?"

"My," said the archbishop at the quantity of the condiment Richard had applied.

"Pah!" said His Majesty, spitting the mouthful of pork onto his plate and grabbing for his wine.

It mightn't have been so bad if she'd had a couple of candles, Arianne thought, or if the smell of roast pork hadn't wafted up—or was it down?—from the Great Hall, where Avalon was no doubt feasting in honor of its newly returned king. But she didn't have any candles, and Thurgood hadn't left so much as a crumb of bread. Like it or not, she'd have to venture out on her own if she didn't want to go hungry.

As for a bath . . . She sighed. No, she couldn't quite face a washing in cold water right now. Tomorrow maybe, when she'd had a chance to find some soap and a towel.

At least she'd offered *him* hot water and soap, while he—

No, best not think of that rotten rat's betrayal.

So this was the way he got even, huh? Well, she'd show him! As soon as her brothers were free of their spell and she could talk again, she'd give His high and mighty Majesty the sharp edge of her tongue. She might even demand that her father declare war on him, just for the satisfaction of it.

Well, all right, so she wouldn't demand a

declaration of war, but it was awfully appealing to think of cutting that arrogant jerk down to size.

She should have let him sleep in the mud. The hearth had been way too good for him.

If she ever got another chance . . .

Fueled by her murderous thoughts, Arianne stormed through the castle corridors, up some stairs, through more corridors, down some stairs, then down yet more stairs, searching for the kitchen. By the time she found it, she was light-headed from hunger and anger and exertion.

Without stopping to tidy her hair or remember that she was no longer the Princess Arianne of Montavia but a common peasant girl named Goldie, she slammed through the double doors like a whirlwind on a rant. The doors banged against the walls on either side with enough force to set the dishes in a nearby cupboard rattling.

Work in the kitchen stopped dead. Two dozen faces, glistening with sweat and a few well-dusted with flour, turned to stare at her.

Arianne stared back, her bravado draining away. Montavia's kitchen was a large, warm, friendly place, and even Cook, who was known to be temperamental, didn't mind visitors so long as they kept out from underfoot.

Evidently it didn't work that way at Avalon.

A giant loomed over her.

"Who are you, and what are you doing in my kitchen?"

Avalon's chief cook looked as if he ate small children for afternoon snacks.

Arianne backed up against a wall, desperately looking around for a friendly face. Here and there she saw sympathy but no one willing to confront the giant.

Someone snickered. "That's the peasant girl King Jim brought back with 'im." It was a raisin-faced old woman who'd been scrubbing pots in a corner. "Must not've been to 'is taste if she's here 'stead of nekkid in 'is bed."

The heat washing up her face wasn't all from the kitchen fires, but Arianne stood her ground, chin high.

"Mrrmm," said the giant. "His Majesty's man said you was to be fed."

As if she were a cow, she thought, disgusted.

His Majesty was going to have an awful lot to answer for.

Chapter Eight

Red room. Blue room. The grand duchess's room. He'd even tried the huge, remote suite with the view and the secondary guest rooms. All one hundred and forty three of them.

Goldie wasn't in any of them.

At least Richard hadn't found her, nor any trace of her knitting, and he'd spent the best part of the past week looking.

Granted, he'd been handicapped by the fact that it had had to be a surreptitious search. He didn't want his subjects seeing him chasing after a peasant girl who didn't want anything to do with him, and couldn't quite bring himself to ask the obviously disapproving Thurgood where he'd put her.

Pride, of course, but there it was. He was a

man and a king. He *couldn't* ask for directions. It simply wasn't done.

He wouldn't have had to resort to such demeaning tactics if Goldie had accepted one of his invitations for dinner. Or breakfast. Breakfast would have been fine. He'd even have settled for afternoon snacks, but she'd refused those, too. She'd also refused his invitations for drinks, for strolls in the park, or a walk around the battlements. He was running out of options.

Thank God no one but the trustworthy young page who'd carried his invitations to her knew about the refusals. It wouldn't help his reputation if anyone found out that a peasant wench had spurned the King of Avalon.

Damned if he knew why he even bothered.

It wasn't just John Paul's tendency to remember her at the most inconvenient times. It wasn't her beauty, either. He'd known hundreds of women as beautiful as she.

Well, dozens, anyway.

A handful for sure.

Pretty sure.

But it wasn't her beauty.

Richard sighed. He wanted to talk with her, that's all. He liked the way she laughed and the challenging look that came into her eyes whenever he said something she didn't agree with.

If he was really pressed, he'd even admit he was intrigued by her independence and her

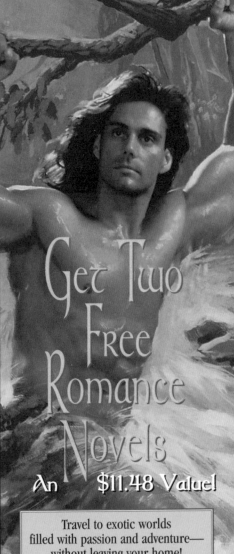

Thrill to the most sensual, adventure-filled Romances on the market today...

FROM  LOVE SPELL BOOKS

As a home subscriber to the Love Spell Romance Book Club, you'll enjoy the best in today's BRAND-NEW Time Travel, Futuristic, Legendary Lovers, Perfect Heroes and other genre romance fiction. For five years, Love Spell has brought you the award-winning, high-quality authors you know and love to read. Each Love Spell romance will sweep you away to a world of high adventure...and intimate romance. Discover for yourself all the passion and excitement millions of readers thrill to each and every month.

Save $5.00 Each Time You Buy!

Every other month, the Love Spell Romance Book Club brings you four brand-new titles from Love Spell Books. EACH PACKAGE WILL SAVE YOU AT LEAST $5.00 FROM THE BOOK-STORE PRICE! And you'll never miss a new title with our convenient home delivery service.

Here's how we do it: Each package will carry a FREE 10-DAY EXAMINATION privilege. At the end of that time, if you decide to keep your books, simply pay the low invoice price of $17.96, no shipping or handling charges added. HOME DELIVERY IS ALWAYS FREE. With today's top romance novels selling for $5.99 and higher, our price SAVES YOU AT LEAST $5.00 with each shipment.

AND YOUR FIRST TWO-BOOK SHIP-MENT IS TOTALLY FREE!

IT'S A BARGAIN YOU CAN'T BEAT! A SUPER $11.48 Value!

Love Spell ✦ A Division of Dorchester Publishing Co., Inc.

Get Two Books Totally
FREE —
An $11.48 Value!

▼ Tear Here and Mail Your FREE Book Card Today! ▼

PLEASE RUSH
MY TWO FREE
BOOKS TO ME
RIGHT AWAY!

Love Spell Romance Book Club
P.O. Box 6613
Edison, NJ 08818-6613

AFFIX
STAMP
HERE

intelligence and her refusal to be impressed by his rank or his wealth. But only if he was pressed.

Thank all the saints and the seven magicians no one knew about his search.

"Still haven't found her, huh?" said Harry, plopping down in the chair beside him.

Richard almost spewed his wine. "What are you talking about?"

Harry reached for the flagon. "Sir Osric's got up a pool on how long it'll be till you give in and ask somebody to tell you where she is."

"Hell."

"Half of 'em didn't think you'd last even this long."

"Half of 'em haven't got the brains God gave a turkey," Richard growled.

Harry studied him over the rim of his cup, frowning. Slowly he put down his wine.

"This isn't like you, Richard. Chasing around after one woman. Passing up sword practice so you can go poking in all those damned drafty rooms looking for her. I swear you didn't even notice the Earl of Mapps's daughter when he was through here last Thursday."

"He had a daughter?"

Harry threw up his hands. "See what I mean? Used to be you'd have noticed a good-looking chit like her right off."

Richard sighed and set down his cup. "So where is she, Harry? Where's Goldie?"

"Damned if I know. Avalon's a big place. Easy to lose a dozen chits like her and never notice."

"*I've* noticed," said Richard very quietly.

"Seen her about though," Harry added, ever helpful. "Coming and going. You know how it is. Hear she's fond of walking out to the pond where that flock of swans has taken up residence."

"Is she?" said Richard, brightening. "When, exactly? Does she go every very day? Which way does she go? Out the main gate or through the postern?"

Before Harry could reply, a servant entered bearing a covered tray.

"Your lunch, Sire."

"Lunch!" said Harry, rubbing his hands together in anticipation. "That'll put you right.

"Or maybe not," he added gloomily when the charred remains of what must once have been a chicken were uncovered.

Richard stared at the blackened carcass glumly, then looked up at the stone-faced servant who had brought it.

"Cook not feeling well lately, Thomas?"

Thomas stared at a spot on the wall somewhere over Richard's left shoulder. "Cook's fine, Sire. Never better."

"Problems in the kitchen, then? Stoves acting up? Assistant cooks getting into the sherry?"

"No, Sire. Nothing like that." The man was so stiff, he looked as if a broomstick had been rammed up his spine.

"I see," said Richard, and sighed.

He covered the remains and waved the tray away.

Harry grabbed for the bread and the wedge of cheese before they were hauled off along with the corpse. "Never seen a chicken quite that . . . uh . . . well done."

"It's been this way for the past couple of days," Richard admitted, morosely considering the gouda. "Food served in the hall's fine, but anything prepared for me . . ."

He didn't need to finish.

Harry poured him more wine.

"I hear Goldie takes her meals in the kitchen," he said very casually.

Richard looked up, suddenly alert.

"From what I hear, Cook's become quite fond of her."

Richard went still. "And she's helping with the cooking, is she?"

"No. Not exactly. Fact is, *everyone* likes her. Kitchen folk. The household staff. At least, that's what I hear."

"Do you mean to say she's turning my staff against me?" He thumped his chest. "*Me*? The King of Avalon?"

"Not exactly, but . . . Well, you did find her in the Dark Woods, didn't you? And you said that hart was enchanted . . ."

Richard was already halfway across the room. He flung open the door, startling the guard posted outside so much that the fellow dropped his pike.

"Bring me Thurgood!" the King of Avalon roared. "Now!"

He slammed the door and started to walk away, then spun back and flung it open again.

"If not sooner!"

Thurgood danced down the hall a half step in front of Richard. The old man was sweating and flapping his hands and doing his best to dissuade him from his search for Goldie.

"Really, Your Majesty, this isn't necessary. I'm sure if you'd only let me—"

"Shut up!" Richard was too furious with Goldie and her machinations to tolerate one more obstruction.

Thurgood reluctantly shut up and concentrated on trying to keep pace with his liege lord, who was so angry he was just this side of leaving scorch marks in his wake.

Burn his chicken, would she? Turn his cook against him? He'd show her!

Just where did she get off thinking she had the right to upset his life this way, anyway? She could have stayed in that cottage of hers if she'd wanted. He hadn't dragged her off against her will, and nobody could say he had.

Hell, he'd even given up his bed and his tent for her, and he'd never done that for *any* woman!

The more he thought about it, the madder he got.

Was it the kisses? Was she really crazy enough to be this upset over a couple of *kisses?*

What kind of woman would hold his attempted seduction against him, anyway? Especially when she'd never given him a chance to get farther than those damned bodice laces!

Richard lowered his head, thrust out his chin, and walked faster.

The bodice laces and what lay under them particularly annoyed him. In fact, they downright pissed him off. They'd been haunting his dreams for days, and all because he'd never gotten beyond them.

All this suffering, and for a woman who'd made him sleep on the hearth, then kicked him out of his own bed!

The consideration of his multiple grievances might have stoked his fury for hours if he hadn't suddenly realized just how far Thurgood was leading him into Avalon's labyrinth.

Richard looked around suspiciously. Then he looked at Thurgood.

"I don't remember any guest rooms in this part of the castle."

Thurgood bared his teeth in what was probably meant to be an ingratiating smile.

"It's so much quieter here far away from the main halls, you see, Your Majesty," he said, eager to explain. "And since she was used to being alone, I thought . . . That is . . . I gave her a quite adequate room! *Quite* adequate."

Richard frowned, and Thurgood sank into himself until he seemed very small. By the time they reached the narrow door at the end of a dark hallway deep in the oldest part of the castle, he was trying hard to be a shadow with the rest of the shadows.

Richard stared at the door, then glared at Thurgood.

The old man shrank back against the wall. "You said—"

"I said to take care of her."

The air in Richard's lungs became a hot, heavy ball in his chest. No wonder he hadn't found her. He was probably lucky she'd hadn't poisoned his chicken instead of just charring it.

"You said to treat her as she deserves," Thurgood protested. "She's a peasant. You're the *King*. I—"

Richard came this close to grabbing him by his scrawny old neck and giving him a shake that would make his false teeth rattle.

He forced his fingers to uncurl. There had to be some way to recover lost ground, to make amends for the insult he'd unwittingly offered her.

"You will go back and prepare the grand duchess's room for Mistress Goldie."

"The gra—Yes, Sire. The duchess's room."

"You will find a maid to attend her and

clothes for her to wear, and you will do it so quickly that everything will be in readiness when I return with her."

"Yes, Your Majesty."

"And you will treat her with all the respect that is due a lady."

"Treat her—! Of course, Your Majesty." Thurgood was getting smaller by the second, folding in on himself like a crumpled piece of parchment.

"Now," said Richard.

Hunched in misery, Thurgood scuttled back the way they'd come.

Richard waited until the old man was out of sight, then raised a hand, steeled his nerves, and knocked on the door to Goldie's room.

Arianne had drawn the stool as close to the window as she could, but there still wasn't enough light. The window was too small, and at this hour of the day the angle of the sun was wrong. If she wanted to keep on knitting, she'd have to work in the dark or give in and go down to the kitchens.

Neither prospect held much appeal. The kitchen folk had been kind to her—even Cook had unbent after she'd shown him a trick with custard sauce and puréed pears—but their little kingdom was a hot, noisy, bustling place, and she didn't belong.

The Great Hall of the castle would have light

and warmth and people aplenty, but she didn't want to run the risk of having His high and mighty Majesty see her, a beggar at his feast. She'd turn nun and take up praying before she'd give him the satisfaction. Yet she didn't want to spend another evening alone in this cold, dark cell of a room, either.

The unexpected knock made her jump.

She opened the door, took one look, and slammed it again. Hard.

"Ow!"

Arianne smiled in grim satisfaction. Served him right. And as far as she was concerned, that was just for starters.

Since the door had neither locks nor wooden bars, she planted her feet, crossed her arms over her chest, and waited.

Three seconds later it burst open and the king limped in.

"Shit!" he said, and glared at her. "You damn near broke my toe."

She met his angry glare with an equally angry glare of her own and considered grabbing a knitting needle.

"Oh, no, you don't!" He hobbled around to stand between her and her basket of knitting.

"Where the hell have you been, anyway?" he demanded peevishly, trying to stand on one foot without looking as if he was.

Arianne sucked in so much air that her eyes

almost popped out. Where had *she* been? As if he didn't know!

For one long, satisfying moment she considered stomping on his other foot, then decided it wasn't worth the effort. If he couldn't walk out of here on his own, she'd have to hoof it a good quarter mile through cold, dark hallways to find someone to haul him out for her.

"And why'd you refuse all my invitations? I thought you'd enjoy having a meal with me, maybe seeing some of the sights."

Her eyes narrowed. The arrogant jerk! Had he really thought she'd grab for the crumbs he'd tossed her? He'd never once bothered to come himself, just sent his page, and then he expected her to be *grateful?*

Maybe that quarter-mile hike would be worth it, after all.

"And why . . ." The question trailed away to nothing as his gaze swept the room.

"Shit!" he said again, only this time his anger wasn't directed at her. "What in hell kind of guest room is this?"

Arianne studied him, puzzled. He was the one who'd given the order to put her here. He had to be. So why did he look so surprised?

His gaze swept back to meet hers, hot with scarcely restrained anger and, she'd swear, not a little guilt.

"I didn't know," he said. "I swear I had no idea Thurgood put you here."

Maybe, she thought. Maybe not.

Which didn't excuse his not bothering to find out, she reminded herself, sternly tamping down the temptation to believe him. Start believing him, and before you knew it she'd be forgiving him, too.

She wasn't about to forgive him. This was one grudge she wanted to nurse for a while.

To her disgust, she found her gaze slipping down his face, lingering on those eminently kissable lips, that small, almost imperceptible cleft in his chin. Several times these past few days she'd seen him striding across the bailey or riding out in the morning for exercise. He'd never seen her, and she'd never risked getting too close, but the memory of those lips, that chin, those dangerous hands of his, had made for some very unsettling moments. It had gotten so bad at times, she'd even caught herself wishing she hadn't stopped him at the bodice laces.

For that aggravation alone he owed her. Big time.

"What?" said Richard nervously. Even nervous he looked big and terrifying and tempting. "Look, I honestly didn't know. If I say I'm sorry, will that satisfy you?"

She eyed his uninjured foot.

He hopped back a step.

"I'm sorry. Really. I never meant for you to end up in a place like this."

But she had, and whose fault was it? Not hers.

"I sent Thurgood off to prepare a proper room for you," he said, a hint of desperation in his voice. "The grand duchess's chamber. You'll like it. Big. Comfortable. Great view."

He caught her bitter glance at the narrow bed she'd occupied these last few days.

"Big bed, too," he said with forced heartiness. "Lots of fat feather pillows."

Before she could object, he grabbed the basket with her knitting.

She snatched the basket from him and protectively clutched it to her chest. There were three and a half finished shirts in there. She wasn't about to trust them to anyone, not even the King of Avalon.

He tried to stifle a sigh of relief, but his smile was a little too wide to be convincing. "I don't mind if you want to carry it. You know me and nettles."

She nodded. She knew him and nettles.

She pointed to the other three baskets in the corner.

He gave a dismissive wave. "Don't worry about those. I'll send someone for them. Though it beats me why you—What?"

Arianne's gaze had hardened into outright menace. She wasn't leaving without *all* the nettles.

187

Kate Holmes

Mashed toes forgotten, the King of Avalon drew himself up to his full, indignant height.

"Absolutely not! I'll carry a basket of knitting—nothing wrong with a man doing that—but I draw the line at turning into your packhorse. There are servants for that sort of thing, you know.

"Besides," he added defensively, "just one of the damned things makes me itch. No telling what would happen if I got near that many nettles."

After a week in this cell of a room, Arianne was a little short on sympathy. Before he realized what she was about, she snatched his dagger from its sheath on his belt, grabbed the blanket off the bed, and sliced it in two.

While Richard watched, openmouthed, she braided strips of cut blanket into a makeshift rope and used the rest of the fabric to cover the baskets so nothing would fall out or rub against him. When she finished a few minutes later, she'd lashed the three baskets together with enough blanket-rope for a man to throw over his shoulder. Clumsy but effective.

She handed Richard his dagger, then the rope.

He opened his mouth to protest, eyed her narrowly, sighed, and took it.

"This is your way of getting even, right?"

She smiled a smile of angelic sweetness,

picked up her basket of knitting, and gestured for him to lead the way.

The baskets didn't weigh much, but they were bulky and awkward and most unkingly. Worse, he flinched every time they bumped against him. The mere thought of hives all over his arse was enough to make him break out in a sweat.

First villein he saw, he grabbed.

"A shilling to carry 'em," he said, which made the fellow grin in anticipation of such easy riches. As far as Richard was concerned, it was cheap at twice the price.

Goldie's look of utter innocence didn't fool him for a minute. She knew exactly what he'd been thinking, and she'd relished knowing it.

For a peasant girl, she had a mighty high-handed way about her. Manipulative, through and through. He couldn't think of any other woman who could have gotten him to serve as her beast of burden without saying so much as a word.

Then again, no other woman had made him feel so guilty. Except his old nurse, of course, but that didn't count.

He didn't like feeling guilty. If it had been anyone else . . .

Richard glanced at her out of the corner of his eye.

His memory, he was pleased to see, hadn't

been mistaken—she was every bit as beautiful and desirable as he'd remembered. More, maybe, which was saying quite a lot, given the lusty nature of his dreams lately.

A feeling of satisfaction washed through him, warm and soothing as a tot of good brandy on a cold winter's day, driving out the guilt. They'd gotten off to a rocky start, but now that he'd said he was sorry, things were going to work out just fine.

Women loved it when a man said he was sorry. Didn't matter if he really meant it or not; they just wanted to hear him say it because they figured he *should* be, regardless.

So he'd said he was sorry, and now he was putting her in the best guest room in the castle, and he'd have a really first-class supper prepared for just the two of them. He'd have it served in his chambers, he decided. A little candlelight, the best wine in Avalon . . .

He smiled. Things were going to work out just fine.

In the corridor they passed a handful of footmen and cleaning women laden with brooms and feather dusters and serving trays. Three chambermaids were scurrying around the grand duchess's room when he led Goldie through the door. Thurgood, he was relieved to note, had had the good sense to make himself scarce.

At the sight of the king and his guest, the

maids curtsied, blushing and tittering like a small flock of sparrows. "Your Majesty. Miss."

Goldie nodded.

Richard checked out the room. Personally, he'd never cared for it much. There were too many ruffles and too much silk for his taste, and no furniture that a man could get comfortable in or put his feet on. But the women seemed to like it, especially the ones who put a lot of store in fancy show, and that was what counted now.

Thurgood and his draftees had done all right in the little time they'd had. A fire crackled cozily in the fireplace. Candles were lit, the bed turned back, a bottle of wine and two cups set out on a table near the hearth, with two armchairs drawn up close.

"We've hung some gowns in the closet for you, miss," said one of the maids. "Master Thurgood said you was to take your pick. Whatever suits."

"We laid out a lovely nightgown on the bed," said the second with a little giggle.

Richard could see a lacy, filmy thing laid out on the bed. An image of Goldie with her hair down and clad in nothing but that scrap of silk roused both him and John Paul to instant attention.

"Master Thurgood, he said we was to wait on you, if you wanted," the third maid added helpfully. "So we was wondering, was there anything? That you wanted, I mean?"

191

"Anything," Richard echoed expansively. Thurgood had finally gotten it right. He couldn't have done better himself if he'd tried.

Arianne ignored him. She ignored the three maids. Pivoting slowly on her heels, she studied this monstrosity of a room he'd chosen for her. Ruffles and silk and chairs that weren't made to be sat on. Fantasy nightgown neatly laid out on the bed, arranged so there was no mistaking its purpose. The wine and goblets by the fire.

With each item she noted, her fury grew.

Did he really think she was that much of a fool? Or that easily persuaded?

She looked back at him and didn't try to hide her scorn.

He flinched as if she'd hit him.

"What? What's wrong?" He looked around him with the slightly puzzled, anxious air of a hunting dog that's lost the scent and is desperately trying to find it again. "You don't like it?"

She shook her head.

"Why? Is there something missing?"

Another shake.

"Is it too big? Too hot? Too cold? You need more candles?"

To each query she gave a shake of her head. Eventually she grew tired of it and simply stood there, stubbornly defiant.

He threw up his hands at last, defeated. "So what *do* you want?"

Arianne rolled her eyes.

The King of Avalon grimaced. He stared at her, then he stared at the three maids. When they didn't offer him any answers, he stared at the floor. She could almost hear the wheels grinding in his head.

"Do you . . . ah . . . Would you like another room?" he ventured at last.

Arianne smiled and picked up the knitting she'd dropped at her feet. The man was thick but not impenetrable.

"Right, then." He marched toward the door, then stopped halfway when nobody followed. "Well?" he demanded irritably, scowling at the befuddled maids. "What are you waiting for? Let's go find the lady a room!"

He stalked out, head high, shoulders set like those of a man going to do battle with the fiercest of enemies. This time, he didn't bother looking back.

Arianne winked at the maids, who giggled, relieved and not a little pleased to be included in the excitement, then set off after him. The maids trooped behind, each laden with one of the baskets the villein had left.

It took half an hour to find what she wanted.

The red room was too big, the blue room too blue, the next three too stuffy or dark or cold. She settled at last on a comfortable, unpretentious guest room with a fireplace and a chair and a view of the gardens.

Ten minutes later the maids had changed the

sheets, gotten a fire going, and brought in all the candles that would fit. Richard himself brought the wine—but only one wine cup, she was pleased to note.

Richard caught the flash of approval in Goldie's eyes as he walked into the room, but it was only as he set the bottle down that he realized she'd been looking at what he carried, not at him.

One bottle of wine. One goblet.

Oh.

He set the goblet down with care. Thank God he'd decided to have a quick swig back in the duchess's digs.

Despite the evening coolness seeping into the castle's halls, he was starting to sweat. Trying to sort out what women wanted was enough to drive a man to drink.

They never liked the sensible, reasonable things a man could be content with. Worse, they'd never come right out and tell you what it was they *did* want but expected you to be a mind reader and figure it out yourself. Yet do your best to guess, and ten times out of ten you'd get it wrong, and they'd get mad, and you'd be the one they blamed.

A man couldn't win. Take them out to dinner, and they'd scarf up all the chocolate in sight, but give them a box of chocolates as a gift and they'd accuse you of trying to ruin their diet. Bring them the finest silk scarf in the kingdom, and they'd wail because you should have known that purple made them look sallow.

Even a dozen roses, which was about as safe a gift as you could get, didn't always work. He'd learned that when he'd given one of his mistresses a dozen red roses and she'd flung them in his face because he'd given his previous mistress a dozen just like them. So he'd gone out and gotten her a dozen yellow ones, but instead of being grateful, she'd shrieked and thrown them on the floor, then stomped them into mush.

He'd never figured out what *that* was about.

Men were so much easier to please. Buy them an ale, and they were happy. Throw in a jousting match or a good round of wrestling, and you were friends for life. When you were around men you didn't have to shave or change your underwear if you didn't want to, and there wasn't a man born who'd even notice, let alone complain about it, if you tracked mud across his floor.

But a woman? Hah!

He looked up to see one of the maids walk in the door with the nightgown draped over her arm. He damn near knocked over the wine getting across the room before Goldie saw the flimsy garment.

Before the maid could squeak, he clamped his hand over her mouth and hustled her out the door. When he turned back into the room, Goldie was watching him.

195

He tugged at the collar of his tunic and tried to look casual.

"Must be getting close to suppertime."

She stared back. He couldn't read a thing in her face.

"I . . . uh . . . I'd be honored if you'd join me."

Her head came up. Her nostrils flared.

Whoops.

"*Us*, I mean," he hastily corrected himself. "In the Hall. Join *us* in the Hall for supper."

She opened her mouth, then closed it. Her gaze dropped. Suddenly intent, she picked at a bit of nettle that had snagged in her sleeve.

"It's very informal," he assured her. "Only a couple hundred people in all. Just family, so to speak."

She shook her head no.

"Would you rather have your supper here?" he asked, brightening. Maybe that intimate twosome he'd planned wasn't impossible after all.

A moment's hesitation, then she shook her head again. He'd swear he caught a flash of sadness in her eyes.

Not in the Hall. Not here.

She wouldn't refuse his invitation just to spite him, would she? No, of course not.

Head down, she tugged at her skirt.

It was, he couldn't help noticing with distaste, the same plain, drab dress she'd worn when he'd first met her. That surprised him. In his experience, women never wore the same dress twice running if they could help it.

Hmmm.

"I guess you would . . . uh . . . like to change first?"

The two maids hurried off to fetch the clothes hanging in the duchess's closet. Goldie stared at the floor, a slight frown on her face.

"Don't worry about having to rush," he assured her. "They'll wait. They'll have to. I'm the king."

Goldie didn't seem nearly as reassured as he would have liked. He looked around him, desperately searching for inspiration. What else would a woman want?

"How about a bath, as well? A nice *hot* bath?"

She smiled, and her eyes lit up.

"And maybe some scented bath oils?"

The smile widened.

"And someone to do your hair?"

Yes, that would work, too.

Richard relaxed. He was getting the hang of this.

Figuring out what a woman wanted wasn't so hard after all. You just had to get back to basics.

Five minutes later, convinced he'd managed to patch things up rather nicely, he set off to find someone to haul up bathwater and carry word to the kitchen that dinner would be delayed until Mistress Goldie was ready to join him.

Comfortably pleased with himself and life in general, he started whistling.

At this rate he'd get beyond those bodice lacings in no time.

Chapter Nine

Richard flopped over onto his back and stared into the darkness, disgusted.

Another sleepless night. More endless hours of tossing and turning and thinking about how big and empty his bed was and how easily it could be filled if only one golden-haired female would come to her senses and realize what she was missing.

He'd been having a lot of nights like this lately, and he was getting very tired of it.

The hell of it was, Goldie appeared oblivious to his sufferings.

Not that she ignored him, mind you, but she didn't seem the least bit concerned that she was ruining his sleep. Either that, or she was a better actress than he'd given her credit for.

He refused to think she was doing this deliberately. Only a cruel and heartless woman would deliberately make him suffer this way.

He'd been wrong about how quickly he could get beyond the bodice lacings. In a week of wining, dining, and dazzling Goldie, he hadn't even managed another really good, deep kiss—one with lots of tongue and teeth—let alone any serious exploration of interesting things like bodice laces and petticoat hooks.

Nobody, absolutely *nobody*, could say he hadn't been trying.

Despite her inexplicable compulsion to spend every waking moment she could on that damned knitting of hers, he'd enticed her out for walks in the castle gardens, induced her to take her meals with him in the Great Hall, and joined her for visits to that flock of swans she'd adopted. He'd brought her flowers and sweets he'd wheedled out of the castle confectioner, taken her up to the top of the tallest tower in Avalon to see the sunset, and kept her company while she knitted, telling her tales of Avalon and his adventures and making her laugh.

By now, with any other woman, he'd have been home or heading there fast. With Goldie, he wasn't even warming up.

What did he have to do? Pounce on her? A man had his pride, but there weren't many options left.

The few kisses he'd stolen simply made his sufferings worse, not better.

It was getting so bad, he and John Paul were on the point of entertaining themselves, something he hadn't resorted to since he was thirteen and a half and had been introduced to more satisfying activities by the Lady Fredericka, who'd been a lusty and amoral sixteen.

If he had the sense God gave a goose he'd give up on Goldie and move on to more productive territory. Unfortunately, the geese were way ahead in the game.

Goldie was becoming an obsession. Even when he wasn't with her, he was thinking of her. And it wasn't just John Paul that got him going, either.

He'd be in council with his ministers and find himself wondering what she might think of this or that proposal—for a peasant girl, she had a surprising grasp of politics. An arched eyebrow was enough to make him reconsider some point he'd overlooked, and nine times out of ten he'd find that he agreed with her. He'd ride out for exercise in the morning and wonder if she was watching the sunrise, or he'd be in the middle of the quarterly tax accounting and find himself adding up her charms instead of his revenues.

And that was just the tip of the trouble heap. Whenever he was with her, he forgot everything and everyone else demanding his attention. Whenever he was somewhere else, he counted the hours until he'd see her again. And let's not talk about the havoc she played with his dreams!

If she'd done a thing to entice him, he might have understood. He'd known one or two women who could turn a man inside out merely by quirking a pinky finger at him. But Goldie wasn't like that. He was pretty sure she enjoyed his company, but she never sought him out and never tried to stop him when he rose to leave. She didn't flirt, didn't primp, didn't even seem to realize how provocative a glance from under those long eyelashes of hers could be, yet somehow she'd managed to move into his mind and take up permanent residence in a way no other woman ever had.

Maybe Harry had it right after all. Maybe there'd been more to that hart he'd chased into the Dark Woods than a damn big rack of antlers.

Growling in frustration, he rolled over onto his belly, pulled the pillows over his head, and started counting sheep.

"Hello there, pretty thing. You looking for some company?"

The burly guard at the gate hooked his thumbs in his belt and swaggered into Arianne's path, his chest was thrust out almost far enough to compensate for his bulging belly.

Arianne grimaced. She'd never seen the fellow before, but she knew his kind—a bit of a bully and convinced he was irresistible to the opposite sex. Every castle had one or two guards like him, and a woman alone, dressed in a plain wool dress and carrying a basket of bread crumbs as if she was a peasant, would be considered fair game for his attentions.

She stepped to the side, ready to go around him. He immediately moved into her path.

"Need help with that basket? I get off duty in an hour."

Her chin came up, and her grip on the basket tightened. She met his gaze with a cool, steady stare.

He came a step closer, close enough that she could smell the garlic and onions on his breath.

"Whatsa matter? Think you're too good to have a word with a man who—"

His question was cut short when a second guard, whom Arianne hadn't heard approach, laid a warning hand on the man's arm.

"Your pardon, mistress," the second man said with a bow. "Ruger is new come from the provinces and a bit lacking in manners."

"Hey!" Ruger protested.

The second guard ignored him. "The king rode out an hour ago," he continued, smiling. "I imagine he'll be back soon if you care to walk out to meet him. No? Do you want me to find someone to carry your basket? No? Ah,

well, then, have a nice walk. It's a lovely morning for it, to be sure."

Arianne gave a little smile and nod in recognition of the courtesy but hurried on before the
two could see the blush rising in her face.
Behind her, she heard the first guard's angry
hiss.

"Who's she, then? Nose in the air like—"

"She's the king's new fancy."

There was a sound of choking, followed by
low, fluent cursing.

"You want to get reassigned to cleaning out
the cess pits," the second guard warned, "you
go right ahead and flirt with her. This king's
never cut off anyone's head for something like
that, but that's not to say he won't start, as
touchy as he is about this one . . ."

She didn't hear any more.

The king's fancy! She hadn't realized—

No, that was a lie. Of course she'd realized
what people were probably saying. She just
hadn't wanted to think about it. This past week
with Richard had been like something out of
the dreams she'd indulged in when she was
younger and still believed in fairy tales.

Being with him, laughing together, sharing
quiet evenings and refreshing walks and odd
stolen moments, she'd almost forgotten her
other troubles.

True, he could set her heart pounding with
one crooked smile. What his slightest touch

could do to her wasn't the sort of thing any decent woman would ever admit to, even to her best friend. But she definitely *wasn't* his *fancy*.

Why, he hadn't even tried to kiss her more than half a dozen times since he'd fished her out of that dank room in the bowels of the castle. He'd never come anywhere close to repeating the all-out assault on her senses he'd made that first night in his tent in the Dark Woods.

And that was the heart of the problem, Arianne ruefully admitted.

He hadn't kissed her, and he hadn't tried to make love to her. What was she suddenly, chopped liver? He'd seemed interested enough not so long ago. What had changed since then?

And why did she care, anyway? It wasn't as if she planned on hanging around Avalon forever. Once her brothers were safe, she'd take them home, and that would be the end of it.

Would Richard be more interested in her if he knew she was a princess? she wondered.

No, don't think about it! she told herself. It wouldn't matter if he did, because she belonged in Montavia. Her brothers needed her. Her father needed her. The castle folk all needed her.

But what did *she* need?

That thought stopped her in her tracks.

She'd never asked herself that question before. It simply hadn't occurred to her. But now . . .

What *did* she need? What was it she wanted for herself?

Her brothers were growing up. Even little Dickie was out of the nursery now, and Rheidwn—Why, good heavens, Rheidwn was almost fourteen years old!

The admission made her head reel. Fourteen! And all the others not so far behind him, really. What would she do when her last fledgling left the nest? By then she'd be—

No, she refused to think of how old she'd be. It didn't matter, anyway, because someone would still have to take care of her father, regardless of how many of her brothers were left at home. The poor old dear got so lost in those dusty old books of his that half the time he forgot to eat and fell asleep with his nose buried in the open tome in front of him.

It didn't matter if Richard hadn't tried to make love to her since they'd returned to Avalon. It didn't matter if his smiles made her heart go pitter-pat or his touch could melt her bones. It didn't matter what she wanted because she had twelve brothers and an absentminded father who needed her, and that, quite simply, was that.

Arianne sighed, then squared her shoulders, shifted her grip on the basket of crumbs, and walked a little faster.

His Majesty the King of Avalon, Darian, Longshore, etc., was having a fine morning.

Goldie had smiled at him at breakfast. He'd knocked three lusty younger knights off their horses in exercise, and he was quite sure they hadn't been trying to make it easy for him. There were no visiting ambassadors or heads of state, no trade delegations, no meetings, and not one single problem that couldn't wait until he got around to it tomorrow.

He would, he decided, take Goldie riding. Just the two of them. He'd have Thurgood pack a lunch for them. Nothing fancy—a bottle of wine and some cheese and bread and sweet-cakes. And a blanket, just in case. A little spot he knew of near the forest would be a marvelous place for a seduction.

At the thought, he smiled. A successful seduction would turn a fine day into a perfect one. Especially since an absolutely perfect day ought, inevitably, to lead to a sweaty, slippery, hard-breathing, absolutely perfect night.

If it hadn't been for Harry leaning over and poking him, Richard never would have noticed the guard at the gate trying to get his attention.

"In case you wondered, Sire," the guard said, "Mistress Goldie went out not half an hour since. To the lake." The amused, knowing look on the fellow's face didn't quite slip over the line, but it came close. "I expect Your Majesty will know the place."

"Oh," said His Majesty.

Damn.

There went that ride he'd planned.

"I'll take your horse," said Harry. "Might as

207

well. For all the company *you've* been, the beast'll probably be more entertaining."

Richard bristled and began to protest.

"Don't be so damned prickly," Harry admonished him, grinning. "Nobody's poking into your business. All they have to do is look at your face to know what you're thinking." He leaned out of the saddle and added in a conspiratorial stage whisper, "As a favor to the rest of us, go find Goldie. You'll be nothing but a pain in the arse if you don't."

"Pack of prying busybodies," Richard muttered, but he tossed his reins to Harry anyway.

By the time he was back across the drawbridge, it occurred to him that there were a number of pretty, secluded spots around the lake that would serve for a seduction, too.

Ten minutes later he'd rounded the far corner of the castle and was belting out a naughty little ditty about a knight and his red-haired wench that he sang only when he was in the best of moods.

His pleasure dimmed considerably when he spotted His Grace, the Archbishop of Avalon, stalking down the path toward him. Strolling, really, but with His Grace, it was hard to tell the difference.

"Your Majesty! Well met!"

Richard wasn't averse to lying, depending on the circumstances, but he was damned if he'd go so far as to say they were well met. "I've never known you to be much interested in exercise, Archibald."

Archibald smiled. It was the kind of smile that gave small children bad dreams. It annoyed the devil out of Richard.

"On such a lovely day," Archibald said, "even an indolent old man such as I can be tempted out of doors. There's so much to see, you know. And hear."

Richard didn't miss the subtle emphasis. He wasn't meant to.

"If you're looking for Mistress Goldie," His Grace continued smoothly, "she's not far ahead. I'm sure you'll have no trouble finding her." His smile widened nastily. "I don't imagine the handsome young man I saw with her will have left yet."

Richard went still.

"I didn't catch his name, I'm afraid," the archbishop added, "but then, I didn't care to intrude. They looked as if they preferred to be left alone."

"No doubt," Richard said dryly. Damned if he'd let Archie's poison work on him. "Privacy's hard to come by at Avalon. All those people sticking their noses into other people's business, you know."

His Grace's nostrils flared. "Someone must when the others manage it so ill. But enough of this chat. I must be off about my own business. So many things can go amiss if you don't tend them carefully, you know."

Richard caught a muffled chuckle as the archbishop walked away, but he didn't respond. He wouldn't give the old fart the satisfaction.

By the time he came upon Goldie, there was no young man, handsome or otherwise, anywhere in sight.

He paused at the edge of the clearing, wary, and angry at himself for it. Goldie was seated on the grass near the edge of the lake, arms wrapped around her updrawn legs, chin propped on her knees, staring at a flock of swans drifting lazily on the lake.

She must have sensed his presence, for her head came up, and a welcoming smile lit her face like sunshine.

Richard grinned and started across the grass to her.

An instant later a cloud obscured the sun— her smile wavered.

His steps faltered.

A handsome young man, Archie'd said.

Surely it was his imagination that her arms tightened protectively around her legs as he came closer. And the shadow he thought he'd seen in her face—that was imagination, too.

Anger rose in him. To hell with Archie and his insinuations.

And yet he couldn't stop the first words that rose to his lips. "I met the archbishop on the path. He said I'd find you here."

He could read surprise on her face but not a trace of guilt.

"You didn't see him?"

She shook her head, then shyly patted the ground beside her.

Relieved, Richard sat. He ought to know better than to listen to a word His Grace said. The man was like a poisonous spider, always creeping out of dark places to sting you for no reason.

Forget about Archie.

"The guard at the gate told me you'd come this way." He flicked on of Goldie's wayward curls. "The way he said it, I wondered if I ought to be jealous."

She blushed and ducked her head.

The urge to touch her was too strong to resist. He dragged her hair back, letting his fingers brush against her cheek and the curve of her ear. The silky curls seemed to float on his hand, rebelling against his effort to control them.

Rather like Goldie herself, he thought wryly.

He let go of the curls. They tumbled back over her shoulder and down her arm. Even with all the natural kinks and waves, her hair reached below her waist. If it were straight, it would fall well below her hips.

For a moment, an image of Goldie clothed in nothing but golden hair blinded him, and he had to fight to get his breathing under control.

Though she was pretending to watch the swans, he saw her glance at him out of the corner of her eye. And *her* breathing quickened.

Good. She'd played hell with his concentration for days. It was only fair he distract her a little, too.

Actually, he intended to do a lot more than distract her. As a place for seduction, this spot held promise.

"I suppose by now those swans are eating out of your hands."

Her blush deepened as she nudged the basket on the ground at her feet. The basket tipped, spilling some of the bread crumbs it held. There weren't very many left.

"Were you saving the crumbs for me?" When she blinked, he tweaked a curl the breeze had blown toward him, then leaned closer. "Not that I want crumbs," he added softly.

Arianne gulped and wondered if air was suddenly in short supply. It happened whenever Richard got too close. When he got even closer, close enough to kiss her, she almost stopped breathing entirely.

It was all the proof she needed that she should be careful what she wished for. She'd been thinking of him, wishing he were there to share the morning with her, and suddenly there he was, standing in the sun-dappled shade at the edge of the clearing as if conjured out of the earth and air by her own longings.

Her first reaction had been bounding delight. Her second, worry and doubt.

Not half an hour earlier her brothers had taken human form for a few minutes. Rheidwn had been the last to regain his feathers. "We miss you," he'd said in that half-boy, half-man voice of his that he couldn't yet trust not to break. "And we're very tired of being swans. Please hurry."

That was all he'd said. There hadn't been time for more chatter.

"Please hurry."

As swans, they'd gobbled up her bread crumbs, then retreated to the lake—an unpleasant encounter with a dog that had left Jonathan James short a few tail feathers had taught them the wisdom of caution. She'd been sitting there watching them, thinking, when Richard had appeared.

Now she couldn't think at all. Richard smelled of sweat and sun and the dirt of his morning's exercise. And suddenly his mouth was hot on hers, robbing her of air and setting her heart to pounding.

Murmuring her name, he gently, inexorably, drew her down on the grass beside him.

She didn't resist. She couldn't.

Her mouth parted, welcoming him. With the tip of his tongue he traced the inner curve of her lips, then the outer, leaving a trail of damp fire behind. The stubble of his beard scraped against her cheek and set her nerve ends tingling.

213

His hand slid over her shoulder and down her arm, then back up again, dragging her sleeve up with it. Even through the weight of the cloth she could feel the shape of his palm, the strength of those long fingers. When they trailed back up her neck to cup her cheek, she shivered.

Vaguely, she was aware of the grassy ground beneath her back and of the sunlight that streamed through the leaves overhead, fracturing into flashes and glints of liquid gold. But those were distant things caught on the periphery of her awareness. Richard filled the rest.

There was a hunger in him she hadn't sensed before. The fire was the same fire she'd felt in his tent, but the hunger . . .

"Ah, Goldie," he whispered in her ear.

The soft sound lanced straight to the sensitive flesh between her legs, making her gasp and the muscles there tighten involuntarily.

"What is your secret, mistress?" he murmured in the hollow beneath her ear. "How can you do this to me so easily?" The words followed his kisses across her cheek and back to her mouth.

Even if she could have spoken, she wouldn't have possessed the words to answer him. She didn't understand what it was *he* did to *her,* and that without even trying. When he was trying—

"Owww!"

It was a cry of exquisite pain.

Richard abruptly rolled away from her and sat up. "What the hell?"

Arianne struggled up beside him, then burst out laughing.

Three large swans stood on the grass at his feet, wings spread aggressively wide, beady eyes bright and hostile. The two largest were Rheidwn and William. She thought the third was Benjamin John, but she couldn't be sure. The rest of her brothers had gathered in the shallow water near shore, watching the proceedings.

They'd been watching when Richard kissed her.

A hot blush burned her cheeks, rising with her laughter.

"Don't laugh," said His Majesty, offended. "Damned thing bit my toe. Hard." He pulled the wounded member back out of reach, then warily got to his feet. "It's all your fault, too."

The laughter stopped. She stared at him, uncertain. How had he discovered her secret? Did he really know about her brothers?

"If you hadn't brought the bread crumbs, they'd have kept to the water, where they belong."

He kicked her basket, sending it tumbling and spilling the last of the crumbs onto the grass.

"Stupid birds can't tell the difference between a bit of bread and my big toe."

The "stupid birds" lowered their heads and charged. Richard danced out of the way, cursing.

Arianne's laughter bubbled up again. By the

time she caught up with her brothers, they had chased Richard halfway across the clearing.

She darted among them, arms flapping to catch their attention.

The swans stopped cold. They eyed her, then Richard. The swan that was Rheidwn spread his wings wider and hissed.

Struggling to control her laughter, Arianne made little shooing motions with her hands, urging them back to the lake.

"What are you doing? Training them to be your guard dogs?" Richard demanded, disgruntled. "They'd better watch it, or I'll make sure roast swan is on the menu one of these days."

The blood drained from her face in a rush.

"Don't worry. I won't really shoot them." He sent the three swans a menacing look. "I *probably* won't shoot them. If they behave."

Reluctantly, hissing in disapproval, the three finally retreated to the lake. They didn't go far, however, but patrolled the shoreline like men-of-war set to guard against marauding pirates.

Arianne sighed. So much for any assaults on her virtue.

Although there *was* that shelter made of willow withies she'd found tucked away in the bushes . . .

No, not that. What was she thinking? Richard's kisses must have addled her brain if she could even consider an assignation like that.

"Don't look so crestfallen." Richard's smile

was wickedly tempting. "The King of Avalon's not driven from the field that easily."

He tilted up her chin, forcing her to meet his pirate's gaze.

"Especially not," he said softly, "when the price is so worth winning."

His thick lashes slid downward, hiding his eyes as he lowered his head and brushed a gentle kiss across her mouth.

Arianne stopped breathing and started hoping anew.

Wasted effort. He dropped his hand and stepped away.

"Come on. I'll walk you back to the castle."

He retrieved her basket, then wrapped his other arm around her waist, drawing her close beside him.

"It's cozier this way," he said, guiding her to the path.

As easily as if she'd done it all her life, Arianne fell into step beside him.

"I didn't tell you," he said with the cheerful air of a man who wanted to talk, "I had a *great* morning. Knocked three of our hotheaded young knights off their horses. Pow! Flat on their arses! You should have seen it! All three of 'em are eager to have at me in the season's jousting, but this king isn't about to yield the field. Not for a few years yet!"

Neither one of them looked back to see the dozen swans who wistfully watched them go.

* * *

Mindful of proprieties, the moment they were in sight of Avalon, Arianne slipped free of Richard's hold about her waist.

His detailed accounting of how those young hot-bloods had come at him this morning and how neatly he'd put them flat on their arses in the dirt, one right after the other, had been the perfect distraction.

She'd needed something to distract her.

Because his kisses lingered. She'd swear they did. She could feel them on her lips and taste him on her tongue like the lingering sweetness of a chocolate drop.

He, on the other hand, seemed completely unaffected. He'd tried to kiss her and been interrupted. He hadn't tried to kiss her since, which had to mean it hadn't been all that important to him to begin with, no matter what he said to the contrary.

She was almost beginning to wish she hadn't been so quick with those knitting needles at the start.

Whatever hope she had of another kiss died the minute they hit the steps leading to the Great Hall and saw the small crowd that had gathered there. At sight of the pair, the crowd surged forward. Richard's secretary, who'd been trying to bring some order to the chaos, threw up his hands in defeat and hastily got out of their way.

"Your Majesty!" a stout burgher called, rushing up. "A moment of your time!"

"*I'm* first," another man said irritably. "I've been waiting longer than you have, and my concerns are far more pressing."

"Oh, yeah?" The merchant lowered his shoulders, ready to bull past anyone in his way.

Behind him, a dozen people jockeyed for advantage and the right to lay their problems before King Jim.

Richard sighed, then raised his hands to call for silence. Beneath his quelling gaze, even the bullying burgher fell silent.

"I will see you all," he said, "but anyone who tries to shove his way to the front unfairly will have to come back another day and wait his proper turn."

The petitioners eyed each other, then reluctantly reshuffled their order in the line.

Richard's secretary rushed up, sweating and red-faced. He blew his hair out of his eyes and said, "We've got everything set up, Your Majesty. Scribes and oath-takers and record-keepers and what not. I know it isn't an Audience Day, but you always see them if you can, and with nothing else on your schedule, I thought—"

Richard clapped him on the shoulder. "It's all right. As you say, I didn't have anything written on my schedule.

"Though next time I may make sure I do," he

muttered under his breath so only she could hear him.

Curious—her father hadn't had an Audience Day for years, let alone this kind of informal session—Arianne found a spot where she could watch and listen but not be in the way. She'd stay for a few minutes only, she told herself sternly, and then she'd get back to her knitting. She didn't have time to sit around mooning over Richard, no matter how much she would have liked to.

"He'll be a while," a woman near her said. "Been gone, you know, the king has, and any number of folk wanting to talk to him in the meantime." She pulled a roll of tatting from her pocket and started working, all the while watching the proceedings. "You ever been here before?" she asked.

Arianne shook her head.

The woman nodded. "Thought not. Well, there's not much to see, usually. Just folks with this problem or that who want King Jim to solve 'em. Most times he does, too. Pretty sharp, our king is. Sharp enough to know it ain't the problems brings folks here but knowin' they can talk to the king. That means a lot to 'em.

Undeterred by Arianne's silence, the woman rattled on.

"The old king, now, King John, he'd as soon kick a commoner as talk to him. But this 'un's different. He listens, you know? And while he likes a good fight as much as the next one, he don't go off startin' wars for the fun of it like his father done."

The chatty woman stopped to check her tatting, made a correction, then picked up the conversation where she'd left off. "Avalon's been lucky to have him. Mind you, he's bein' a little slow about takin' a wife, but I guess bein' a king makes it a bit tougher. Just because a girl's born a princess don't make her pretty or smart or kind, and I'd say the king's holdin' out for someone who's all three. And who's to blame him if he does? Hard as he works, he *deserves* a good woman!

"They do say he'll be running out of prospective princesses pretty soon, though. Don't know what he'll do if he can't find one before that happens. Start lookin' at the daughters of the dukes, most like. Can't have him marryin' just anyone. Wouldn't do. Not for the King of Avalon and whatnot.

"Not that he hasn't had plenty of entertainment while he's been looking!" she added with a knowing wink. "Chits by the dozen, and every one prettier than the last, I hear. But then, chits're one thing, a wife is quite another.

"Take old Martin Dallingsworth over there, for example." She cocked her chin in the direction of a dour-faced fellow waiting his turn to speak. "Had half a dozen chits before he got married, though you wouldn't think it to look at him. But he has money, and that helps—there's no one saying it don't. Anyway, there he was, happy as a clam, until he ups and marries that Doody Roberts. Nobody knows what made him do it, 'cause she weren't any prettier than the rest. Myself, I think it was 'cause she wouldn't agree to anything less than marriage, and he weren't smart enough to see what was comin', so when he couldn't get what he wanted . . ."

The woman's chatter faded into the noise of the crowd. Arianne was no longer listening. She was looking.

At the far end of the hall, Richard sat and heard two farmers argue their case. He wasn't wearing a crown—he almost never did—and he was still dressed in the dusty, sweaty clothes he'd worn to exercise that morning, yet he looked every inch a king.

"Can't have him marrying just anyone," the woman had said.

Of course they couldn't. Kings never married just anyone.

Neither did princesses, for that matter. It simply wasn't done.

But she wasn't just anyone, and she could marry a king if she wanted.

Actually, she didn't care if he was a king or not. And it didn't really matter that she was a princess.

What she cared about, what really, really mattered, was that there was nothing, absolutely *nothing*, she wanted more than to marry Richard.

That shocking cry came from her heart.

Against all good sense and in spite of her responsibilities to her brothers and her father and the people of Montavia, she had fallen in love with Richard. It was as simple as that.

And it wasn't simple at all.

The audience seemed to drag on forever, though Richard did his best to keep things moving along. Concentrating on his subjects' troubles wasn't easy when he was so intensely aware of Goldie at the back of the Hall, silently watching him. He knew the instant she slipped away, and he had to fight to keep from going after her.

Eventually, however, his subjects ran out of things to complain about. He scrawled his name and titles in the record book—the clerks wouldn't let him scribble King Jim or Richard and let it go at that—ignored the secretary with his pouchful of papers, and hurried out of the Hall in the direction Goldie had taken.

She wasn't in her room. The door stood open, and her basket of knitting was gone. The maid who was straightening the chamber said she was very sorry but she hadn't the slightest idea where miss had got to, and could she help His Majesty with anything else?

Richard didn't bother answering, just turned and stalked away.

So much for that perfect day he'd hoped for. Until that damn swan bit him, things had been going along just fine. Now look!

It was enough to make a man weep in his ale.

He'd see her at supper, he told himself. There were lots of things to keep him busy until then. Maybe he'd grab Harry, and they'd ride out to see how that new bridge the royal bridge-makers were building was coming along. Two hours' ride there, a couple hours to inspect the work—which made it about an hour and fifty-five minutes more than necessary—two hours' ride back. Hell, he'd easily kill the afternoon and then some.

He didn't need to worry about Goldie. She was off with her damn knitting and wouldn't be worrying about him.

The thought did nothing to soothe his festering temper.

When he finally slammed into his rooms, he found Harry flirting with the chambermaid and drinking up his wine.

Harry's mustache twitched. He patted the maid on the bottom and smiled and told her to run along, then poured some more wine and handed Richard the cup.

"Didn't get any, huh?"

If there was any justice in the world, Richard thought sourly, taking the wine, Harry would have developed a severe case of boils, at the least, as punishment for his impertinence.

Impervious, Harry grinned and refilled his own cup.

"I'm guessing one kiss, maybe," he said, "and that's probably pushing it. And then what happened?"

Richard growled and considered the possibility of strangling his boyhood friend. Unfortunately, even kings had a hard time getting away with murder, though, under the circumstances, chances were good the courts would call it justifiable manslaughter and let it go at that.

"Well?" said Harry. "What happened next? She slap you? Fall over in a faint?"

"Damned swan bit my toe," Richard admitted reluctantly. "Came right up out of the water and bit my toe!"

Harry snickered and deliberately settled in Richard's favorite chair.

"Couldn't do a thing about it, either. I said something about serving roast swan, and Goldie blanched and almost keeled over. She's as batty about those birds as she is about those damned nettles she knits."

Harry nodded sympathetically, but the corners of his mouth were quivering. "I've noticed."

Richard paced, ignoring him.

"Then we came back to the castle, and I got

caught in a mob of people wanting to complain about something or other . . ."

"Told you it was a bad idea to listen to 'em. Give 'em a minute, I said, and they'll take an hour."

". . . and by the time I got free she was gone again, off with her damned knitting." He slammed his wine cup down. "Her knitting, damn it!"

"Awfully fond of her knitting, our Goldie."

"I'll be damned if I'll spend my time hunting all over Avalon for a woman who prefers her knitting to me!"

He was roaring by now, but even that didn't offer much relief to his wounded sensibilities.

"I am the king!"

"No doubt about it."

"I'm more important than some silly knitting!"

"Absolutely."

Richard turned on him in a fury. "Would you shut up?"

Harry laughed and lifted his cup in a mocking toast.

"Aaaargh!" said Richard.

Propping his feet on the table, Harry tilted back in his chair and watched Richard wear a groove in the carpet. "You know what your trouble is?" he said at last.

Richard growled and kept on pacing.

"I'll tell you what your trouble is. It's that vow you made. Remember? You swore to marry the first woman you saw who wouldn't be forever jabbering in your ear."

"That's ridiculous. I didn't mean it. It was a— a, what do you call it? A figure of speech."

"On your honor, you said. I heard it."

Richard snorted in disgust. "Come on, Harry. Don't be an ass. You know I wasn't serious."

Harry shrugged. "Maybe not, but somebody seems to think you were. It's the only reason I can think of that you haven't managed to get Goldie's knickers off by now." He hesitated, clearly troubled. "You do want to, don't you? Get her knickers off, I mean?"

Richard's glance shot daggers through his heart.

Harry relaxed. "That's what I thought."

Defeated, Richard threw himself into the other chair.

"It's more than that, Harry. It's not just sex. It's—I want to be with her, you know? I worry about her—all that knitting, even when her fingertips are bleeding. I want to help her, but I don't know how, and she can't tell me and . . . Well . . ."

He sighed and picked up his cup and glumly took a drink.

Harry frowned and set down his wine cup. "No help for it, my man. You'll have to marry her. Word of a king and all that."

Richard choked, spewing wine.

"*Marry* her?"

"You could do worse."

Richard stared.

Marry her?

He smiled. Of course! Why hadn't he realized? It was so simple when Harry put it that way.

Marry her!

There was nothing, absolutely nothing, he wanted more than to marry Goldie.

It was as if the sun had suddenly risen in his private chamber and dragged out all the secrets hiding in the dark.

To hell with protocol and political marriages. To hell with the Princesses Graciella and Alice and Thessia and all the rest.

He wanted Goldie.

And if the only way he could get her was to marry her, then that's what he'd do. He'd marry her.

It was as simple as that.

Chapter Ten

Supper at Avalon was an informal affair when there were no visiting dignitaries or important guests—never more than a couple hundred people, give or take a dozen or so, and served in the Great Hall without much ceremony. People were as likely as not to wander in from their gardening or practice in the lists still garbed in their soiled, sweaty, workaday clothes. Nobody had ever objected to the lack of pomp, and it was likely nobody ever would, given the convenience of the arrangements.

For that reason, King Jim's order that everyone would be expected to clean up for that evening's affair was greeted with a great deal of consternation among those who regularly supped with him. When further word reached them via the servants who carried in their baths and shaving water that the king had decreed a seven-course meal be prepared, thereby throwing the kitchen into turmoil and the head cook into a fury of fluent curses and mad cries for more partridges, Avalon's finest turned to one another in perplexity and wondered what the devil was going on.

They didn't get any hints when they sat down to eat. Other than the freshly starched tablecloths and clean napkins set at each place and the promised extra courses, nothing much had changed. The tables were arranged as they always were, side-by-side down the long walls and the center of the room. The high table stood on a dais at the far end, where everyone could see what the king and his closest friends and distinguished guests were up to.

The king didn't give them any indication of what he planned. He looked, they thought, much as he always did. A little pale, perhaps, but that was due, no doubt, to the glare from all those starched white tablecloths. Otherwise, he was just what a king ought to be—tall and handsome and properly regal, which, besides his tax cuts, was one of the things everyone in Avalon could agree they liked about him. Kings were supposed to look like kings, though few of them ever did.

Their only real complaint was that he hadn't yet taken a wife. A man his age, they grumbled, ought to be properly leg-shackled by now and well on his way to producing a royal heir. At least, that's the way the men put it when their better halves weren't around to hear. The ladies were more inclined to sigh over those luscious eyelashes and that wicked mouth and the cleft in his chin, not to mention all the rest of him, and say that if only they were younger, *they'd* know how to catch his eye. Pity there wasn't a princess in any kingdom worth the mention who was good enough for *their* king, but what could you do? He needed a wife, he needed children, and that was that. It was long past time he got on about the business.

Mind you, the men added (but only when the women weren't listening), no man in his right mind would take a wife when he had a charmer like the golden-haired beauty King Jim had brought back with him this last time. They'd heard about the Princess Graciella's breasts and her chattering tongue, and, frankly, save for the fact that Graciella was a princess and this Goldie wasn't, they were of the opinion that the king had come out ahead on the deal, which was just the sort of thing he was always doing, the clever dog.

Really, the women said (but only when the men weren't listening, which was pretty much most of the time), it was just like King Jim to come home with that pretty package of his instead of the princess he'd gone to inspect. Separate bedrooms indeed! Just whom did he think he was fooling?

There were a few ladies, however, who said they thought Mistress Goldie was actually quite nice, well-behaved and kind, and hadn't she taught Cook about those puréed pears—or was it poached peaches?—and given Dr. Arbustis the recipe for that marvelous unguent and patched up Lady Ellen's Tommy when he'd scraped his knee? And they had it on good authority that the part about the separate bedrooms was *true*! To be sure, this passion for knitting nettle shirts was a little strange, but otherwise . . .

Not that it mattered one way or the other, everyone agreed—the king needed a wife, and all this fuss over supper must mean he'd found one somewhere. Either that or he'd taken a little too much sun at exercise today, and they'd gotten all dressed up for nothing.

When he rose and admitted that he had, indeed, decided to take a wife, a rustle of excitement filled the room. He definitely looked pale, some said to their neighbors. "You think *he* looks pale," the neighbors said, "check out the girl." Why, they'd seen ghosts who had more color to 'em!

And then the whispering died down, and the king said something about having sworn on his honor to marry the next woman who met certain . . . uh . . . conversational criteria (*"Conversational criteria"*? everyone said, looking blank) and how fate had led him to the perfect woman and the wedding would be tomorrow evening at six precisely, and they were all, of course, invited.

Everyone kept looking blank. A wedding was all fine and good, a few muttered, but who the devil was he marrying? Fortunately, the Earl of Sunnyvale, who wasn't always quite as dense as he sometimes seemed, tugged on His Majesty's sleeve, then whispered something urgently.

"Oh, yes," said the king, turning a little red. "I'm marrying Goldie."

That floored them. They might have been even more indignant if it hadn't been so apparent that Goldie was a great deal more surprised than they were.

In fact, a lot of them said afterward, when they'd had time to consider the matter, she'd looked absolutely devastated. Not devastated, others objected, stunned. Definitely stunned. Only a few of the most mean-spirited ventured to suggest that she might have looked a little pleased, as well.

One thing they all agreed on, however, was that, instead of standing up and taking a bow or whatever one ought to do in circumstances like that, she'd stared at the king so hard that you'd think he'd grown an extra head, then she'd jumped to her feet, kicking her chair over in the process, and run out of the room without a word to anybody.

Only the favored few who were seated near the king heard his comments on the subject, but they were more than willing to pass the royal words on.

"Doesn't change a damn thing," His Majesty had growled to no one in particular. "I'm still getting married tomorrow evening."

With that he'd thrown his napkin into the middle of his puréed pears and stomped off after her, leaving the others to digest their supper and the astounding news.

"Goldie? Goldie! I know you're in there. Let me in!"

Richard hammered on her bedchamber door. He'd been hammering a whole lot longer than the King of Avalon ought to have to, but that was Goldie for you.

Hammering wasn't working.

All right. Try another tactic.

"Goldie? Please?"

That got the same response the hammering did—total silence.

"Please?"

A moment of silence, then the sound of a bar scraping against wood and the metallic click of a latch. Slowly the door swung open.

Head high, eyes wide and starry with unshed tears in a face gone pale as moonlight, Goldie gestured for him to come in.

Without a word, Richard edged past her. He'd never walked on eggshells, but this was how it had to feel—every nerve strung taut, knowing that with one misstep you'd ruin everything.

Instead of closing the door, she pointedly swung it wide.

He grimaced. She'd heard the rumors, then. He should have thought of that, but his thoughts—and John Paul's—had been on other things. The sort of things that would have made the rumors true.

Now here he was, and things weren't quite that simple anymore.

"I suppose I should have told you earlier," he said. "About the wedding, I mean."

Her eyes widened even farther, and her chin came up another fraction of an inch. Her mouth thinned into a terrifyingly small, straight line.

"What? I shouldn't have told you?"

The fire in her eyes was beginning to drive out the unshed tears.

"I couldn't find you! Nobody could find you! You went off with that damned knitting, so I didn't have a chance—"

He didn't finish the sentence.

He'd seen a look like that before. It took a moment to realize he'd seen the same expression on the face of that big dragon he'd slain, landing himself back in the record books. Eyes sparking, nostrils flared, lips pulled back to show the teeth.

Except for the fact that Goldie wasn't spouting fire out her nose, and she had golden hair, not scales, on the top of her head, he'd swear the two of them were twins.

And, of the two, he'd rather face the dragon.

"Look," he said, trying to be reasonable, "I didn't want to wait. I want to marry you. I want to make you my queen. Is that so terrible?"

His eyes narrowed. That wasn't smoke coming out her nose, was it?

All right, he'd try the rational approach. Goldie was a very rational woman. She'd like that kind of thing.

With one eye on her, just in case, he shut the door and checked that the latch caught. He didn't care to make everyone in Avalon privy to this private conversation.

When she didn't try to stop him, he relaxed a little. Enough to take her hand and lead her to a chair in front of the fire. Fires were calming sorts of things. Might make her see things a little more serenely. It sure as hell couldn't hurt.

While he marshaled his arguments, Richard poked at the fire, then pulled up another chair. Not too close to hers, but close enough. Success on the battlefield often depended on getting the details right.

"It's like this," he said, propping his hands on his knees and leaning forward earnestly. Under his fine tunic, he was starting to sweat. "I've been looking for a wife for months. Years, almost. Not that I really wanted to get married, you understand, but when you're a king, you don't have much choice. Everyone expects you to get married and produce an heir or two, so that's what you have to do. You know what I mean?"

He couldn't be absolutely sure, but he thought he caught a gleam of sympathy in her eyes for a moment. Encouraged, he plunged ahead.

"I've visited damn near every kingdom around—well, most of 'em, anyway. All the ones that count and a bunch that don't."

She didn't seem too pleased with that for some reason, but that might be his imagination. It wasn't as if he'd had much experience with this sort of thing, after all.

He didn't dare dwell on it. Never give the other side a chance to regroup.

"I'm telling you, Goldie, I've met just about every princess around who's past the age of ten. There may be a few I missed, but not many, and I imagine I'd have gotten around to them, eventually, and still not found anyone like you."

He slanted a glance from under his lashes. That was better. There was definitely some softening of her defenses.

"Some of those princesses were pretty"—best not to go too far in that direction—"and some were clever, and some were kind, but I swear to you, Goldie, on my honor—"

Suddenly the eyebrows shot up to dangerous heights.

He stared at her, confused. At this rate, he'd

get so tangled in explanations that he'd forget why he was here in the first place.

"On my honor—"

Oh, *that* was the phrase she didn't like. But why?

Richard chewed his lower lip. This was worse than arguing with his council of ministers when they were in one of their moods. A man's honor—

"Oh! You're wondering about that swearing on my honor to marry, right?"

She nodded warily.

"It's like this . . ."

No, that wouldn't work, either. He couldn't tell her about swearing to marry the first woman he met who didn't chatter all the time, and he definitely couldn't tell her about Harry's theory about the knickers.

He couldn't lie, either. Not to Goldie. Not about this. He sighed and tried again.

"The vow was something I said in jest, Goldie. I didn't mean it. But I did swear, and they expect me to marry a princess, not a woman I found by chance in the Dark Woods, but I want to marry *you*. I thought if I told my people that the vow obliged me to marry you, they'd be more willing to accept you. Does that make sense?"

She was so still, it frightened him. No lifted eyebrow. No quiver at the corner of her mouth. Nothing to tell him what she was thinking.

With the fear came anger. He was trying to explain, damn it! Why did she have to make this so difficult?

"Look," he said, desperate now. "I know this doesn't sound all that good, but it's not always easy being a king. If you're a king, you get to live in a castle, true, and order folks around and never have to worry about starving, but you don't always get to do what you want. No matter how much you want to do it. Wearing a crown means you have to fight wars and worry about finances and marry a woman everyone else thinks you ought to marry, whether you want to marry her or not. A queen or a princess or someone like that. That's the way it works."

He stopped, fighting for calm. He hadn't meant to say any of that, but it had poured out anyway.

"All those princesses, Goldie," he said, more calmly this time, "and I haven't wanted to marry any of them. *They'd* be delighted if I wanted to marry them. Why aren't *you* delighted that I want to marry *you?*"

A horrible thought struck.

"It's not . . ." He sucked in air and anxiously leaned closer. "That is, don't you *want* to marry me?"

That got through her defenses! She flinched. He was sure she'd flinched.

Richard breathed a little easier.

When you're ahead in the fight, step up the

pressure. His father had taught him that maxim, and he'd always found it a good one. Goldie wasn't the enemy, but this *was* a fight, and it was a fight he was determined to win, no matter what.

He stepped up the pressure.

"So you *do* want to marry me?"

Arianne was having a hard time breathing. In the short time since Richard had publicly announced that he was marrying her, she'd gone through every emotion in the book and a half dozen she hadn't even known existed. Shock, fury, fear, doubt, suspicion, resentment—she'd felt them all. Yet there were two things she was absolutely sure of—that she loved him, and that she wanted to marry him.

If only it were that simple! Even putting aside her concern for her father and brothers, she had her pride.

She wasn't a piece of furniture to be bought and sold, nor a dog to be told what to do and when to do it. She was a woman and a princess, and she wasn't going to marry a man just because he said she was.

Not even the King of Avalon. Not even though she loved him.

Why couldn't he just *ask* her, like any normal man?

Richard watched the play of emotions across her face. He couldn't decipher the half of it, but of one thing he was sure—she wouldn't refuse to marry him.

Which didn't mean she'd marry him, either. He had to remember that.

Scootching forward in his chair, he took her hand in his. To his relief, she didn't resist. She didn't show much interest, either, just let her hand lie in his, passive and cool and uncommunicative.

Softly, he stroked his thumb along the edge and across the tips of her fingers.

Poor fingertips, so worn and tender from the nettles.

There was nothing planned or studied in the way he gently kissed those maltreated fingertips.

If she was his wife—no, *when* she was his wife—he'd find out why she was so consumed with the nettles and her knitting. He couldn't bear to see her work like that. If it took all the magi and wise men and scholars in the kingdom to free her from this obsession, he'd do it.

"I met so many princesses," he said gently, "and not one of them made me laugh like you do, Goldie. None of them argued with me, either," he added with a wry little smile.

None of them haunted my dreams or made me crazy with wanting them, either.

Without letting go of her hand, he slid out of his chair and onto his knees at her feet.

"Marry me, Goldie. Please."

The tremor in her hand gave him the courage to go on.

"That's what I should have said from the beginning, isn't it? Not tell you that you were marrying me, but ask you if you would. It's just—I want you, Goldie. Will you marry me?"

Want. Not *love.*

Arianne felt as if she were poised on the brink of a precipice. He wanted her. For him, that was enough.

But she *loved* him.

She thought of her brothers and her father, of Montavia and all the years that lay ahead. And she nodded. Slowly, up and down. Yes, she would marry him.

He laughed. She looked down into his beautiful face, alight with pleasure and smug, masculine satisfaction, and felt her heart constrict.

Avalon's great chapel was bursting at the seams with flowers and all the castle folk who could crowd through its doors. The available dukes and earls and their wives took up the most important rows in the front, of course—there hadn't been time to invite the kings of any neighboring kingdoms—followed by a large but miscellaneous collection of viscounts and barons and assorted odd titles. In the rows behind them were the knights and their ladies, followed, in descending order of importance, by the senior scholars and wise men and magi and witches, the ladies-in-waiting, the wealthy burghers and merchants, the castle officials, and, for the few still able to find a seat, a handful or two of distinguished but untitled travelers who chanced to be in the area. Standing room was allotted to any of the squires, pages, secretaries, stewards, and senior castle servants and junior magi and witches who could squeeze in the doors. Everyone else had to make do with finding a spot in the courtyard in the hope of seeing the procession coming and going.

To Arianne, the world had become an indistinguishable blur of faces and a low, dull roar that blocked out every other sound except the beating of her heart.

Even that stopped when she caught sight of Richard in all his finery. He looked a little pale, which was only fair, since she wasn't feeling quite the thing, either. A person was entitled to a few misgivings at a time like this.

Harry was beside him, pop-eyed and sweating. He caught her eye, grinned, and winked. Arianne tried to ignore him and almost broke into nervous giggles instead.

She was a bundle of nerves, every one of them raw and on edge. She was terrified, excited, sad, lost, euphoric, and dangerously dizzy, convinced one minute that this was the most wonderful thing in the world that could possibly happen to her, the next equally convinced she'd gone mad.

She was in love.

And she was marrying Richard.

When he reached for her, his fingers trembled ever so slightly. Then his hand closed around hers, and the trembling stopped.

Together they turned to face His Grace, the Archbishop of Avalon.

Arianne's stomach dropped. His Grace's eyes seemed small and dark and dangerous—malevolent, almost—but that was probably just her imagination. His manner was all bland unctuousness.

Don't think about him, Arianne told herself. All that mattered was that she was marrying Richard.

Nervous, she glanced at him and found him watching her. There was a faint sheen on his forehead, as though he was sweating, and an unaccustomed tautness about his jaw, but his eyes were alive with unspoken promises.

For an instant he simply looked at her; then the tautness eased, and he smiled suddenly, just for her.

Somehow, they made it through the ceremony.

She clung to his fingers and nodded in all the right places. He held on to her, his hand warm and solid around hers, and said "I do" loudly enough that everyone could hear.

When he kissed her, the crowd burst into cheers.

The kiss lasted longer than was strictly necessary, and there was a little more hunger behind it than was proper, but Arianne didn't mind. If he hadn't been holding her, she'd either have floated out the door or collapsed on the floor at his feet—she wasn't sure which.

"We did it, Goldie," he said, and grinned. "We did it! They may not know it yet, but I've given 'em a queen to remember!"

With the possessive air of a man determined to make sure no one stole his treasure, he tucked her hand into the crook of his elbow and turned to face the crowd.

The crowd went wild. Richard grinned and waved, utterly sure of himself, magnificent in his power. Light flashed from the jewels in the crown that sat so easily on his head.

Arianne fought to keep her knees from giving out beneath her.

Queen! And married! Had she gone mad?

Sudden desolation swept through her, driving out the joy. There were hundreds gathered in the chapel, hundreds more awaiting them outside, and not one soul among them was a friend or relative of hers. No one from Montavia was there to share the moment. Among all these hundreds and hundreds of people, she was alone, and not even Richard seemed to notice.

Just then shouts came from the crowd outside. A moment later a dozen swans swooped through the open chapel door.

"Look! Look!" the people cried, surging to their feet, laughing and pointing and gaping in wonder.

"It's a sign!"

"A blessing!"

"It means a dozen sons for Avalon!"

"Hooray for Avalon! Hooray for our new queen!"

The swans soared over the altar, dipping their wings as though saluting the king and his new queen, then circling higher and higher until the sunlight pouring through the uppermost windows of the chapel shone blindingly on their white feathers.

Just when it seemed they might fly right through the roof, they swooped down, one after the other, and brushed the tips of their wings against the queen's outstretched finger. One fleeting touch, no more, before they flew back out the open door and disappeared.

The crowd went wild with excitement, drowning the curses of His Grace, the Archbishop, who was dancing around like a madman, swearing and cursing and mopping at the mess in his eye.

Arianne couldn't help it. She laughed out loud and threw herself into her husband's arms and kissed him until they were both so dizzy from lack of air that they almost collapsed right there in front of the altar at Avalon.

Chapter Eleven

"Thank you. Really. That's very kind of you. Thank you. Thanks. Yes, thank you. You're welcome. Thanks. Uh-huh. Yes, thanks. Thank you. You're welcome. Thank you. Thank you."

Richard was growing hoarse from acknowledging the good wishes of his subjects, but the rasp in his voice was the only outward sign that he was wearying. Looking every inch a king, he stood at the door of his outer chambers and bade farewell to each of his distinguished guests.

Arianne didn't want to know what she looked like beside him. Her head hurt, her back ached, and her legs were a mass of pins and needles. Her feet had gone numb hours ago. Every now and then she had to look down to make sure

Kate Holmes

her right hand hadn't fallen off from all the shaking.

At least the line was growing shorter. They'd made it through the wedding supper and the longer line of well-wishers in the Great Hall a couple of hours ago. Unfortunately, tradition declared there should be another, smaller reception in the king's chambers for close friends and all the most senior people of the kingdom.

Small, in this case, had meant enough people to pack the room as tightly as a barrel of dried cod.

Fortunately, the cod were emptying out. Most were tired enough and sufficiently primed with the king's wine that they forgot to leer or make suggestive good wishes for Their Majesties' more immediate pleasures as well as their future happiness.

"Good night." Richard nodded at the tipsy old duke who was the last in line. Under pretense of giving him a friendly pat on the back, he shoved the fellow into the corridor and shut the door so fast that the tapestry on the wall billowed.

Arianne collapsed into the nearest chair.

"Whew!" Richard locked the door, then snatched the crown off his head and dropped it amidst the litter of used wine cups and mashed wedding cake and empty wine bottles adorning

248

a nearby table. "Damn thing gains five pounds for every hour you wear it."

He waggled his head from side to side, then tucked in his chin and shoved his shoulders down, trying to straighten the muscles in his neck.

"Take a look. Is my neck shorter? No? You're sure? Way it feels, I'd swear my head's been rammed down atop my shoulders."

Rubbing the back of his neck, he flopped into the chair beside her. "God, I'm tired. All this formality wears me out. Rather fight a dragon any day."

Arianne nodded wearily. And she'd thought running a castle and keeping up with a dozen troublesome, active brothers had been hard work!

She stretched out a leg, trying to grab hold of a footstool without getting out of her chair. The thing was just out of reach. She was debating whether she wanted it badly enough to get up when Richard leaned forward and dragged it closer. Instead of offering it to her, however, he picked up her feet and set them in his lap, then propped his own feet on the stool.

He sighed and leaned back in his chair, every inch the contented, self-satisfied male. "There. That's better, isn't it?"

Define *better*. Arianne forced herself to breathe. Having her feet up felt great. Having her feet up in Richard's lap was disrupting normal bodily functions like breathing and thinking and keeping her heart beating. She'd never realized so simple an act could be so thoroughly unsettling. It didn't seem quite ... decent, somehow. Not at all the sort of thing that well-brought-up princesses were supposed to do.

It doesn't matter. You're not a princess anymore. You're a queen—and married.

Married!

Somehow, in the confusion of the last few hours, she'd forgotten that fact. With an effort, she dragged in air and tried to keep from twitching.

If Richard's hands hadn't been lying atop her leg in casual, intimate possession, she would have jerked her feet off his lap and fled. But his hands were there, and running away wouldn't accomplish anything.

Besides, this was her wedding night.

At the thought, her muscles and bones melted into mush. So much for running.

Gently, Richard ran his left hand down her leg to her ankle. His right hand remained possessively atop her knee. His head was bent, his gaze lowered to follow the movement of his hand. She couldn't read his expression, but she had the sense he wasn't quite as tired as he'd been a moment ago.

His fingers reached the hem of her skirts and slid under them to circle her ankle.

Arianne stirred uncertainly. She wanted to jerk her foot away, out of his reach. At the same time, there was a sudden, eager tightness in her chest that made her want to see what would come next.

Beneath her concealing skirts, Richard worked at the laces of her shoes, first the left, then the right. There was a casual yet sensual aura about the hidden intimacy. It was very unsettling.

Or maybe that unsettling feeling came from the way the fingers of his right hand were stroking the inside of her knee. Even through the layers of skirt and underskirt she could feel that slow, rhythmic touch against her skin.

Scarcely breathing, she closed her eyes and concentrated on the sensation of being touched, pampered. When he slipped her right shoe off, she stopped breathing altogether. When the left came off, her heart stopped beating. His fingers slid over her ankle and around her unshod foot. With the sureness of a man who was master of the situation—and of her— he kneaded the sensitive sole and arch.

She gasped, and her eyes shot open. A glance, half-hidden under his dark lashes, and the faint, smug, upward curve of the corner of his mouth said he was aware of her reaction.

He transferred his attentions to the other foot.

Again he kneaded her sole and arch. This time her heart and lungs took up the rhythm of his fingers as he slowly worked out the ache in her foot, stroking, probing, pressing.

She'd had no idea a foot could be so sensitive. Or was it his touch alone that could rouse the tingling warmth seeping up her leg? And why, she wondered vaguely, was his touch on her foot able to stoke a damp, aching heat between her legs without even coming close?

Slowly, tormentingly slowly, his left hand worked its way upward, over her instep, past her ankle, up the swell of her calf, still stroking, kneading the tension out of her muscles until they were as warm and soft as melted wax. Inch by tormenting inch, he came closer to that aching, needy point at her center.

But it was only when his fingers tangled with the lacing strings that held up her stockings that she realized just how his hand had progressed. And when the tips of his fingers slid over the top of her stocking, grazing the incredibly sensitive skin of her inner thigh, Arianne bit her lip to keep from crying out at the fire that flared through her.

Still moving slowly and deliberately, he unfastened the strings, then carefully rolled the stocking down her leg. A tug here, a glide there was all he needed to strip off the length of silk. That was all *she* needed. Her nerve endings tingled. Her skin burned wherever he touched it.

An eternity later he'd stripped off the other stocking, and Arianne wondered if she'd ever be able to breathe right again.

"Feels good to take off your shoes and socks after a long day on your feet, doesn't it?"

His soft, deep voice slipped across her skin like liquid heat.

"It feels even better when you slip out of all the rest of your clothes. Trust me."

That last "trust me" was scarcely more than a whisper, yet Arianne could swear it rumbled through her bones and set her body vibrating.

Light as the drift of an errant breeze, his fingers skimmed back down her leg, sending a fierce, hot shaft of longing shooting through her. When he lifted her feet off his lap and put them on the stool, she almost cried out in protest at his abandonment.

Seemingly oblivious to what he'd wrought, Richard casually got to his feet. "Want some wine?"

Without waiting for an answer, he wandered off to rummage through the rubble for a clean cup. He lifted a bottle and frowned at the dregs visible through the dark glass.

"Damn! You'd think they'd have left *something* for a man to drink. Worse than sailors set loose in a grog shop, the pack of 'em."

He set the bottle down and kept rummaging.

Fighting for control, dizzy with desire and a lack of oxygen, Arianne watched his desultory actions and considered murder.

Then she considered rape.

At the thought of him naked and at her mercy, she dug her fingers into the arms of her chair, clawing for support.

She felt as if she stood at the edge of a precipice. One step farther and she'd plunge into unfamiliar and dangerous territory. Still, it was tempting.

If she had the nerve, she'd fling herself across the room and into Richard's arms, and to hell with propriety. She'd just sweep the mess off that table, hop up onto it, hike up her skirts, and offer herself right there like a hussy out of the lowliest tavern in Avalon.

Deep inside her, muscles she hadn't known she possessed contracted in an involuntary spasm of raw lust, making her squirm in her chair, vainly searching for some relief.

Across the room, Richard stopped digging in the clutter and watched her, a smug little smile on his lips. In his dark gaze Arianne read a male satisfaction that said, more clearly than words, that he knew *exactly* what he'd done to her and what she was suffering.

Heat flooded her face as she snapped upright in her chair. How *dare* he?

Furious, she flew out of the seat and across

the room at him. Too late she saw the glint of triumph in his eyes.

With a growl, he swept the table clear in one great crash of broken crockery, then grabbed her and swung her up onto the table in front of him.

Arianne grabbed for support and somehow found her fingers clutching his tunic, pulling him closer. His mouth closed on hers in one hungry swoop.

No hesitation. No slow, delicate torment. This time he forced her lips open and plunged his tongue into her mouth, probing, exploring, tasting.

His hands slipped down her sides and along her legs, then back up again, dragging her skirts up with them.

Without thinking, she slid her legs apart until he could stand between them, close to that hot, aching center of her, though not quite close enough to touch.

"So sweet, little Goldie," he murmured, and he swept the tip of his tongue across her teeth and under her tongue.

Vaguely, she was conscious of his hands shoving her skirts higher until the heavy fabric mounded in her lap, leaving nothing but the delicate linen of her underskirts to protect her. His body so massive, so solid, so intimately close, made her muscles tense.

Instinctively, she closed her legs until she

gripped his waist between her thighs. The fine, heavy cloth of his tunic rubbed her skin and made the heat and hunger worse.

So *close* . . .

Richard's head bent. He abandoned her mouth to trail hard, demanding kisses down her neck. He nipped her once, twice, then soothed the bites with his tongue.

As his tongue circled the small hollow at the base of her throat, his left hand slid up to claim her breast, his fingers closing around the curve of it with a possessive sureness that drove out any lingering thought of resistance. She could feel her nipples peak into hard points, so sensitized that even the silky linen that covered them seemed unbearably rough.

With a groan, she arched her back, forcing herself into his hand. His fingers dug into her. His palm pressed harder, grinding the linen against that sensitive peak until she cried out in protest and delight.

It was only when he lightly brushed the curls at the juncture of her thighs that she realized that his right hand had sought another destination entirely.

She stopped breathing, poised on a knife point, shocked and excited, waiting for what came next.

He didn't leave her waiting long. His left hand slid down to her waist as his head came up. His heavy-lidded gaze held her suspended, so open and vulnerable that he could see her every reaction.

All she could see in *his* eyes was her own reflection. She didn't care. More than anything, she wanted him to touch her . . . *there.*

If only he would, she knew she'd be able to breathe again, think again.

She was wrong.

With the first delicate brush of his fingers through those hidden curls, she gasped and automatically clamped her legs more tightly around his waist even as she tried to pull away from him.

He wouldn't let her go. His left hand slid around her back, pulling her toward him, while the fingers of his right hand went farther, touching her . . . *there.* Touching, then stroking, sliding over flesh that had grown wet and swollen and so sensitive that she wanted to scream if she could have gotten the air past the constriction in her throat.

She couldn't scream, couldn't move. It was as if every muscle in her body was suddenly paralyzed, all voluntary action suspended beneath his sure, implacable exploration.

She'd thought the brush of his fingers against her inner thighs had been dangerous and exciting, but she'd been wrong. *This* was danger and fulfillment, all at the same time.

Dazed, she looked down, trying to see what he was doing to her, but his hand was hidden beneath the mounded mass of her skirts, leaving everything to her imagination and the inexorable power of the sensations he was rousing within her.

With an effort of will, she dragged her gaze back up to his chest.

At least he seemed to be having as hard a time breathing as she was.

The thought was distant yet satisfying. But only distantly. The sure stroke of his fingers against her flesh and the eager thrumming of her blood through her veins were everything now.

Arianne raised her gaze farther and found him watching her, eyes hooded beneath their thick lashes, lips parted as though he was caught on the edge of a breath.

Their gazes locked, just for an instant, then he smiled and bent to kiss her. As his mouth claimed her, his fingers slipped inside her. In, then out, then in again.

He moved slowly, confident in his power. With each movement he pressed against the small, hot nub of flesh at her center. Out, then in. Deeper. Harder.

Tremors shook her. Somehow the universe had constricted until it held only the two of them. Rational thought was impossible. With his touch, he had reduced the world to raw impressions and pure sensation.

If it wasn't for his mouth on hers and his hand at her back, she might have leapt into the air like a frightened bird or collapsed, trembling, on the floor at his feet. She did neither, for he held her and refused to let go even as he drove her to the very edge of that precipice, then over.

Helpless, she plunged downward, tumbling, tossed, crying out in fear and a strange exultation. She shivered and shook and rocked in his arms, driven by the unfamiliar sensations that made her body buck like a wild thing beyond her control.

When she collapsed at last, sagging against him, shaking, he drew her closer still. Only then did she realize that he was trembling almost as much as she was.

"Damn." He drew in an unsteady breath and laughed. *"Damn!"*

He laughed again and swept her off the table.

As easily as if she were a child, he carried her into his bedchamber, then tumbled down onto the great bed with her. Arianne was conscious of a tangle of arms and legs and of the weight of him.

He tugged at the fastenings of her gown. She ripped at his tunic. He kissed her eyes and forehead and the tip of her ear, then pulled her hair free until it was a loose, wild mass that engulfed them both.

She moaned and struggled beneath him, not to escape but to get free of her encumbering clothes. She wanted to feel his bare skin against her bare skin, wanted to feel his mouth on her breasts and his hands all over her, devouring every inch of her.

Through the many layers of their clothing she could feel his erection pressing hard against her. And when he took her hand and pressed her palm over it, she had a moment of panic. He was so *big*. Surely—

"He'll fit. Trust me, John Paul will fit. He'll provide pleasure for both of us." Richard's voice was rough, raw with need.

Hand pressed over hers, guiding her, he urged her to explore the length of him, unmistakable even beneath several layers of fabric.

His groan of pleasure at her touch seemed to reverberate through her bones.

Richard dragged in air, fighting for control. The feel of her hand pressing on him almost unmanned him.

He pulled her up, tugging off her clothes, heedless of the sound of ripping seams and laces. One by one he threw the things aside until she lay before him, naked and glorious, clad only in the spun gold of her hair.

For an eternity she simply lay there looking up at him, eyes wide and wondrously blue in the candlelight, kiss-swollen lips half parted. Her breasts rose and fell with each rapid, shallow breath, tempting him with their perfect peaks. The short, ruddy-gold curls he'd explored glistened with the dampness his touch had left on them.

Then, almost unconsciously, she parted her legs, opening for him in mute invitation. John Paul damn near poked through his tunic in his haste to be set free.

Like a wild man, Richard ripped off his clothes and flung them away in all directions. It took every ounce of will he possessed to keep from throwing himself on top of her in answer to her mute entreaty.

Make love to me, she said.

I am uncertain and hungry and aching, all at the same time.

And, *I want you.*

He doubted she would have put it all into words so clearly even if she could have spoken, but he knew.

An immense gentleness filled him, sharpening the ache of wanting her.

Muscles taut with the effort at restraint, he stretched out on the bed beside her, then lightly brushed his hand over her chin and down her throat, all the way to one sweet pink peak. She watched his face and quivered at his touch.

He meant to go slowly, despite John Paul's insistent demands.

It was Goldie who decreed otherwise.

Blushing yet eager, she rolled against him, head tilted to demand his kisses even as her hands flattened against his chest. Her fingers sifted through the curling hairs there, unerringly finding his nipples, which instantly sharpened into hard nubs while John Paul waved his approval . . . and his hunger.

"The last time I thought to try this, I had to use my sword, to protect myself from your fury." He nipped at her lower lip, deliberately teasing, fighting the urge to lose himself entirely in the exquisite pleasure of making love with her.

He tasted the hot, sweet hollow at the corner of her jaw.

"This time," he said, "I've a different sword in play."

She shifted closer against him, and one hand slid down toward his waist, dangerous provocation.

"Will you try it, lady? Now?"

He felt rather than saw her nod.

Gently, he rolled her onto her back. She was clumsy yet eager, not quite certain what was expected of her.

"Let me," he murmured in her ear.

Slowly, breath held, struggling for restraint, he entered her.

She was wet and hot and far too tight. When his first tentative thrusts managed little more than to make her whimper in frustration, she dug her fingers into his back and arched to meet him.

Too quickly. His groan as he ripped through the hidden barrier muffled her sharp cry of pain. He heard it, though, and it sliced through his heart.

Cursing, arms taut with strain, he hung above her, waiting while her body adjusted to accommodate him. Sweat popped out on his forehead with his effort at self-control. Gently, he kissed her and felt her relax beneath him.

He pulled out—not too far—then thrust again, slowly but without hesitation this time. Then again, and again.

Her eyes widened, and her mouth formed a small *o* of wonder as pleasure slowly drove out the pain.

Awed, Richard watched the change and reveled in it. To find that she wanted him as much as he wanted her, that she was all fire and heat and hunger within that perfect golden body, was like finding Christmas and fireworks and the first perfect day of spring bundled into one explosive thrill.

All these weeks of wanting her, all the nights spent dreaming of her, coalesced into an urgent need to possess her.

He wasn't sure just how or when his control shattered. He couldn't help it, not when she met his thrusts with such innocent, untutored joy.

Whatever shyness or reserve there'd been about her had burned away until she drove him as hard as he drove her, matching him thrust for thrust, making him wild with her need. His groans and grunts mingled with her cries of pleasure until they were both consumed, one right after the other, in the convulsive release of climax.

Chapter Twelve

"Was it as good for you as it was for me?"

Richard's voice rumbled in his chest, Arianne discovered. At least it did when her head was pillowed on that broad mass of curl-softened muscle. His laughter made his flat stomach shake beneath her splayed hand.

She raised her head to meet his amused gaze with a questioning one of her own.

"An old joke," he explained. "You wouldn't have heard it."

She grinned, then caught her breath as he traced the tip of one finger down her nose and around her mouth. With their bodies pressed so close, their legs still intimately tangled together, the gesture had enough sensual

Kate Holmes

power to make the muscles of her belly contract in a spasm of pure lust.

His eyes darkened with answering desire, but their corners crinkled with amusement.

"Not yet, my hungry wife." He tapped the tip of her nose, then deliberately disentangled himself from her. "The king needs a bit of sustenance if he's to face the long night ahead."

When she made a small sound of protest, he grinned and leaned to kiss her. "Don't be so greedy. We've hours ahead of us yet, and I'll wager you've had scarce anything to eat today despite the feasting. Am I right?"

Her stomach growled.

His grin widened. "That's what I thought."

Graceful as a cat, he swung out of bed, then crossed the room to throw more logs onto the fire.

Fascinated, and blushing for her shamelessness, Arianne shoved herself up on one elbow so she could watch his every move.

He was a beautiful creature, all raw male power, yet with a wild grace about him that made it impossible to tear her gaze away. The firelight gleamed on his bare skin, casting his body in a ruddy glow that highlighted every line and angle of him.

When he turned, the fire lit his face and outlined his half-roused sex.

At the sight of it, something lodged in Arianne's throat. Awe, perhaps, and not a little

266

fear. He was so *big,* in every way. If it weren't for the satisfying ache between her legs and the dampness that still coated her thighs, she wouldn't have believed it possible they could ever have been joined.

He glanced at the bed and caught her watching him. The smile he flashed her was alive with understanding and a heart-stopping promise.

Blushing fiercely, Arianne pulled up the sheet to cover herself. Surely it was only a trick of the firelight that made it look as if his sex stirred in response. A moment later he'd disappeared through the door that led to the outer chamber.

Hands knotted in the sheet she clutched to her chest, Arianne sank back into the pillows and stared at the dancing shadows the fire cast on the ceiling.

Wedded and bedded, she was. And in love, though she couldn't tell him that.

Her head spun at the thought of it.

Later, perhaps, the doubts might creep back, but right now nothing seemed impossible. Not when Richard was there to help her through it.

"It's a damned mess out there, but I found enough to get us through to morning!"

Grinning in triumph, Richard kicked the door closed behind him, then crossed to the bed. In one hand he bore an open bottle of wine and a plate of cake, in the other, two cups.

Arianne glanced at the cake. A mere piece of

Kate Holmes

cake, when her stomach suddenly seemed as hollow as a cavern?

"What? You don't like cake? Or you'd rather have a good ham, maybe? Well, so would I, but cake is all there is, so that's what we're having, like it or not."

He set his trophies on the chest beside the bed, then, with an arrogant sweep of his hand, tugged the sheet from her grip and slid in beside her. When she tried to pull the sheet back up to cover her breasts, he ripped it out of her fingers and leaned to kiss first one breast, then the other.

Her nipples peaked instantly. When he drifted lower to place a kiss beside her navel, a shaft of heat ripped through her.

"That's better." That irritating note of smug masculine pride was back in his voice, lurking just beneath the laughter.

Blithely ignoring her confusion, Richard plumped the fat pillows and piled them against the vast carved headboard of the royal bed, then stretched to retrieve the wine and cups.

"Have some wine. It's probably the last bottle left in the castle. I'm damned sure these cups are the last clean ones."

Arianne clutched a cup in one hand, the sheet in the other. They'd made wild love, and she'd never once thought of her nudity, but now, like this . . .

"To my wife," he said softly, and he chinked his cup against hers.

She felt caught in his gaze like a fly in honey. Her hand trembled as she raised her cup to her lips. When she tried to sip, wine slopped over the rim onto her breast.

"Hmm. Deliberate provocation."

Richard dipped his head and lapped up the wine, then grinned and kissed her. If she hadn't wrapped both hands around her cup, she would have spilled the rest of its contents over both of them.

"Perhaps we ought to try the cake instead," he murmured against her lips.

He didn't offer her the plate, just broke off a piece of cake and brought it to her lips. She giggled and flinched and ended up with frosting of thick whipped cream and sugar smeared at the corner of her mouth.

Richard bent to lick it off, and it slipped across their lips and melted on their tangled tongues.

With a low growl of satisfaction, he dabbed the cake on the point of her chin, then licked off that evidence, too. When he pulled back, there was a wicked gleam in his eye and a dangerous tilt to his sugar-frosted smile.

Arianne dipped the tip of one finger in her wine, then ran it across his lips. She wasn't sure if it was the wine or his tongue chasing her finger that wiped away the frosting.

Again she dipped her finger, then brushed at the trace of white that marked the cleft in his chin.

When she leaned forward to lick both wine and frosting away, Richard froze like a man poised on the brink of battle, waiting to see what would happen next.

She gave a quick flick of her tongue to the end of that strong chin, then a longer, slower lap up the cleft, scraping over the first rough traces of beard. The sugar and wine melded into a heady mix of sweet and dark.

But beneath the wine and sugar was the taste and smell of the man—a headier elixir by far.

She dipped three fingers, then trailed them under his jaw and down his neck, watching the excess trickle down in tiny rivulets. He turned his head, and firelight shone on the trace of red glistening against his sun-bronzed skin.

She'd swear he stopped breathing when she reclaimed her wine in little laps and kisses and licks, all the way down to where droplets pooled in the hollow at the base of his throat.

"My turn." His voice was low and roughened by desire.

Sweeping a finger through a bit of frosting, he painted a line of whipped cream from the hollow of *her* throat down her breastbone to one breast, circling its rosy peak.

Arianne clutched her cup and fought for air. Her gaze flicked from that tormenting finger to his intent expression and back again.

His finger hovered over her nipple, then gently brushed the aching tip. At her gasp, he looked up and grinned a triumphant pirate's grin.

"Whatever you want"—he lightly flicked her nipple—"just show me. Whatever you need . . ."

It wasn't she who made that choked little squeaking sound—Arianne would swear it wasn't she.

He laughed and pulled the wine cup out of her hands, then delicately drizzled wine along the fluffy trail of white that marked her breast.

The wine slid across her skin and under her breast. Cool and wicked, it made her skin prickle into goose bumps and her center contract in a sudden, disconcerting squeeze of flesh and heat.

Richard bent and lapped at the frosting on her nipple. A moment later he retreated, grabbed the sheet and flung it back, exposing her to his hungry gaze.

She caught the swift intake of his breath. Fascinated, she watched as the tip of his tongue flicked out to wet his lips. For an instant, their gazes locked. His eyes glittered with raw, unabashed desire.

A sense of power filled her, dazzling in its intensity. This was the King of Avalon—her husband—and he wanted her. Her!

Then he drizzled more wine across her belly, into her navel, and lower. At the feel of the drops trickling through those intimate curls and across her even more intimate flesh, her sense of power vanished, swept away by her own flood of raw desire.

Here in this vast royal bed, she realized suddenly, there was no king and no queen, no conqueror and no conquered, only a man and a woman and the mutual hunger that burned between them.

As she sank back into the pillows, helpless beneath his exploring mouth and hands, the thought melted away in the heat rising within her.

In its wake came another, more dangerous thought.

Her fingers knotted in his dark curls as he lapped at the wine pooled in her navel.

There *was* one thing she needed.

She needed to hear him say he loved her.

The thought blazed brightly for an instant, then faded in a greater heat as he followed that trail of wine down her belly and into a realm of wonder.

Arianne's first drowsy thought was that it was very warm this morning. Something, a feather perhaps, tickled her nose.

She batted at it sleepily, then shifted, trying to find a softer spot on a mattress that had turned unaccountably solid in the night. Her nose twitched. The scent wasn't right, either, and something heavy lay across her back, pinning her to the bed.

Her left eye opened.

It was a curly chest hair, not a feather, that had tickled her nose. Several of them, in fact.

The chest hairs were attached to the extraordinarily broad chest on which her head was pillowed. By a somewhat laborious reasoning process, she deduced that she was half sprawled atop His Majesty, the King of Avalon, and the weight on her back was the royal left arm.

Her heart rate quickened as the rest of her woke up.

Her breasts—her bare breasts—were mashed against his chest. His hipbone poked into her stomach, and her legs were so tightly wrapped around his left leg that she could feel his thigh pressing against that sensitive center he'd explored so thoroughly the night before.

At the top of her thigh she could feel something silky stirring, brushing against her skin, growing harder and bigger.

Scarcely breathing, she shifted to find Richard, head propped up on a pillow, watching her.

"Good morning, Your Majesty," he drawled, dark eyes alight with amusement and a darker, more intriguing interest.

With his free hand, he shoved the mass of her hair back from her face, then gently tapped her nose. "I'm glad to see we're all awake at last."

Her eyes widened in silent query. We *all?*

He smiled. "You, me, and John Paul."

Kate Holmes

John Paul, now fully at attention, grazed her thigh in greeting.

Arianne shivered with the answering response inside her. Instinctively, she pressed herself against Richard and was startled to see him suck in his breath.

"Glad to see you don't like good things going to waste either," he murmured.

With the ease of a man who knew exactly what he was doing, he gently rolled her back into the pillows. His first kiss was as gentle as the touch of his fingers sliding down her breastbone. The second was hotter, and his hand slid farther, palm flat against her belly, moving lower. With the third kiss his magic fingers found her center and penetrated, making her cry out in surprise and sharp pleasure, making her arch into his hand.

After that she lost count of his kisses.

The morning's heat was slower, less frantic and demanding but no less stirring than the driving hunger that had consumed her the night before. He brought her to an arching, gasping climax, swallowing her cries, driving her harder.

And then she collapsed back into the pillows, trembling and weak and, somehow, still hungry.

She opened her eyes to see his face above her, pirate dark and dangerous, alight with satisfaction at the pleasure he had given her. Her breathing was still unsteady, her body still shaking with the tremors of her climax when she reached up to cup his face between her hands and pull him back to her.

This time he rolled over and into her. She spread her legs wider, welcoming him, lazy and satisfied and hungry all at the same time.

When he drove deep, she laughed and thrust her hips to meet him.

With him to guide and drive her, they fell into a slow, steady rhythm, thrust and arch, pull back, and thrust again. Not the wildness of last night but a deliberate savoring of each tug and slide and plunge.

His climax caught her by surprise as he drove deeper, then deeper still, his big body suspended above her, poised on the brink, then, with a groan, sinking, melting into her so that the pulse of him inside her was enough to free her, too.

There were no wild cries this time, no panting, just a sigh of satisfaction and then he sank down beside her on the bed and slid free.

His face seemed softer somehow, the hard lines of it melted away. His eyes closed as a small smile curved his lips.

Without thinking, Arianne pressed a soft kiss on first one eyelid, then the other. And then she kissed him on the mouth. She almost laughed out loud in triumph and pleasure when he simply gave her a soft kiss in return.

Satisfied and very, very pleased with herself and this new husband of hers, she settled into the curve of his shoulder and drifted back to sleep.

* * *

The next time Arianne came awake it was to the distant sounds of a door banging and feet shuffling across a stone floor, followed by the splash of water and muffled giggles.

"Bath time," Richard murmured in her ear.

He gave her a quick kiss on the cheek, then freed himself and rolled out of bed. Instead of walking away, he stood there, unabashedly naked, staring at her.

"God, you look wonderful," he said. "Hair tumbled, lips swollen, totally naked under that sheet. The answer to a king's prayers, I swear."

She blushed but couldn't stop her gaze from sliding down his glorious, naked body. Even limp, John Paul was impressive, but not half so impressive as the whole man, perfectly formed, pride and raw, masculine power in every line of him.

He grinned. "I know. I look pretty damned good, too. The answer to a queen's prayers, no?"

Still grinning, he leaned down to whisper in her ear, "Aren't you lucky you're a queen?"

The brush of his breath in the hollow of her ear sent fire shooting through her.

Before she could catch her own breath, he snatched the sheet out of her fingers and bent to nip at her left nipple. When his tongue flicked over the point, she gasped and arched, offering herself to him.

Instead, he straightened, laughing, knowing

276

exactly what he'd just done to her, and ripped the sheet off the bed, leaving her totally exposed.

"Drastic measures are called for when a woman does nothing but lie in my bed and drive me crazy," he informed her. "I have my limits, much as I hate to admit it."

Laughing and blushing, she slid off the bed on the other side, safely out of his reach, and slipped on the warm wool gown one of the servants had left there yesterday.

Her mistake was following him into the dressing room where his bath was laid out. The place seemed filled with people, all of them carrying buckets.

Thurgood was there, supervising the filling of the big wooden tub that had been set before the fire. At the sight of her, his withered old cheeks darkened. He pointedly looked away, scolding one of the maids to hurry with those buckets of hot water before they turned to ice.

No one paid him any heed. Their attention was fixed on her.

Arianne had lived all her life in a castle and had thought she was accustomed to the inescapable interest that everyone took in everyone else's business, but this was different. Her cheeks burned.

One of the maids waggled her fingers at Richard in greeting. "Hi, Yer Majesty!"

Richard smiled. "Nelly. How are the bunions?"

"Better." She lifted one foot to show him the bulge at the side of her shoe. "Yer Majesty," she added, curtseying to Arianne, "we all want t'wish ye the best."

That set off a round of curtseying and bowing and hearty good wishes, which Richard acknowledged but which set Arianne blushing all the harder.

No one seemed to notice that Richard was stark naked.

Arianne recognized two boys from the scullery. She'd slipped them sweets a couple of times when no one was looking, though she suspected they were quite capable of snitching the treats themselves.

The littlest, Tim, grinned up at her happily. "Hiya, Goldie."

Jimmie, perhaps a year older, poked him with his elbow. "Ain't Goldie no more. She's Queen Goldie, stupid. Don't you know nothin'?"

Tim's eyes widened. Arianne ruffled his hair and thought of little Dickie and wished she could ruffle his hair, too.

Soon. Soon she would be able to.

And then what?

The thought struck like a blow.

What would happen to her little brothers when they were boys again? Who would take care of them now that she was the Queen of Avalon? Who would take care of her father?

She couldn't go back to caring for her father

278

and brothers and running the castle as she once had. By marrying Richard, by following her heart, she'd suddenly made life more complicated, not less.

Shaking off the worry for the moment, she gently shooed the boys away, sending them scurrying after Thurgood and the departing maids.

Finish the shirts first, she told herself, then worry about what comes next. The click of the door closing behind the last water carrier seemed unusually loud in the sudden silence.

Distracted, she turned to fuss with the towels and soaps that had been laid out on a bench beside the tub.

When Richard came up behind her and pulled her against him, she jumped.

"Relax. I won't hurt you."

Obediently, almost gratefully, she leaned back against him. He wrapped his arms around her, warm and comforting and strong.

"Whatever it is that troubles you," he said softly, "We'll work it out. I promise you, we'll work it out."

He kissed the top of her head, then let her go. "Scrub my back?"

Arianne blushed but bent to pick up the cloth. Over the years she'd given her brothers their fair share of baths. She could manage this, surely.

Jaw set with determination, she started to roll up her sleeves.

Kate Holmes

He laughed. "No, not that way."

Before she realized what he was about, he'd whipped off her robe and tossed it aside, then picked her up and set her in the bath. When he settled between her legs, his back to her, water slopped over the side of the tub. He didn't seem to notice.

"*This* way," he said, flashing a teasing grin over his shoulder. "I've got all sorts of interesting things to teach you about the art of taking a bath."

He was as good as his word. There was more water on the floor than in the tub when they finally emerged a good half hour later.

But it wasn't just the bath or the lovemaking that had soothed away the uncertainties the thought of her brothers had roused, Arianne realized. It was his promise that they would work out her troubles together.

Richard of Avalon, she thought as she watched him pull on his shirt, would always be as good as his word. The thought bolstered her courage when, properly dressed and her hair decently combed, she followed him out of their chambers and into the new life awaiting her.

Chapter Thirteen

Married! Two weeks wedded and it still surprised him. Yet with each passing day, Richard found he liked this new state more and more.

It would have been different if he'd made the mistake of marrying the Princess Thessia or the Princess Graciella or any of the other blue-blooded females who'd been trotted out for his inspection over the last few years. If he had, he'd probably be out starting a border war by now, just to escape.

But he hadn't married them. He'd married Goldie. And that made all the difference.

Bless that big hart. Bewitched or not, the beast had led him to the one rare creature in all the land who made marriage a joy instead of a burden.

Even his people were pleased. Without saying a word, Goldie had managed to enchant
them almost as much as she'd enchanted him.
Her passion for knitting those damned nettle
shirts continued unabated, yet somehow she
managed to find time to go about Avalon, getting to know his people and seeing to the duties
that naturally befell her as the queen. Every-
where she went, his people stopped grumbling
about his having married a nameless commoner and started singing the praises of their
beautiful, gracious queen.

Well, almost everybody. Thurgood still grumbled every now and then, though Richard suspected even he was beginning to fall under
Goldie's silent, golden spell.

His Grace the Archbishop was none too
happy about the situation, but he wasn't rash
enough to suggest that a marriage over which
he'd officiated was anything less than legal.
Which didn't stop him from stalking around in
his usual squinty-eyed funk and arranging
clandestine meetings with the disgruntled few
who were willing to listen to his poison.

Despite Harry's continued urgings to get rid
of old Archie, Richard had long ago chosen to
abide by his deathbed promise to his father to
maintain the peace between them. He'd set
men he trusted to watch the archbishop and
his followers, but until Archibald made an
overt move against Avalon, he wouldn't do

more than watch and wait. If anyone broke the uneasy peace, he was determined it wouldn't be he.

One thing he insisted on—he didn't want Goldie learning about Archibald and his threats.

Harry told him he was a fool. Harry was probably right, but Richard couldn't bring himself to cast even that much of a shadow over his marriage. Not yet. He'd worry about such things later. For right now, all he wanted was to explore the unexpected pleasures of being a married man.

There was one slight gray cloud on the horizon, however. Richard had never minded Harry's sometimes contrary views about politics, but he was starting to be annoyed by his friend's enthusiastic championing of the new queen. Foolish though it was, Richard didn't like having another man paying so much attention to his wife. And Harry *was* paying attention.

For instance, it wasn't until Harry mentioned it that Richard had realized how easily Goldie had slipped into her new role. As if she'd been born to it, Harry had said. But then he'd leered and said it was a damned shame Richard had snagged her because half the young bucks in the kingdom were falling in love with her. Richard had made a point of knocking him off his horse in jousting practice as punishment for his presumption.

Of course, Harry hadn't really meant anything by it, but the thought of all those handsome, hungry males eyeing his beautiful Goldie didn't sit well with Richard. The thought of *Harry* eyeing her made him downright bilious.

Not that he suspected Harry or anyone else of stepping over the line, of course. They wouldn't dare, and Goldie wouldn't let them if they tried. But still . . .

No, he refused to think about it. Why waste energy on something as foolish as irrational jealousy? Especially when he had more interesting things to do—such as teach his new wife the pleasures of sex in the afternoon, or sex in a hidden meadow, or a quick, hot, hungry bout of sex while courtiers waited for them in the antechamber.

Not to mention all the other pleasures available to a king and his lovely queen. The jousting season was coming up, after all, and then there was the last of the summer fishing, the fall boar and goose hunts, ice fishing, the winter hunt for wild gryphons and manticores, and of course the annual skirmish between the knights of Avalon and the knights of neighboring Grimaldi. He was looking forward to that. Last year Grimaldi had unaccountably walked away with the pennant, and everyone in Avalon was eager to get it back. It was bound to be a rough, wild fight guaranteed to keep spectators

on the edge of their seats. And that was just for
starters.

Yes, Richard assured himself, there were
tons of things to keep his Goldie entertained.
He needn't worry about her being distracted by
any male other than her husband. Really he
didn't. No matter *what* Harry said.

Arianne was knitting when Richard swept into
the room like a whirlwind. "Ready?"

Startled, she dropped a stitch. She glanced at
him, annoyed, then dug for the stitch.

"Come on. Don't just sit there. Let's go! It's a
beautiful day out. Couldn't ask for a better one."

The stitch reclaimed, she folded up her knitting and put it carefully aside, then raised one
eyebrow in silent query.

He grinned. "Guess I forgot to tell you. It's
Monday afternoon jousting, of course."

Jousting? Scarcely two weeks married and
he wanted to risk his neck *jousting?* Arianne
frowned, pointed at him, stuck out her forefin-
gers and stabbed them at each other, then
raised that inquiring eyebrow again.

He laughed and bent to kiss her. A quick kiss
on the mouth with just enough tongue to send
sparks shooting straight to her toes.

"Don't worry. *I'm* not jousting. The king
never jousts at these pre-season things."

He claimed her hand and drew her to her
feet. "It's just a few of the local knights, you

know. No one killed, no serious maiming, and the winner doesn't get to keep the loser's horse and armor, like in the regular season."

Arianne eyed him doubtfully.

"You'll like it, trust me," Richard said with the same sort of enthusiasm her brothers used when they tried to convince her that she'd like petting snakes or carrying a frog around in her pocket, if only she'd give it a try.

She'd been able to resist the snakes and frogs, but there was no resisting Richard. Arianne didn't really try. She'd learned long ago that males, no matter what their age, had the most inexplicable enthusiasms, and it was usually best for the females who loved them to smile indulgently and go along with them, regardless. It only hurt their feelings if you didn't.

The jousting field had been set up in a nearby meadow. Pennants flapped in the breeze, moving splotches of color against the bright blue sky. Dozens of gaily colored tents dotted the grass where knights and their squires and pages prepared for the coming competition.

The royal box was huge and provided with all the comforts a king and his queen could possibly want. By the time they arrived, it was already crowded with the gentlemen and ladies of the court, all dressed in their weekday best and determined to have a good time.

Richard settled her into the chair beside him, solicitously ordered wine and a cushion for her feet, then promptly forgot her existence. Two older, portly knights on his other side, obviously good friends, wanted his opinion on the new crop of contenders who would be making an appearance on the field this year, and he was soon lost in a spirited debate on the young men's rival merits.

Left to her own devices, Arianne looked around, curious. There'd been few tournaments in Montavia and never anything as organized as this. The tournament area was marked off with roped fences, and wooden hustings had been erected to keep the crowd back. Along the sides of the hustings, crudely painted in the brightest colors the would-be artists could find, were advertisements for a number of local businesses. DRINK PORTER'S ALE and SCHWARTZ'S—THREE GENERATIONS IN MONEYLENDING. CHECK OUR RATES!

A SAMPSON SWORD SWINGS! shouted yet another in bright red letters. Arianne wondered if the red paint trickling off the letters like blood had been deliberately applied.

An eager crowd had already gathered, the poor folk packed around the barriers that marked off the field, the richer citizens with an extra penny to spare crowded into the tiered stands opposite the royal box. Vendors wandered through the crowd shouting out their wares—ale and roasted chestnuts and pork-on-a-stick. They were doing good business, as the prospect of a fight always made folks hungry.

Arianne was actually beginning to enjoy herself when Archbishop Archibald suddenly appeared at her side.

"Your Majesty."

Her pleasure in the day vanished. Thurgood was bad enough. She could make allowances for old servants who were jealous and overly protective, but the archbishop made the hairs at the back of her neck stand on end.

"I hope you don't mind if I join you."

Without waiting for an answer, he crooked a finger, and two servants set his chair beside hers. With a soft rustle of his silken robes, he settled, then looked about him. She couldn't help noticing that the other occupants of the royal box hastily looked away rather than meet that piercing gaze.

"I imagine a spectacle such as this is a little outside your experience," he said, turning back to her. "I shall be most pleased to explain things—though, with my being a man of the cloth, not of the sword, my knowledge is necessarily limited."

His knowledge, it turned out, was extensive but of a rather peculiar kind.

"A blow like that, properly applied, ought to draw a great deal more blood," he informed her at one point, when two young knights were enthusiastically whacking away at each other. "If he'd brought the blade down at a steeper angle and with a little more force, it would have sheared through his opponent's shoulder instead of just sliding off."

And, "Frightfully unscientific. A mace can ram a man's head right down on top of his shoulders, but that blow just glanced off. Of course, the defender had one of those new-fangled helms with no edges to catch on, but still . . ."

And, "Tsk. His use of the lance is impossibly bumbling. He should have had the other fellow off his horse at the first pass. If he'd done it really well, he would have broken his rival's shield and buried the tip in the man's chest. Of course, they're only using wooden-tipped lances this early in the season, which necessarily limits the bloodshed." His face was pinched tightly with distaste. "Pity."

Half an hour later, Arianne was fighting a queasy stomach and an absolute loathing of His Grace, the Archbishop of Avalon. She carefully avoided looking at him when he rose to take his leave.

"Your Majesty will forgive me for departing so early, I know," he said, bowing to Richard. "The press of work, you understand."

"Leaving? Already?" Richard reluctantly dragged his attention away from the competition. "Nice you could make it. Come any time. Will you look at that! What an arm!" he shouted as one of his knights made a particularly skillful pass on the field. "Go, Gareth!"

Archibald's thin lips pulled back ever so

slightly, revealing those sharp white teeth. As Arianne watched him stalk away, she shuddered.

Harry claimed the archbishop's empty chair. "Damned slimy, bloody-minded fellow," he muttered so only she could hear. "He gives me the creeps."

Arianne gave a shaky laugh. Harry had taken the words right out of her mouth.

"Here, have some wine." He refilled her goblet and shoved it at her. "Always need something to settle the stomach after Archie comes around."

The wine helped.

"So," said Harry, settling deeper into the chair and propping his feet up on the rail in front of him, "what do you think?"

She tilted her head inquiringly.

"About Richard. About being a queen. About"—he waved a hand vaguely—"this."

How did she feel? Confused. Elated. Scared.

She glanced at Richard. He was on his feet, shouting and shoving a fist into the air, his face alight with excitement. "Get 'im, Reedabeck! Don't let him under your guard!"

In love. Above everything else, she loved him.

"Did you see *that?*" he yelled, punching the middle-aged knight beside him in the arm. "What a hit! And I taught him that!"

The knight grinned and punched him back. "Two to one Umbert takes him."

Richard hooted in derision. "Done! Unless

he's come out of his slump from last year, Umbert won't last to the melee."

She loved him, and, for the moment, at least, Richard had forgotten she even existed.

Ah, well. She knew enough of men and their ways to realize it had nothing to do with her. From the cradle men were as different from women as night is from day. It was the way the world was made, and not even a queen could change it. And still she loved him.

But what, she wondered, did he really feel for her?

Her hands were shaking as she reached for her wine.

Harry eyed her thoughtfully when she finally came up for air. "Feel better? Good. Having to listen to old Archie for more than two minutes at a stretch would rattle anyone."

He frowned like a man weighing some decision, then glanced around them. No one was paying them any heed; all eyes were on the jousting. You couldn't have heard a word five feet away unless it was shouted, and everyone was yelling and cheering too loudly to be listening to anyone else.

Satisfied, he leaned closer. "Richard probably wouldn't like my telling you, but he and Archie aren't exactly the best of friends."

Arianne stifled a small smile. She hadn't needed Harry to tell her that.

"Archie's been after the throne for years. Him

and old King John—Richard's father, you know—went to war a couple of times. Damn near tore Avalon in two, I can tell you. Not that all that many folk are on Archie's side, but back then . . ."

He hesitated, his handsome, guileless face revealing the inner struggle between loyalty to his friend, who also happened to be the king, and the need to warn his friend's wife to be on her guard.

"Truth is," he said at last, so low she had to strain to catch his words, "nobody much liked Richard's father, either. Back then it was pretty much a case of six-of-one, half-dozen-of-the-other. But then John died, and Richard became king, and—"

The king chose that moment to jump to his feet, cheering madly. "Two to one, you said! So much for Umbert!"

The middle-aged knight grumbled good-naturedly and dug into his purse. "All right, then. Here."

Richard snagged the coin from the air. "A copper tuppence?"

"Twice the worth of a copper penny." The knight grinned. "Next time, if you're so sure of winning, make sure to set the stakes."

"I'll remember that, you old cheat," Richard said, laughing and pocketing the coin.

"You see?" said Harry, nudging Arianne. "People like him as well as respect him. Anyone'll tell you, he's been a good king. Killed a few dragons that were becoming damn nuisances, settled a couple of border wars—that sort of thing. Lowered taxes, too, which folks always appreciate. More'n his father ever did. Now *there* was a man for tax and spend, tax and spend. If I was to tell you—But there, I'm not talking about John."

Arianne watched as Richard leaned over the rail to talk with some of the castle servants who'd been granted permission to watch from the ground in front of the king's box. He did it as naturally as if they were nobly born or he a commoner like them, she thought.

A king who not only killed dragons, lowered taxes, and restored peace but also remembered the names of the scullery servants who carried up his bathwater was a king who'd earned the respect and loyalty his people gave him in such great measure.

"Trouble is," Harry continued confidingly, "Richard promised his father on his deathbed that he'd settle things with Archibald. He's done it, too, but . . ."

Frowning, Harry chewed on the tip of his mustache, then glanced around again. They might as well have been on a distant mountaintop for all the attention anyone paid them.

"Archie still wants the throne. He keeps more men on his payroll than an archbishop has any right to, and there are a few nobles—

mean bastards, the lot of 'em—who'd rather have him as king than someone who believes in the rule of law.

"Richard refuses to quell him, says he won't go back on his word to his father unless Archie does something obvious, like try to kill him, but me . . ." He shook his head, disgusted. "I don't trust the bastard, nor should you."

Arianne's stomach turned over. She stared at her hands, clutched so tightly together in her lap that the bones stood out like wires beneath her skin. Montavia was a peaceable little kingdom, too small and out of the way to tempt would-be conquerers. What little she knew of such political rivalries she'd learned from history lessons, not real life.

Life, it seemed, had a way of teaching new lessons, even when one didn't want to learn them.

Shadows stretched across the churned ground when the last event, a general melee that anyone could participate in, finally came to a close. Those still on their feet congratulated each other and called for ale while stretcher-bearers hauled off the injured. Cleanup crews were already starting to tackle the litter even as the crowd filtered out of the stands.

"Great show," said Richard, yawning and stretching. "Best pre-season match I've seen in years."

"That Reedabeck's got a great future in front of him," his betting partner agreed.

"Not to mention Umber—"

Harry's elbow stopped Richard's comment mid-word.

"You idiot," said Harry under his breath. "Have you forgotten Goldie?"

Richard gaped stupidly. "Goldie?"

Harry gave a quick tip of his head to indicate what he meant. "Your wife."

"Oh!" said Richard. Hot with guilt, he looked up and found her watching him, eyebrows arched in amused inquiry. He forced a wide smile. "Goldie!"

How could he have forgotten a woman that beautiful? And her smile!

"Best take Her Majesty down to congratulate the winners, don't you think?" said Harry, louder this time.

"What? Oh!" Richard cleared his throat and silently willed John Paul to keep his thoughts to himself. "Oh, yes. Yes, of course. You won't mind, will you, love?" Was that a blush on her cheeks, or the coloring of anger? "I . . . uh . . . I imagine the fellows rather expect it, your being their new queen and all, and—"

Another sharp elbow to the ribs stopped the stammering explanation mid-sentence. Richard grimaced and offered his arm to his wife. "Shall we?"

Thank God she couldn't talk! Any other

woman would have chewed his ear off for having forgotten her like that. Goldie not only didn't say a word, she didn't frown or pout or sulk, either. Let his advisers say he'd gone mad to marry a nameless nobody he'd found in the middle of nowhere; he knew he'd found a wife in a million.

His knights adored her.

"Your Majesty," said Sir Gareth, flashing a smile Richard had seen him use on any number of impressionable maidens—always successfully, damn his ogling eyes. "It was an honor to fight knowing you were watching. We—"

"Are delighted to have so beautiful a queen." Sir Reedabeck smoothly edged past Gareth to claim Goldie's hand.

Goldie beamed on them both.

Why, Richard wondered, had he never noticed how damnably good-looking those two young men were? And surely Reedabeck was holding Goldie's hand a great deal longer than courtesy required?

And how in hell had the two whelps managed to shove him to the side like this? He'd have to kick half a dozen of the dogs away just to get to his own wife!

He cleared his throat with magisterial authority.

His knights ignored him. He wasn't sure they even remembered he existed. All their attention was focused on the golden-haired beauty in their midst.

"I wrote a poem to you," said a pushy little upstart named Warfield or Warford or some such nonsense. Goldie didn't seem to notice how squinty-eyed the fellow was but smiled at him as sweetly as she had at the rest.

Somehow Umbert managed to force the others aside and claim the best spot right in front of her. He swept her a flourishing bow.

"May I beg the favor of your token when we go against Grimaldi, Your Majesty? I'm sure the honor would spur me to even greater achievements."

Richard's gaze narrowed. He stretched on tiptoe to peer over the crowd that now separated him from Goldie. If that bastard was looking down the front of her dress—

"Jealous?"

Richard spun, hand on sword hilt, to find Harry beside him. "Damn you! Since when have you turned into a sneaking little spy, creeping up on a fellow like that?"

"Since you became so besotted with your wife that nothing short of a good joust can take your mind off her." Harry grinned and rocked back on his heels, smugly amused. "Was I right when I told you to marry her, or was I right?"

"Hah!" said Richard, and he turned to keep an eye on the leering, strutting, ill-mannered males crowding around his wife. He wouldn't have been so annoyed if she hadn't so clearly been enjoying herself. It was one thing to be appropriately gracious and kind and condescending and . . . and whatnot, but did she have to smile so brightly at every single one of 'em?

He watched as she bent forward solicitously to check one young would-be knight's arm sling while the boy recounted his heroic battle and the vicious blow that had struck him down. There wasn't a speck of truth in any of it—the boy had dodged a clumsy swing from another lad his age and dislocated his shoulder when he'd tried to keep from falling off his horse—but Goldie looked as impressed as if he'd battled a half-dozen ogres single-handedly.

Richard crossed his arms over his chest and glared.

Damned upstart puppy. And damn Goldie for looking so concerned. She hadn't been half that worried over *his* injuries the night he'd landed on her cottage doorstep—all frowns and snippy sneers and not a speck of sympathy for his sufferings—yet here she was cooing over a clumsy oaf who hadn't the good sense to know how to fall off his own horse!

"Got a way with her, our Goldie has," Harry said complacently.

"*Our* Goldie!" Richard turned on him, furious, hands clenching into fists. "Damn you! What do you mean, *our* Goldie?"

"Whoa!" Harry laughed and threw his hands up in surrender. The laugh infuriated Richard even more. "Didn't mean anything by it. Aren't you our king? Well, then, Goldie's our queen. Don't be so damned touchy," he added as Richard reluctantly forced his fingers to uncurl.

"Then be more respectful next time."

Harry thrust out his lower lip thoughtfully. "You know, I'm beginning to think you've fallen in love with your wife.

"What?"

Harry grinned.

Richard cleared his throat, embarrassed by that unkingly squawk. "Don't be ridiculous."

"What's so ridiculous about being in love with your wife? Especially if she's a girl like Goldie?"

Richard opened his mouth to retort, then closed it without saying a word.

"You show all the signs," Harry informed him with the air of One Who Knew. "It's always Goldie this or Goldie that until a fellow can hardly get a word in edgewise. If she's around, you've got eyes for no one but her and don't hear half of what anyone says to you. If she's somewhere else, you're always fretting and fidgeting and wondering what she's doing."

"That's absurd! What about the jousting today? Did you hear me say one word—"

"Monday afternoon jousting doesn't count,"

said Harry, waving a hand in airy dismissal. "No man who has any right to the name would be fool enough to let anything get in the way of *that*. No, it's all the rest of the time I'm talking about. Like looking murder at any man who so much as smiles at your wife, let alone flirts or kisses her hand or—"

Richard had grabbed the front of Harry's tunic with one hand and drawn back his other hand in a fist before he realized what he was about. He wasn't sure what he would have done next if Goldie hadn't suddenly appeared at his side.

Eyes wide with concern, she laid a hand on his arm. It took a few seconds for him to realize that his knights were clustered behind her, watching with interest.

Reluctantly, Richard let Harry go and stepped back.

Harry snickered, unabashed, and tugged his tunic back into place. "Richard hates it when I'm right."

Goldie frowned, puzzled, but a few of the knights—Reedabeck, Gareth, and Umbert among them—had guessed at least some of what had happened. Richard spotted a few quickly stifled grins, which only increased his irritation.

"Time to go," he told Goldie more curtly than he'd intended. "I've work to do."

She flinched, clearly hurt by his harsh tone,

but simply nodded her agreement. Two dozen knights instantly volunteered their services as escort.

Richard wasn't sure if it was chance or by deliberate choice that she ended up riding in the midst of an adoring herd of knights, leaving him to ride at the front of their small cavalcade, alone.

The arrangement wasn't uncommon, but that didn't mean he had to like it. Even though he tried to appear unconcerned, he couldn't help hearing the laughter behind him. He also couldn't stop the odd burning feeling that had settled in his chest, right beneath his breastbone. Too much ale and too many fried turkey wings, no doubt, though a small voice inside his head kept hissing, *Jealous! Jealous!*

Which was absurd. He didn't have a jealous bone in his body. Never had.

You've never been in love before, that nagging voice whispered.

Richard guiltily glanced to the side, expecting Harry to be there, grinning knowingly. He needn't have worried. Clever Harry was riding at Goldie's right. From the looks of it, he was flirting outrageously, and she was enjoying every minute of it.

Jealous? Him?

In love?

With his *wife?*

That was crazy. Wasn't it?

Love wasn't something he'd bargained for. He hadn't even considered it, actually. From the minute he was old enough to understand the concept of political marriage, he'd known he'd have to marry someday. He could, he'd been informed by his father and his father's advisers, hold out for reasonably pretty and, with luck, not too stupid, but that was about it. When he'd become king, he'd decided he was going to hold out for a hell of a lot more than that, but not once had he ever considered the possibility of *love*.

After so many excruciating months of inspecting first one princess, then another, he'd about given up on the idea of marriage altogether, and to hell with his subjects' expectations. And then he'd found Goldie.

Granted, he'd taken a risk in marrying a nameless woman he'd found in the forest, but it had worked out all right after all. Even old Sir Morton Tilbeck, who didn't approve of much of anything, approved of Goldie.

And Richard *liked* Goldie. He liked her a lot. She was smart and pretty, and she made him laugh. She was the only woman he'd ever met whom he could relax with so completely. And what she could do to him and John Paul in bed was the stuff of dreams.

But *love?* What in hell did he know about being in love?

There wasn't anybody around to give him an

answer. Even John Paul wasn't chiming in on this one. Which meant love, whatever it was, wasn't just about sex.

And that only made things more confusing. Sex was simple. This wasn't simple at all.

By the time they rode through the gates of Avalon, his head had begun to ache. There'd be feasting tonight in honor of the combatants. In the past, he'd been among the most eager carousers, but right now what he really wanted was to retreat to his private chambers with Goldie and shut the door on the rest of the world. He didn't even want to take her to bed. Well, he did, but not as much as he wanted to just sit with her by the fire and forget about all these damned unanswerable questions, like what love was and whether he was suffering from it.

Goldie's escort seemed to have forgotten he existed as they vied for the honor of helping her down from her horse. Only Harry and the groom remembered he was there. The groom took his horse as Harry sauntered up, a knowing smirk on his face. Together, they watched Goldie walk up the steps, regal as the queen she now was, with two dozen fawning knights in her wake. She never once looked back to see what had become of her husband.

"They like her, don't they?" Richard said at last, still staring at the open doorway through which she'd disappeared. "The people of Avalon, I mean. They really do like her."

"*Like* her?" Harry laughed. "She goes on like this, and she'll soon be topping you in the opinion polls." His eyebrows tilted dangerously. "You mark my words, Richard, if you don't take care, you're going to have to beat 'em off with a stick."

Chapter Fourteen

"You've gotta do something about Archie." Harry wrenched a leg off the roast duck, then waved it at Richard to emphasize his point. "I'm telling you, he's up to something."

Richard shrugged irritably. "Archie's always up to something. Eat your duck."

He didn't want to talk about Archie. He didn't want to talk to Harry. Right now, he didn't want to bother with anyone except Goldie.

He watched, fascinated, as she neatly sliced off a piece of the breast meat and put it on her plate, then spooned some plum sauce over it. When she delicately licked off a drop of sauce that had spilled on her finger, John Paul stirred to attention.

One could do a lot with plum sauce and sweet, hot flesh. To hell with the duck.

Not half an hour earlier he'd enticed her away from her knitting long enough for a quick, hot tumble on the rug in front of the fire. It was sheer good luck that they'd been decently dressed, if a little rumpled, when the servants had walked in.

Under cover of the table, he worked the toe of his boot beneath her skirts and gently nudged her ankle. Just a friendly little bump to remind her. The sudden wash of rose across her cheeks couldn't hide the conspiratorial twinkle in her eyes as she glanced at him from beneath those long lashes.

John Paul stirred anew with interest, but Harry chose that moment to ask for the peas, effectively squelching things before they even got started.

Richard had to turn his attention to his plate to keep from glaring at his friend. If it hadn't been for Harry, he could have gone for the plum sauce and to hell with everything else.

Unfortunately, the good-looking ox had ambled in unannounced just as the servants were laying supper in his and Goldie's private quarters. Before anyone had a chance to say hello and good-bye, he'd pinched the maid's bottom and invited himself to stay. Goldie had rapped his hand with her knitting needle and made him apologize to the maid, but by then the damage was done—short of bodily pitching him out the door, there hadn't been any way of getting rid of him.

Richard grumpily watched his friend further dismember the duck. Was it just his imagination, or did Harry show up more often than he used to? It wasn't his imagination that his friend spent more time flirting with his wife than he did talking to him.

The hell of it was, Goldie flirted back.

Richard watched from under lowered brows as she passed Harry the peas. Harry winked, which made her smile.

All right, maybe not *flirted*. Not the way most women did, anyway. She was simply being nice. She couldn't help it, Richard reminded himself. That was just the way she was.

But why did she have to be so damned attentive, or so willing to laugh at every stupid joke Harry told, or to listen to whatever wild tale he happened to be telling? *He* could tell she wasn't really flirting, but he wasn't all that sure about Harry.

Not that he was worried his wife would look at another man the way she looked at him! Why should she, when she was married to the king?

Trouble was, he couldn't be sure that hot-blooded men like Harry or Sir Gareth or that preening peacock, Sir Umbert, understood how innocent she really was. After all, none of them had had the sense to find a wife of his own. They could easily mistake Goldie's natural friendliness for something far more deliberately enticing.

Not that they'd ever try to cuckold their king, of course, even if she were inclined to let them, which she wasn't, but there was no denying they were getting to be damned nuisances.

Seemed his best men were always underfoot these days, talking Goldie's ears off with overblown tales of their adventures and quarreling over who got to lead her in to dinner or carry her basket of bread crumbs when she went out to feed those damned swans of hers. Things had gotten so bad, he'd even considered sending them off to fight dragons or rescue kidnapped maidens or something similarly useful, even if it meant having to hire somebody else to rouse the dragons and kidnap the maidens to begin with.

On top of it all, there was Warfield making an utter ass of himself with the poetry he'd taken to writing lately. In honor of Her Majesty, or so he said. Poetry!

Just the thought of it gave Richard indigestion.

"Richard?"

Richard looked up to find his wife and friend staring at him.

"You look like hell," Harry said helpfully. "What's the matter? Liver turned upside down? Don't like duck anymore?"

"Nothing's the matter with me." He glared at Harry, then he glared at the duck. Then he picked up his knife, stabbed the carcass, and savagely wrenched off the remaining leg.

"Glad to hear it," said Harry, watching the process with interest. "Hate to think what you'd do to the thing otherwise."

Richard snarled, sank his teeth into the leg, and ripped off a huge chunk of meat. To hell with the plum sauce.

What had she done? What had made Richard so angry over supper?

Arianne poked at the dwindling pile of nettles in her basket, but what she saw was Richard's frowning face across the table, staring at something only he could see. Something, she was sure, that had to do with her. But what?

She'd seen no hint of his displeasure an hour earlier when he'd pulled her down on the rug in front of the hearth, but then, she never did see it when they were alone together. Whenever they were with others, however, she'd swear she sensed a growing hostility in him.

Was he, she wondered, disappointed in her? In these past few weeks she'd tried her best to learn all she could about Avalon and its people, tried to be a good wife and a good queen. Since she couldn't speak, she worked extra hard to be as friendly as possible to everyone she met, even the silly knights who'd taken to vying with each other for her favors because they evidently hadn't anything better to do.

Perhaps it wasn't enough, or not good enough. If that was the case, though, wouldn't he tell her?

Thank Heaven she was almost finished with the nettle shirts. Ten and a half done, going on eleven—if only the nettles held out. Once she could speak again, she'd explain everything to Richard, then do something special that would make him laugh and forget whatever it was that bothered him. But what?

As she bent to her knitting, Arianne's thoughts spun, searching for an idea of something that might make her husband laugh again.

A week later Richard found himself staring at the closed door of his small reception room and thinking about murder.

Ever since the incident of the roast duck, he'd tried to keep his thoughts and his temper under control—God knew he'd tried!—but there were limits to everything, including self-restraint, and he'd just reached the end of his.

It was the troubadour who'd started it. Richard was sure of it.

Gregory of Tours had showed up at the castle gates not two days ago, begging entrance and offering to pay for his room and board with his songs and storytelling. Since he'd been through Avalon any number of times in recent years, the guards hadn't hesitated to let him in, and the castle steward had readily found him a comfortable room and a place at table in the Great Hall.

Richard hadn't minded any of that. He liked a little music and song as well as the next man, and Gregory was a great deal more talented than most of his kind. He'd even ordered the servants to offer the fellow some extra wine and see to it that the castle laundresses washed his clothes and fetched hot water for a bath.

But that was before the evil little bastard had taken to seducing his wife. Goldie would never have met with a rat like him in private if he hadn't tricked and tempted her to it in the first place. He was a sly, smarmy fellow, thin and ferret-faced, with a shock of pale yellow hair that constantly fell in his eyes and a voice to match his looks. For some reason, the women thought him handsome. Adorable, one giggling matron had informed him.

Adorable!

Bile rose in Richard's throat.

If he'd had his way, the fellow would have been tossed into the nearest lake after that first private session with Goldie. Trouble was, he couldn't throw the bastard out, no matter how much he'd like to, without loosing the tongue of every ill-natured gossip in the kingdom.

So what if he'd enjoyed the fellow's performances well enough in the past—and paid handsomely for the entertainment, too? That was then. This was now, and right now the fellow was closeted alone with his wife.

Richard didn't like it, but he couldn't quite bring himself to break into the room like a barbarian storming the castle. Instead, he paced the hall outside and wondered what in hell was going on behind that locked door.

Locked, damn it! What in hell were they up to that Goldie thought she had to lock the door behind her?

"Your Majesty?" Thurgood was the first person in an hour rash enough to venture anywhere near him.

With a prune-faced calm polished over years of practice, the old man planted himself in the middle of the corridor, clasped his hands in front of him, and waited until Richard came within speaking range—Thurgood never raised his voice, not even if it meant delivering his messages in bits and pieces.

"The representatives from the merchants' guild are waiting for you in the Great Hall," he said. "The meeting was scheduled for a good half hour since."

Richard glowered at him and kept on pacing. Not a hint of movement behind that door.

Once he was back in range, Thurgood continued, "Your accountants wondered when you might have time to go over the latest tax records. You demanded the records six days ago and haven't yet seen fit to glance at them."

Hunching his shoulders and shoving his fists deeper into his pockets, Richard stalked back the way he'd come. This time he stopped and pressed his ear to the door. Gregory was singing, but the thick wood swallowed sound so that he could scarcely make out the tune, let alone the words. The instant the singing stopped, Goldie laughed. There was an indecipherable murmur, then the singing started again.

God help Gregory of Tours if he ever let the silence stretch too long.

Richard stalked back up the corridor.

"At this rate," said Thurgood, pinch-faced with disapproval, "you'll be the laughingstock of Avalon. Anyone would think you suspected Her Majesty of inappropriate behavior, which we all know is absurd."

Richard ignored him. "What's she want with that slick fool, anyway?"

"Perhaps Her Majesty is taking music lessons."

"Lessons? With *that* one-note dog? Hah!"

"You do Her Majesty a grave injustice to be so suspicious."

Richard threw up his hands in frustration. "You, too? Isn't there one man in all of Avalon who hasn't fallen in love with my wife?"

Thurgood's wrinkled cheeks turned a dull shade of pink. He sniffed and drew himself up with dignity. "I would never be so presumptuous as to fall in love with anyone's wife, let alone yours. But Her Majesty has several times been so gracious as to entertain my little niece when she's wandered in while I was working. I cannot help but be grateful for her kindness to the child."

"Your *niece!* What about my *wife?* Alone like this with that scrawny little fop of a—"

"You," said Thurgood with patent disgust, "are a fool."

Hell of a note, Richard thought grimly a few hours later. First insults from his valet, now this! A damned troubadour spends hours closeted with his wife, singing her God alone knew what kinds of songs and making up to her with his slick, fashionable ways, and then *he* has to spend another couple hours listening to the fellow and trying to look as if he liked it!

Seated in his great carved chair on the dais, head sunk on his hand, Richard gloomily surveyed the people assembling for the performance. If he'd had a grain of sense he'd have called the whole thing off and sent sly Gregory packing, but Thurgood had talked him out of it. People would talk, he'd said. As if they weren't already!

Last time he listened to that old fussbudget! Harry plopped into the seat to his left.

"Enjoy your stroll past the small reception room this afternoon?" he inquired cheerily.

Richard turned on him, teeth bared.

"Hey! Don't look at *me* like that. *Everyone's*

talking about it. You didn't really think we wouldn't hear about it, did you? The King of Avalon, crazy in love and jealous to boot! It's got everyone laughing up their sleeves."

"I am *not* jealous."

"Oh, yes, you are," said Harry, nodding wisely. "Love will do that to a man. Or so I'm told. Never suffered from the malady myself, but watching you—"

"You talk so much, your teeth rattle," Richard growled. "Damned shame you have nothing to say worth listening to."

He might have said more except that Goldie entered the hall, and every thought except how beautiful she was went right out of his head. He watched as she made her way through the gathering crowd. A smile here, a nod there. Her progress was slow—it seemed everyone wanted to drop a word or two in her ear. Asking for favors, no doubt, Richard thought glumly. Goldie, with a soft heart and no experience in the ways of a royal court, would probably give them everything they asked for if she could.

His eyes narrowed when that insolent, poetry-writing puppy—Sir Warburn, or Warfop, something like that—grabbed her sleeve, then, blushing, slipped a folded sheet of parchment into her hand.

Harry saw it, too. "Now, don't start growling all over again. Silly fool's always writing poems to the rainbow in her eyes or some such nonsense. Nobody takes it seriously. Not him and certainly not Goldie."

Richard might have believed him if he hadn't seen the way Warburp watched her walk away. When Goldie took her place beside him at last, she was flushed, her eyes alight with excitement.

Was it just his imagination, or did her glance hold the tiniest trace of guilt?

Breathe deeply, he told himself. Don't be a fool. Maybe Harry was right. Maybe he was just a little bit jealous. Yes, surely that was it. A simple little case of unreasonable jealousy, nothing more. Certainly nothing so complicated as love.

Goldie stretched out a hand and, blushing, rested it atop his where it lay on the arm of his chair. Without thinking, Richard turned his hand over and gently laced his fingers through hers. Her answering smile made his heart turn over.

Nothing so complicated as love, he'd said?

Thurgood was right. He *was* a fool.

And he really was in love Goldie.

His Majesty groaned and sank back in his chair and wondered if anyone would notice if he dragged his wife to the floor and made love to her right there in front of God and everybody.

Chapter Fifteen

Eleven shirts finished! The only one left to do was little Dickie's. Unfortunately, she needed more nettles.

Arianne frowned at her half-empty basket. What few nettles she had left simply weren't enough to finish even Dickie's small shirt. Like it or not, she'd have to gather more.

Fortunately, tomorrow night would be the full moon. There was a nettle patch not far from the castle that could provide what she needed. All she had to do was slip out of the castle tomorrow night late, cut the nettles, then somehow slip back in without anyone seeing her.

Richard was the only real worry. He'd been so difficult these past few days, so horribly unreasonable, that she wasn't sure how he'd react to her sneaking out like that.

But she *had* to have the nettles. And it would have to be tomorrow night. Another month and the first frosts would kill off everything until spring.

Carefully, she laid the nettles back in the basket, thinking hard.

A hooded cloak would cover her hair and disguise her figure. There was always someone up and wandering around in a castle, no matter what the hour. No one would pay any attention to one more sleepless person wandering through Avalon's hallways.

No one, that is, except the guards at the gate. The drawbridge would be up by then, but there was still the postern. There wouldn't be a regular guard on that. If she avoided the patrols on the battlements, it shouldn't be a problem. A bit difficult scrambling over the rocks outside, maybe, but not impossible. Stuff a rag into the lock so the gate wouldn't shut, and that would be it. Well, that and gathering the nettles.

And Richard? She could mix a sleeping potion into his wine after dinner. Once he was sound asleep, she could slip out, gather the nettles, and slip back into the castle. By the time he awoke the following morning, she would have what she needed, and he would be none the wiser.

* * *

Goldie was up to something. Richard was sure of it. She'd been on edge all day. No one else seemed to notice, but he could tell.

Had that damned troubadour slipped back into Avalon? He tried to push the thought away, tried to concentrate on the day's accumulation of paperwork, but it kept coming back, sneaking under his defenses and ruining his appetite.

Was this what love did to you? Ruined your life and your appetite and turned you into a jealous fool? If he'd had any idea it would be like this, he'd have left Goldie in that damned cottage in the Dark Woods and never looked back.

It was only by chance that he saw her slip the powder into his cup of wine. He pretended to be deep in some dull report on the increased production of the barley crop when she set the wine beside him. He could see her hand tremble ever so faintly.

Pain stabbed through him. Had she added a sleeping draught to the wine? Or poison?

That he had to wonder made him sick and angry. He'd never been much of an actor, but she didn't seem to notice anything amiss when he glanced up at her and forced a smile.

"Why don't you go to bed?" He'd almost added "my love" but stopped himself in time. "I'll join you shortly. Wait for me."

She went white and refused to look at him as she nodded, then quietly walked away. The sound of the door to the bedchamber shutting behind her seemed to echo in the silence.

Cold with anger, Richard picked up the cup and sniffed, then dipped the tip of his finger in it and tasted. There was a familiar, slightly bitter flavor just beneath the stronger taste of the wine.

Not poison, thank God. A sleeping draught.

That made him feel a little better, but not much.

He didn't come to bed. For an hour Arianne lay staring into the dark, straining for any sound from the room beyond. At last, unable to endure the silence, she got up and went to see.

The candles had sunk to flickering stubs. Richard was sitting in his chair, his head pillowed on his arms. She couldn't see his face, but she could hear his soft snores. He was sound asleep and likely to remain so for some time to come. Her potion had worked its magic, as she had planned.

The knowledge brought little satisfaction. Sternly ignoring the guilt pricking her, she went to get her shoes, her cloak, and the basket.

Richard followed Goldie across the bailey, careful to keep to the shadows where she wouldn't spot him. The full moon was rising, bathing the ground in silver.

He had to give her credit; she was clever

enough not to try to sneak through the shadows as he was doing. Anyone seeing her would assume she was about her proper business, a midwife, perhaps, called out for a midnight delivery.

Only when she neared the postern did she show any caution, pausing in the shelter of an archway until the guards passed, then hurrying forward to lift the bar and swing the door open.

He gave her a few minutes to get clear, then silently followed her.

It was hard going across the rocky ground beyond, but at least there was plenty of cover. He had to wait at the far side of the dry moat that surrounded Avalon, hovering in the shadows of the last rocks while she took a well-worn path across the open field and into the copse beyond. As far as he could tell, she never once looked back.

He lost her in the copse. He hadn't been in here since he was a boy and had forgotten how many paths wound through it, crossing and recrossing until it was impossible to tell which way you were going in the dark. Silently cursing, he strained to catch any sound that was out of place, but all he could hear was the faint rustling of leaves in the breeze.

It was more by luck than skill that he finally found her a half hour later. This time, his curses weren't all silent.

She was cutting nettles. Nettles!

For this he'd banged his knee and torn his sleeve? Had he fallen in love with a madwoman?

Why this obsession with nettles? None of his wise men or magi or seers could explain it, and he'd driven them mercilessly with his demands for an answer.

Careful to make no sound, he took a seat on a fallen tree trunk, safe in the shadows, and watched her work. She'd shed the cloak she'd worn. Her hair gleamed silver in the light of the full moon that now stood high in the sky, drowning out the stars. He could hear the scrape of the nettles against her skirts, but she never uttered a sound, too intent on her work even to lift her head when an owl flew past.

Eventually, she filled her basket. She had to cast about for a moment to find her cloak. When she put it on and drew up the hood, she became little more than a shadow herself. Her path, he was pleased to see, would take her past his tree-trunk seat.

She came toward him, head down, her body canted to balance the weight of the nettles, picking her way with care. When she was only a foot away, he stood up, blocking her path.

Any other woman would have screamed and run away. Goldie gave a choked "Eep!" and backed up. Moonlight glinted on the knife she held in her gloved hand.

"You can put that away. I won't harm you."

She gasped. Her basket hit the ground with a thud.

"I suppose I should apologize," he said, gingerly taking the knife from her. "Your sleeping potion went out the window instead of down my gullet."

He tossed the knife in with the nettles. She probably wouldn't use it against him, but the blade was stained with nettle juice. When it came to nettles, better safe than sorry.

"You'll forgive me if I say that I had some rather grim suspicions. I wasn't expecting you to lead me to a nettle patch. By now you'd think I'd have learned not to expect the expected where you're concerned."

She didn't move when he stretched out a hand and threw back her hood. He let his fingers brush her hair, spun silver in the moonlight.

"There, that's better." His voice seemed to come out of his chest, somewhere beneath his breastbone. Or maybe it was just that he was having a hard time breathing. She did that to him. Often.

He said, more softly, "It's rather disconcerting, talking to a shadow."

In the moonlight she was a fairy creature cast in silver and black velvet. The moon itself became two drops of liquid silver in her eyes.

Gently he traced the line of her cheek.

Dragons, warring knights, treacherous arch-

323

bishops—he could deal with all of them, but this one woman was beyond him. Never had he wanted anything as much as he wanted her, yet always she eluded him, slipping through his fingers like smoke and leaving him empty-handed.

It had been a hell of a lot simpler when all he thought about was making love to her and not about loving her.

And still she stood there, silently watching him, waiting.

Suddenly he wanted to grab her, wrap his cloak around her, and shelter her from the night and whatever it was that had driven her out into it. But what was it he'd be protecting her from? If only she'd had enemies he could see, flesh-and-blood creatures he could slash with a sword and pound with a mace, it would be so much easier.

Unfortunately, the best he could do right now was get her back to the castle. He'd worry about that damned sleeping potion trick of hers later.

Grimacing, he wrapped the edge of his cloak around his hand, then bent to pick up the basket.

"I hope you don't mind walking. I let the postern shut behind me." He couldn't help but smile at her start of surprise. "I didn't want you getting back into the castle if you managed to sneak around behind me. Unfortunately"—he hefted the basket to get a better grip—"the main gate is another half-mile hike around Avalon."

Arianne didn't mind the extra half mile. It would give her a chance to think.

Unfortunately, her brain didn't seem to be working. Guilt, fear, and unadulterated lust were playing havoc with her thought processes.

He'd scared the devil out of her, popping up out of the shadows like that. Once her heart had dropped back from her throat, she'd realized she felt safe with him standing there, so big he seemed to touch the stars.

If he'd yelled at her, it would have been easier. If he'd grabbed her and shaken her till her eyeballs rattled, she could have handled that. Maybe.

Instead, he'd thrown back her hood, then touched her face so gently that it was more a whisper than a caress. With that one tender touch, fire had shot through her. If he'd kissed her, she wouldn't have been responsible for the consequences.

But he hadn't kissed her. He'd simply picked up her basket and set off for the castle. He hadn't once looked back, not even when they were out of that copse.

His silence was more terrifying than overt anger ever could have been. She couldn't bear it if he turned her away now, just when she was so close to being able to tell him the truth.

Lost in dark thoughts, she didn't notice how far they'd gone until they rounded the corner of the castle and spotted the main gate ahead. She could see the shapes of the guardsmen, dimly limned against the moonlight, on the battlements above the gate.

For the first time it occurred to her that it might be a little embarrassing to explain why the King and Queen of Avalon were trailing into the castle on foot at a time like this.

On the other hand, when did a king have to explain himself? Especially to his guardsmen. And if ever there was a king for just sailing in, blissfully unaware that anyone might think to question him, that king was Richard of Avalon.

The thought was oddly cheering.

"Halt! Who goes there?"

The guard's challenge made her jump, but Richard didn't even flinch.

"The king. Open up!"

"The king, is it?" One of the black lumps leaned over the battlements to peer down at them.

Richard dumped the basket, fisted his hands on his hips, and glared up at the man. "That's right. The king. Now open the gate and let us in."

"Sure. As if I was a half-wit pig and didn't know the king don't go wanderin' around by hisself at night."

The shadow craned for a better look, and a couple more shapes popped up beside him. At this time of night, the sentries no doubt welcomed any diversion from the boredom of standing guard.

"That your doxy? You got some nerve, wantin' t'bring her into the castle like this, ye wanderin' knave."

Richard exploded. "She's not my—" He choked back the last word. "Let me in, damn it!"

There came the sound of laughter from above, then something fat and soft splatted against the ground at his feet. Richard hopped back, cursing.

Another splat. Arianne giggled. Tomatoes, she thought, remembering her brothers' occasional forays through the kitchen gardens.

She tugged on his sleeve, urging him away. They weren't going to get into the castle tonight. It was as simple as that.

Richard grudgingly gave in. Even the king couldn't charge Avalon's gate single-handedly. Still cursing, he grabbed the basket and marched off. She had to trot to catch up with his long-legged, angry strides.

"We'll go into the village," he muttered. "The inn will have room. They'll *make* some if they don't," he added darkly.

The inn didn't hold much appeal, a villager's house even less. Richard would be recognized even if she wasn't. Their prospective hosts would be flustered and excited and so anxious to ensure Their Majesties' comfort that they'd make things worse and make her, at least, feel guilty for turning them out of their beds at this time of night.

But there was another possibility . . .

She tugged on Richard's sleeve, dragging him to a stop. For a moment he simply glared at her, a tall, angry silhouette in the darkness. The King of Avalon was not accustomed to having tomatoes thrown at him.

Arianne could tell the instant the anger drained out of him.

"Don't worry," he said. "I know old George at the inn. There won't be any problem." He paused. She could feel him studying her, trying to grasp what she couldn't tell him.

"You don't want to go into the village, do you?"

She shook her head and tugged again on his sleeve.

"You have someplace else in mind?"

At her nod, he sighed.

"Why is it when you're around I so often end up sleeping someplace I don't want to?"

The moon, slowing sliding down the sky, still cast enough light for Goldie to find the wattle shelter tucked in its walls of greenery. Inside it smelled of the sweet dried grass that some shepherd had heaped in the corner for a bed. They couldn't stand up in it, but with their cloaks, they'd be warm enough.

Richard's irritation with the guards—he'd been muttering about them all the way back—vanished at the sight of a warm, dry shelter with no one nearby to bother them.

"Better than your old hearth," he teased, spreading his cloak on top of the mounded grass.

When he moved to unfasten her cloak, she turned and came into his arms. Her hands slid up, pulling him down to her.

He let her cloak fall away, forgotten, as she kissed his mouth, his chin, his jaw, nibbling down his throat and back up again. He tried to capture her face, but she nipped his chin and ran the tip of her tongue up the edge of his jaw and around to his ear so that he forgot all about trying to kiss her and concentrated on trying to breathe instead. Her fingers slid through his hair as she licked the curve of his cheek, flicking at the corner of his eye, the edge of his nose, and back to his mouth.

He caught her there, arching her back, plunging his tongue into her mouth, provoking her. Their breaths blended, heated, quickened.

He tugged at the laces on her gown. She pulled at his tunic, yanked on his belt. They collapsed on the grass bed, still locked together, laughing at their clumsiness. Somehow their clothes came off, flung aside as quickly as they could untangle them.

Richard rolled, intent on pulling her under him, but she squirmed out of his grasp, laughing, planted her hands on his shoulders, and pinned him to his cloak.

"All right, then," he murmured. He slid his hands down and claimed her nipples, gently squeezing them between thumb and forefinger. She sucked in air and shivered. Her breasts hung forward, their weight a warm softness against his hands.

Slowly, he relaxed into the cloak, while she remained suspended above him, her hands pressing hard into his shoulders. She swayed forward, silently urging him on, so he lifted his head and gently took first one hard nipple, then the other into his mouth, nipping, sucking, tickling the very tip with his tongue.

As he sucked, he let his hands roam lower, sliding down her sides, over the curve of her hips, down the long, sweet length of her outer thighs. Even now, with only the night air to clothe her, her skin was warm—hot, even. He gently tickled the sensitive skin at the back of her knees, then slowly dragged his hands back up.

When she moved, clumsily, to mount him, he guided her, tugging at her to show her what to do. He reached up and grabbed her hand, forcing her to shift her weight, then pulled it down to close around John Paul.

At her touch, they both suddenly stopped breathing.

Gently folding his hand over hers, he guided her down, squeezing gently, then up again, then down. When he was sure she had the rhythm, he freed her and reached to claim her center.

A quick brush of a fingertip through the

thick curls, then deeper, probing for that soft, sweet nub.

Even that was almost too much. She cried out, a wild, animal cry, and bucked against him.

And all the while he kept tormenting her by showering attention on first one breast, then the other.

Before he could venture farther into her feminine secrets, she shifted her hips. He was so dazed and aching that it took him a moment to realize what she was after.

With a low, gasping laugh, he let go of her breast, then claimed her mouth just as she found the right angle and drove herself onto him. He swallowed her gasp of pleasure as she pulled away, too focused on the sensation of their joining to be able to think of anything else. He let her go and shifted to hold her hips, centering himself under her, then thrusting upward to meet her downward slide.

She sucked in air, and her body arched, driving him deeper still.

In the faint moonlight that filtered in from the shelter's doorway, she was all silver and black, her hair a wild tangle of silver threads floating free in the night, her body all heat and black velvet and need.

Another thrust, and another, and then he couldn't breathe, couldn't think. The world was centered in that one exquisite point of union and the hot, wet slide of her against him.

He came first. He hadn't meant to. He'd been sure he could control himself, keep back the release for her sake. But she was implacable and hungry, yielding nothing, demanding surrender without realizing it, so shaken by her own plunging need that he was helpless against the force of it.

With a strangled cry, he pulled her hard against him, pinioning her while he gave one last, mad thrust and exploded inside her.

Dimly he heard her cry of protest, but he was too far gone in his own climax to help her over.

Yet even as he relaxed inside her, he felt her muscles squeezing around him, crushing him, dragging her own release out of him.

And then she was shaking, caught in the throes of her climax, clinging to him for support and flying away from him all at the same time. She shook, rocked, shivered, then slowly collapsed over him.

Slowly she stretched out on top of him, careful not to force him out of her, her breasts, slick with sweat, hot against his own sweaty chest. The inner tremors that shook her matched the last aching spasms that claimed him.

With a soft, satisfied "Mmmm," she slid off him and onto her side on the cloak, her legs still tangled with his, her breasts pressing against his chest. He gently ran the tip of one fingernail down her side, making her shiver and ease closer against him.

He would have laid there like that forever, or for as long as he could before drifting into sleep, but the night air was cool against their hot, wet skin. Gently, he kissed her, then pulled her cloak over them and tucked in the edges.

Moments later, with her pressed close and warm against him, Richard drifted into sleep.

Chapter Sixteen

They roused to the song of a lark and made slow, languid love while the world came alive around them. Afterward, Richard enticed her into a swim in the lake. Since her brothers were nowhere in sight, Arianne gave in and plunged in after him.

The lake was so cold it made her skin prickle, but Richard, laughing, taught her a new approach to water sports that soon had her blood racing.

Even that wasn't enough to overcome the chill for long, however. Eventually he led her out, laughing and teasing, glorious in his nakedness.

The laughter died when he stopped on the grass, close to their discarded clothes. She couldn't read the shadows in his pirate eyes, but she met his gaze with an open, trusting gaze of her own, hoping he would see the truth in her eyes.

I love you.

He gently drew her to him.

Arianne went willingly. She couldn't tell him that she loved him, not yet, but what she could say without words she said.

Did he understand? Did he realize that making love to him last night was one way of saying she loved him? That by giving back to him some small part of the pleasure he'd given her, she was offering her heart?

His lips were cold and wet, his kiss infinitely gentle. When he pulled away, she murmured a wordless protest. He grinned and teasingly swatted her bottom.

"Enough of that. You're insatiable, but I'm a king, not a satyr. If I'm not fed soon, I'm likely to collapse, and *then* where will you be?"

He snatched up her discarded shift and tossed it at her. Arianne laughed and, shivering, started to dress.

Hunger drove them back to Avalon. This time the main gates were open, but the usual workday bustle had an edge of tension to it that they could feel even from a distance.

There were different guards at the gate than usual. At the sight of the two of them straggling in, rumpled and afoot like any peasants, the men—rough-looking sorts who made Arianne nervous—moved as if to bar their way.

Fortunately, one of the undercooks chanced by just then. At the sight of them, he set up a cheer.

"They're here!" he shouted. "Their Majesties are here!"

That brought a dozen anxious courtiers running from all directions.

"Your Majesty! Whatever—"

"Where—?"

"Why—?"

"We were so *worried!*"

Impossible to get a word in amidst the tumult, but Richard tried. Everyone ignored him, more intent on drowning out the next person than in listening to anything the king actually had to say.

In the confusion, the crowd pressing around Richard shoved Arianne aside. With everyone intent on Richard, she was the only one to spot His Grace, the Archbishop of Avalon, hurrying across the bailey toward them, his eyes burning with scarcely suppressed fury.

She glanced at Richard, then looked back at the archbishop. In that short time, Archie had gotten hold of his emotions and hidden his fury behind a spurious mask of concern. He threw a warning glance at the guards, then pushed his way into the crowd around Richard. The eager courtiers quieted, then reluctantly backed away, opening a path for him. Archibald sailed through like the king Harry had said the man wanted to be.

"Your Majesty." He sketched a faint, almost respectful bow. "We are delighted to see you."

Richard's smile faded. He eyed the archbishop coolly. "You see me most days, Your Grace."

Archibald gave a small, twisted smile that carried no hint of amusement. "True, Sire, but this morning, when a servant found you had not slept in your bed, and a search of the castle could find no trace of either of you, we feared the worst."

"Did you?"

Arianne wondered if she was the only one to catch the knife edge of suspicion in Richard's voice.

"Of course, Sire. Your welfare is always our concern. Yours and Her Majesty's," he added with a narrow-eyed glance at Arianne.

"I'm touched," said Richard dryly. "I'm also curious as to why my regular guards are not at the gate this morning. Two of these fellows are from your own personal guard, if I'm not mistaken. I don't recognize the other two."

"Your Majesty is always so . . . observant," Archibald murmured. He bowed again but not quickly enough to hide his irritation. "The guards are mine. When we could not find you, I thought it . . . prudent to replace the regular guards with trusted men of my own."

"Prudent?"

"Of course, Sire. If you *had* been spirited out of Avalon, the regular guards would have had to be in on the plot. How else would anyone have slipped by them without a cry being raised?"

"Yes, how else? And how . . . convenient."

Archibald eyed Richard from under his thick eyebrows. "Convenient, Your Majesty?"

The gathered courtiers had gone absolutely silent as they nervously followed the exchange.

"That's right. Convenient for . . . any number of things." Richard met the archbishop's stare with a piercingly direct one of his own. "I trust you will never again find cause to trouble your men for such needless duty."

"I assure you, Sire, in the future, I shall see to it they are never *needlessly* . . . troubled."

Someone in the crowd gasped at the scarcely veiled threat.

Richard was unmoved. "I hope you will, Your Grace. I sincerely hope you will."

For a moment, the two locked gazes in a silent challenge that sent shivers down Arianne's back. Richard deliberately turned away first. He pushed past the silent courtiers and extended a hand toward her.

"Breakfast, my dear?" he said, and he led her into the Hall.

Goldie had long since finished her breakfast and retreated with her basket of nettles, but Richard lingered, thinking hard.

Archie was preparing to move against him at last.

The remains of a substantial meal littered the table, but Richard saw none of it. Frowning, he dragged the butt of his fork across the table, making the cloth bunch and ripple.

He'd known it was coming. Despite all his efforts to keep the peace as he'd promised his father, he'd known the archbishop was too hungry for power to be content with second-best. Archie wanted the throne, and it appeared he'd grown tired of waiting.

Richard dragged the fork back across the cloth, stopping beside the litter of bread crumbs he'd left near his plate.

He should have realized it sooner. Should have been watching more closely. Harry had warned him often enough. But first there'd been the hunt for a wife, and then Goldie . . .

Richard lifted the fork and deliberately brought the butt down on the crumbs, one after another, crushing them to powder.

That's what he ought to do to Archie and his followers, he knew. It's what Archie would do to him the moment he had a chance.

A deathbed oath was a deathbed oath, however. He would double the guards at the gates, give instructions that no one was to yield his post except at the king's explicit command, and make whatever other preparations he could that he hadn't already, but he would not be the first one to strike.

339

Not that it mattered. In any confrontation with the archbishop, Richard would win. He was sure of it. His forces were greater, his people behind him and willing to fight if they had to. Short of poison or a knife in the back, there was no way Archie could triumph, and he'd taken precautions against those contingencies.

Nothing new in any of that. Ever since he'd inherited the throne he'd known he'd have to face down Archie one day, and he'd made his plans accordingly.

What *was* new was the wife he now had to factor into the equation, the wife he had to keep safe at all cost.

Richard frowned at the powdered crumbs on the cloth, then angrily tossed the fork aside.

Damned fool! He'd been so besotted with Goldie these past few weeks that he hadn't given any thought to her safety or to how Archie might use her against him.

When it came to her, he was vulnerable, and the archbishop knew it. But how to keep her safe without putting a guard on her at all times? He knew enough of his proud wife to realize she'd resent that, but he might not have any choice. When it came to Archie and his ambitions, he couldn't take anything for granted.

Of one thing he was sure, however: He'd give

his life before he'd let Archie touch one hair on
her golden head.

Another few stitches and she'd be done!

Fingers clumsy with eagerness, Arianne hurried to finish joining the last sleeve to little
Dickie's shirt. When she cast off the last stitch,
she gave a crow of triumph and tossed the
thing into the basket with the other eleven.

Her hands ached, her fingertips were cal-
lused, her palms scratched and rough, but she
didn't care. She didn't care about any of it
because she was done!

All that was left was to find her brothers, toss
the shirts over their heads, and voilá! A dozen
princes where white swans used to be.

And she could speak! Sing!

She could finally tell Richard she loved him.

At the thought of Richard, her smile died. Ever
since the confrontation with the archbishop two
days earlier, he'd been distant, preoccupied with
his own concerns. She hadn't needed to ask why.

At least he'd stopped watching her every move
like some jealous, suspicious hawk. He'd been
so surly over Gregory the troubadour that she'd
stolen some coins from his purse to give to the
poor fellow. Even Thurgood had expressed his
amazement at Richard's having kicked Gregory
out of Avalon like that. When the subject had
come up, Harry had grinned and walked away,

hands in his pockets, whistling, for all the world as if he had a good secret he didn't intend to share with anybody.

Arianne giggled, remembering. Soon she'd be able to give Richard the little surprise she'd made Gregory teach her.

Now that she'd finished the shirts, neither Archibald and his plots nor Richard and his moods had the power to upset her.

The shirts wouldn't do any good sitting there in the basket, however. So busy completing the garments had she been, she hadn't gone out to the lake since she and Richard had spent the night in the shepherd's hut. Wouldn't the boys be surprised to find that their long enchantment was finally at an end!

Joyous laughter bubbled up inside her. She quickly changed her slippers for more practical shoes, then snatched up the basket. The guard in the hall outside the royal apartments looked as if he'd like to stop her, but she smiled and breezed past him. Surely it was just her imagination that hidden eyes watched her progress through the castle corridors and across the bailey.

It wasn't her imagination that the guards at the main gate blocked her passage, however.

"Sorry, Your Majesty," said one. "We're not to let you outa the gate without the king hisself goes with you. Orders. You know how it is."

"That's right. Orders," the second guard echoed solemnly.

Arianne sighed and went to find Richard.

"In a meeting with his advisers," said the solemn page outside the council chambers.

"Said we weren't supposed to knock for nothin'," the guard informed her. "But they'll be done in an hour or two," he added helpfully. "If you like, Turvey, here, he can tell His Majesty you were lookin' for him. Soon as he's free, that is."

Arianne shook her head and retreated. Once advisers started arguing, an hour or two could easily stretch into four or five. Now that the shirts were finished, she didn't intend to waste a minute she didn't have to.

As she made her way back to her chambers, the back of her neck again prickled with an uncomfortable awareness of unseen eyes peering out of the shadows. It *hadn't* been her imagination that she was being watched, then. But by whom? And why?

Had Richard set men to guard her? If so, he'd never mentioned it. She couldn't believe she was in any danger from Archibald. The archbishop might have designs on Richard's throne, but she was no threat to him, and he had to know it.

No matter. She wasn't going to let anyone stop her now, no matter what. If she couldn't get to Richard, she would find another way out. Alone.

The guard posted in the hall outside the royal apartments visibly relaxed when she reappeared.

Twenty minutes later, when the maids arrived to clean the rooms for the day, Arianne was ready. She'd dug her old work dress out of the closet where it had been buried. With her head covered by a scarf and the shirts bundled into a sheet like so much dirty laundry, she easily slipped past the guard.

A quarter of an hour more and she'd made it through the postern and was heading toward the lake and her brothers.

All his advisers agreed—he should arrest the archbishop and his followers before they had a chance to act. Confiscate his lands and wealth, kick his mercenaries out of the country, and break the back of his rebellion before it *was* a rebellion. No, they had no *proof* the archbishop was up to no good, but they hadn't forgotten the turmoil during his father's reign.

Richard had listened to them for hours, but in the end he'd refused to act. "I swore on my father's deathbed that I would keep the peace, and so I shall. Until His Grace actively moves against me, I won't touch him."

They had grumbled and shouted and argued, to no avail. When he dismissed them, they were still grumbling. Harry shut the door after them, then strolled back to claim the chair across the table from him.

"Don't say it!" Richard warned.

"All right, I won't." Harry's usual good humor had vanished hours ago. "But let me ask you a question instead. Do you really think your father's worth it? The man wasn't much better than old Archie when it came to lying and cheating and stealing. Does he really deserve that kind of loyalty from you? Why risk an open fight with Archie when you could cripple him by striking first?"

It was a question Richard had asked himself more than once. "Because it's *my* honor that's at stake, not my father's. If the king's word isn't any good, then what is?"

Harry didn't look convinced, but he didn't try arguing. Instead, he put his feet up on the table and, after a moment's thought, proceeded to trim his fingernails with his knife. Whistling tunelessly, he trimmed each nail, then held his hands out to admire his work.

Richard glared. "The council meeting is over, Harry."

"Hmmm," said Harry, impervious. Still whistling, he slid his knife back into its sheath and idly picked up one of the many rolls of documents awaiting Richard's attention that had been piled at the end of the table, then forgotten in the press of more urgent business.

"More proclamations?" he said. "Keep the lawyers busy, don't they, all these proclamations?" Heedless of propriety, he broke the seal and unrolled the parchment. "Says here . . . whereas . . . and wherefore . . . Hmm."

"I trust you find my private mail of interest?"

Harry was as unimpressed by sarcasm as he

was by glares. "Huh. Nothing worth reading here." He casually tossed the thing over his shoulder.

"How disappointing for you. What were you looking for? A nice little declaration of war?"

"A warrant for Archie's arrest would be nice."

"Harry . . ." said Richard, but Harry wasn't listening. He was frowning at the next parchment he'd just unrolled.

" 'Missing,' it says. 'Reward offered.' Hah!" He skimmed down the parchment. The farther he got, the more he frowned. "Would you believe it? The king of Montavia has misplaced his sons and daughter. All *twelve* of 'em. Thirteen, if you count the princess. Damned stupid thing to do, if you ask me."

Richard shrugged. He wasn't interested in another king's problems. He had more than enough of his own.

"Says here they may be ensorcelled. Ensorcelled! I ask you! In *this* day and age!" Harry skimmed to the bottom. "Huh! Losing all his heirs doesn't seem to have bothered the old king overmuch. In the middle of all his worrying, seems he's managed to get married again."

Harry snorted in disgust and tossed the parchment aside. It rolled across the table, fetching up against the inkwell in front of Richard. "How the devil do you lose twelve princes and a princess? Must have taken a bit of doing. I don't think I could have done it without—"

"Twelve?" Richard sat up abruptly. "Did you say *twelve?*"

He snatched up the discarded proclamation and started reading. When he'd finished, he rolled the parchment with care and carefully set it aside.

It was absurd to think that his wife might—

No, absolutely not.

And yet . . .

Montavia was a rather ordinary little kingdom, its king, if he remembered right, a vague little fellow more interested in his books than in affairs of states. An unimportant little kingdom that lay at the edge of the Dark Woods.

He thought of the dozen swans that had flown over that cottage in the Dark Woods, then caused such a stir on his wedding day. The dozen swans his wife visited every day.

And then he thought of the dozen shirts Goldie had knitted from nettles that stung her fingers and made them bleed. Twelve shirts that had consumed her waking hours to the exclusion of almost everything else.

Above all, he thought of his wife. His silent, beautiful wife . . .

Richard picked up the parchment again, but this time he only unrolled the end, just far enough so he could read that one vital paragraph.

Lost, it said. *The Princess Arianne of Montavia. Of average height and figure. Yellow hair, blue eyes. Likes to sing. Laughs often. A reward is offered.*

That wasn't his wife. There was nothing average about his Goldie!

She was as tall as his heart, with a figure to make the angels weep. And her hair was spun of sunlight and gold, not made of dull, drab yellow.

Blue eyes. Yes, she had those. Blue as the sky at morning.

She didn't sing, though.

Or was it, perhaps, that she couldn't? Had her songs been silenced in the same way her voice had been? Was that why she'd taken such an interest in the troubadour he'd unceremoniously booted out of Avalon? Because Gregory still had the gift of song that had been taken from her?

He quickly voiced his thoughts to Harry.

"You don't think . . . is it possible? *Goldie? A princess?*" Harry's eyes popped at the thought.

"Why not?" Richard snapped, suddenly defensive. "Have you ever known a peasant girl who could make such a natural queen as she has?"

"No, but . . . There's no chance this will change things, is there? With your marriage, I mean?"

"Change things?"

Harry winced. "Well, princesses don't usually get married just like that, you know. Not even to the King of Avalon. Gotta have treaties and agreements and . . . and stuff. What if her papa doesn't like it? Have you thought of that?"

"What can her father possibly have to say about a marriage that's already been consummated?" Richard glared, fighting the urge to leap across the table and throttle Harry for having put his own fears into such blunt words.

"Quite a lot, I imagine," Harry persisted. "If he wanted."

Richard snarled at him. When he kicked back his chair, Harry's feet came off the table with a crash. He inched away.

"Now, Richard . . ."

Richard ignored him. He had to talk to Goldie. *Now.*

He tracked Goldie to their quarters and found the rooms empty, the nettle shirts gone. The fool of a guard swore no one had left except the chambermaids and the girl from the laundry with her bundle of dirty linen. When the chambermaids swore there'd been no one with any laundry, the guard turned pale and started gabbling excuses.

Richard cursed and shouted for his horse.

Harry shouted for his horse and more guards. "You're not going alone. Not with old Archie up to his tricks again."

Fifteen minutes later Richard started out the main gate with Harry at his side and a dozen armed men at his heels. They were barely across the drawbridge before wild cries from the village drew their attention. Black smoke plumed from a stable, then more smoke from the shed beside it. Against the smoke, they could see peasants armed with staves and pitchforks fighting men with swords.

The village . . . or Goldie? The answer to that was easy.

Richard held his plunging mount with an iron hand. "Harry! Take the men! And call for reinforcements! I'm after my wife!"

Before anyone could stop him, he set spurs to his steed and galloped off across the meadow, up the path that led to the lake and the twelve enchanted swans.

Chapter Seventeen

Where *were* they? Arianne paced at the edge of the lake, eyes shaded against the sun. She was early, but not *that* early. They'd known of her departure from the cottage and of her marriage. How could they not know she'd finished the shirts at last?

When a low voice behind her said, "Arianne?" she turned without thinking. As he had before, Richard stood at the edge of the clearing, watching her.

Arianne caught her breath at the sight of him. Joy filled her. Now that he was here, everything would be all right. Her brothers would come. The shirts would break the enchantment. And she could tell him everything. *Everything.*

She was halfway across the clearing when he said, "Princess Arianne of Montavia?"

Arianne stopped dead in her tracks as the meaning of his words sank home.

A muscle at the corner of his mouth twitched. "And the twelve swans ..." He glanced at the empty lake and the pile of nettle shirts on the shore, then back at her. "Your brothers, right?"

She nodded. The somber look on his face tugged her heart into her shoes.

He stopped an arm's distance from her. "I didn't know. If I'd known ..."

There was such darkness in his voice that Arianne clapped her hands over her mouth to keep from crying out. If he had known ... *what?* What would he have done? Returned her to Montavia? Left her there in the Dark Woods? *Forgotten her?*

Anything but that!

He stretched out his left hand, and for the first time she saw that he clutched a crumpled roll of parchment. "This came several days ago, but I didn't see it until today. I swear if I'd seen it ..." The words trailed away.

Reluctantly, Arianne took the parchment. The wording was standard for this sort of thing. *Missing. Last seen. Reward.* Etc., etc., etc. Other than the fact that twelve princes and one princess had all disappeared at the same time, there was nothing unusual in it.

Richard cleared his throat. "I'm sorry about your father. Marrying so unexpectedly like that. I . . . I imagine it must be a shock."

Her father! *Married?*

At the end of the proclamation was a short notice that His Majesty the King of Montavia had wed the widow of Sir Matthew Kelling. Finally! Arianne had been trying to talk her father into marrying Kathryn for years. The lady was plump and kind and motherly and had long been comfortably in love with her father, though her father had never taken his nose out of his books long enough to notice. Left on his own, and with his children missing, he'd probably turned to Kathryn for comfort and ended up marrying her because sensible Kathryn could help him through his troubles when no one else could.

Arianne slowly rolled up the parchment. No, her father's wedding was the good news in the whole thing. What she wanted to know was, what did this proclamation mean for Richard and her?

Silently, she handed the notice back to him. He savagely threw it away, then grabbed her arms and dragged her to him.

"I don't care if you're a princess or your father is a king!" The shadows in his eyes had burned away in his sudden fury. His fingers dug into her arms possessively as he shook her.

"You're my wife now—*mine!*—and no one can take you from me. Do you hear me? No one!"

And then he wrapped his arms around her and crushed her against his chest, claiming a kiss that seared her to the soles of her feet.

One kiss led to another, then another. To Arianne, it felt as if the world had settled back into place at last. She was laughing and crying, dizzy and half drunk on the joy of knowing that he loved her, even if he hadn't said it in so many words.

Richard loved her. Her brothers would soon be free. And her father was wed to the one woman in the world who would know how to make him happy. She thought her heart might burst from the sheer joy of it.

"How . . . charming."

It took a moment for the coldly mocking voice to cut through her haze of happiness. Richard wasn't so slow. With one rough motion he shoved her behind him and turned, sword drawn.

A half-dozen armed men ringed the clearing, weapons drawn. His Grace, the Archbishop of Avalon, stood in the middle of them, like a huntsman surrounded by his hounds.

Arianne felt her skin grow cold.

"Archibald." The way Richard said it, it was a curse.

Archibald gave a mocking bow. "Your

Majesty. You can't imagine how pleased I am to find you here."

"Oh, I can imagine." Richard raised his sword point in warning to one of the brutish mercenaries who'd ventured a step nearer. The man growled, but a sharp glance from his master sent him back. Even from this distance Arianne could see the hungry gleam in the soldier's eyes.

Richard ignored him. All his attention was focused on the enemy he'd inherited from his father. "The fight in the village. Those were your men?"

"Of course. I thought to create a diversion, but I confess, I didn't expect to be so fortunate as to find you so readily caught in my trap like this."

The archbishop smiled at Arianne. Like a snake, she thought, and shivered.

"You and your good wife," he added. His smile showed too many sharp white teeth.

Richard growled, deep in his throat, "You leave Goldie out of this."

"I'm afraid she's already in it, and very conveniently, too, I might add."

Without taking his eyes off them, Archie raised a hand. His hired brutes strained forward, hungry hounds on a short leash. Then the cleric's hand lowered slightly, as though pointing the way. "Sic 'im," he said.

With a roar of satisfaction, the men charged.

"But save the girl for me!" Archie added gleefully.

Even though the men weren't mounted, Arianne would have sworn the earth rocked beneath her feet from their thundering charge. Richard shoved her away an instant before he moved forward to meet his attackers.

"Run, Goldie! Get help! Now!"

She ran. Almost directly into the arms of a grinning, black-haired beast whose eyes gleamed balefully behind his face guard. He laughed and grabbed for her. Arianne dodged, but not quickly enough. His mailed hand closed over her shoulder. He dragged her to him, still laughing.

Behind her, she could hear the ring of steel against steel as Richard closed with his attackers. Not to save himself, she realized in a sudden, blinding flash, but to give her time to escape.

Desperation gave her courage.

The beast who held her was so sure of his victory, he didn't notice when she slid his knife out of the sheath on his belt. His scream of pain when she plunged the weapon into his unprotected armpit was one of the most satisfying sounds she'd ever heard. Never mind the hot blood that sprayed her face and breast.

He let her go and staggered back, grabbing

for the spurting wound. His sword fell from his now useless right hand.

Arianne snatched it up and spun back to help Richard. He was fighting fiercely, but he was outnumbered five to one and, with the lake at his back, without an avenue of retreat. If she couldn't help him, he didn't stand a chance.

Gripping the heavy sword in both hands, Arianne gritted her teeth, then swung at the nearest man. She didn't aim for his armored torso but for the unprotected backs of his knees.

The shock as the heavy sword bit through muscle and tendon, then glanced off bone was sickening, but the man's scream as he collapsed was grimly rewarding.

Panting, she pulled the sword back and struck at the next man. Alerted by the first man's fall, he turned at the last moment so that her sword sliced the side of his knee instead of the more vulnerable back. He staggered but easily sidestepped her next swing and grabbed for her wrist.

Her sword went spinning. Mercilessly, the brute wrenched her arm up and around, forcing her to her knees.

Faintly, as from a distance, she heard the sound of a dozen pairs of wings urgently beating across the sky. She screamed, warning them away.

"Goldie!"

Richard's cry knifed to her heart. Through a tangle of arms and legs and straining bodies, she caught one last glimpse of his anguished face.

Her scream had been his undoing. That momentary distraction was enough for one of his opponents to slip through his guard. She caught the flash of an upraised sword, then the violent downward arc. She didn't see the blow fall, but she heard her husband's groan, quickly choked off, and saw his body fall.

Again she screamed, this time in grief and fury and fear.

Twelve swans lanced down out of the sky. They swooped among the armed men, drawing their attention from the fallen king, diving at her captor and the cursing, flailing archbishop. Arms upraised to protect himself, Archibald screamed for his men to kill the damned swans. Kill them! Kill them!

Terrified for her brothers' safety, Arianne wrenched free of her captor, who was too distracted by his winged assailants to care, and lurched to her feet. Sobbing, she waved her arms above her head to drive her brothers away.

Reluctantly, they retreated, several of them bleeding and shedding feathers from chance wounds, but none so injured that he couldn't fly.

Through tear-filled eyes, Arianne watched them go. She couldn't bear to look at her husband or the nettle shirts that now lay scattered, trampled into the dirt. At least they were safe— swans now, possibly forever, but safe.

Dimly she heard Archibald shouting orders, screaming invective at the wounded men and urging haste because he had to get back to the castle. It was only when he ordered them to throw Richard's body into the lake that she came back to life—too late. Rough hands grabbed her, holding her helpless while another man bound her arms to her sides with a rope.

She scarcely noticed. Her world had narrowed to the battered body that lay so still and silent amidst the trampled shirts.

Richard. Oh, Richard.

A lake of unshed tears burned her throat. She would have given her life to be able to say his name, but stubborn hope kept her silent. There was nothing she could do for her husband now except mourn. But her brothers . . .

Somehow she would find a way to return and free them. Somehow.

That silent vow was the only thing that kept her on her feet when her captors, mounted on the horses they'd hidden in the woods, led her toward Avalon, trussed like a beast for the slaughter.

* * *

"The witch has killed our king! Her sweet looks are nothing but a mask for her evil. With her tricks she ensorcelled him and led him to his doom!"

Bound to the whipping post on the punishment block at one side of Avalon's bailey, her hair a tangle, her gown blood-spattered and torn from her struggles with the archbishop's hired thugs, Arianne stared blindly out over the ravening crowd while Archibald whipped them to greater fury.

"I blame myself!" he cried, beating his breast in a moving display of grief. "It was I who married them. I suspected from the start, but I had no proof, and nothing I could say would sway our beloved king, for he was already caught in her coils. But we have her now! You see the stains where our great monarch's blood drenched her clothes! You see the evil in her face! You see what she has wrought!"

The man's ranting was like a distant storm, audible but unimportant beneath her grief. She had thought Archibald would throw her into Avalon's dungeon or boot her out of the kingdom. Not once had she guessed that he planned to use her this way to consolidate his stolen power over Avalon.

Harry had been right. The man couldn't be trusted, and Richard had been wrong to cling to his honor in the face of the man's ambitions.

But Richard was—had been—too honorable to cheat, and he had lost his kingdom and his life because of it. His Grace the Archbishop held Avalon now, and no one, it seemed, had been able to stop him from taking it.

A pall of smoke hung in the air, witness to the fire that had launched the treacherous plot. Neither Harry nor any of Richard's loyal knights were anywhere in sight—dead, perhaps, or imprisoned as she had expected to be, felled by trickery and deceit. The sentries at the gate when they'd returned had been Archibald's guards, not one of Richard's good men anywhere to be found.

The archbishop had planned his coup well.

She had fallen into his trap as easily as had Richard. Too obsessed with freeing her brothers and too much in love with Richard to give any heed to the politics of the castle around her, she'd ignored Archie whenever she could, endured him when she could not, and tried not to think about Harry and his warnings. More fool she! If Archie had his way—and it seemed very clear he would—she'd pay for her blindness with her life, just as Richard had paid with his.

"Burn her, I say!" Archibald shrieked. "Put her to the stake for the witch and the murderess she is! *Burn her!*"

His mad shriek carried even above the roaring of the confused and chaotic crowd.

Arianne looked out over the sea of hostile

faces but couldn't find it in herself to blame them. Few of them knew her, and none knew her well. They were simple folk for the most part, their king dead, their village half burned, and here was their own archbishop exhorting them to vengeance without one voice of authority they might recognize raised against him. What else were they to do except follow his lead?

"Burn her!" the crowd roared. "Burn her! Burn her! *Burn her!*"

Richard came awake by slow and very painful degrees. His head ached like forty devils. His ribs shouted protests at their mistreatment, his shoulder screamed for attention, and there were a dozen other ills that, combined, made him wish he were still unconscious.

Unmoving, his eyes still firmly shut, he tried to figure out where he was. In mud, for one thing. He was pretty sure it was mud.

The fingers of his right hand clenched, digging into the ooze.

Definitely mud.

He was also wet and damnably cold. At the thought, he shivered. The shivers roused his ribs and shoulders and head to even more strident protests. Maybe he'd just go back to sleep and—

Something hard poked his sore shoulder. Richard grunted and reluctantly forced his eyes to open.

Not a foot away, a huge swan stood in the tall marsh grass, eyeing him out of round, black, unblinking swan eyes. The creature stretched out its neck and again poked his shoulder with its bill.

Richard yelped at the sudden jolt of pain—he couldn't help it—then slowly, teeth gritted, levered himself out of the muck and into a sitting position. Grouped around him, floating in the lake or standing in the grass on the shore on either side of him, were a dozen white swans, and every one of them was staring at him.

The biggest, the one who'd poked his shoulder, came a step nearer, then thrust out its head and eyed him worriedly.

Dimly, memory returned to Richard, bit by tiny, aching bit.

"You're Goldie's brothers, aren't you? *All* of you."

The biggest swan bobbed its head, then made an anxious, clacking noise with its bill.

"Arianne, I mean," said Richard thickly. "Princess Arianne of Montavia. My wife."

And she was in Archie's hands. The thought made him groan. He had to get to her, rescue her from Archie, and right now he was about as powerful as a babe in arms.

The biggest swan nudged him again, beady eyes bright and anxious.

"All right, all right. Gimme a minute, will you?"

Wincing, he took stock of his injuries. A possible cracked collarbone—he could move his right arm, but it hurt like hell to do it. Bruises enough for a dozen. A cut on the brow, which accounted for the headache and the blood. It wasn't nearly as bad as it felt, though, which was fortunate, because it felt like hell.

He probably owed his continued existence to that cut. Archibald must have been too eager to get back to Avalon and the mutiny he'd set in motion to make sure his enemy was really as dead as he'd looked.

Richard cursed, fluently and with feeling. In going after Goldie alone, he'd provided Archibald with the perfect opportunity to get him out of the way without the troublesome bother of witnesses. The archbishop and his men had set the fire, then hidden, ready to take advantage of the confusion to overthrow the castle. When they'd seen him ride off by himself, they'd simply had to follow him.

Archie had always been a clever opportunist, primed to seize the advantages that chance and others' bad judgment presented him. Right about now the bastard was probably accusing Goldie of his murder and grabbing the role of hero and savior for himself.

What a fool he'd been! So damned attached to his own honor that he'd put his wife and his kingdom at risk. He should have listened to Harry while he'd had the chance.

The big swan nudged him again, harder this time. The other eleven stirred restlessly.

"Right. You're right." Groaning and gritting his teeth, Richard hauled himself to his feet. Once the world stopped spinning, he got his bearings, then set off for the clearing where he'd lost Goldie. With any luck, they'd have left his sword behind. If not . . . well, at least there was an easy path back to the castle from there.

His boots squelched with mud and water; his clothes clung to him in a heavy, sodden mass that chilled him to the core. Every muscle and bone in his body ached, and his head pounded so hard that he thought his eyeballs might pop out.

His spirits rose.

Not so bad after all. He'd been in worse shape once or twice.

His spirits fell again when he reached the clearing. No sword. No knife. Nothing except the trampled sheet and the twelve nettle shirts it had held. He would have left them where they were if it hadn't been for the dozen swans that suddenly barred his way, hissing and flapping their wings in agitation.

Richard glared at them in disbelief. "What? You're crazy! If you think I'm going to put those shirts on you and risk puffing up to—"

The biggest swan shook its head, then grabbed for a corner of the trampled sheet.

"You expect me to wrap those damned things

and carry them all the way back to the castle? *Now?*"

He glared so hard at the big swan that he didn't notice the littlest one darting in for a hard nip to his left knee.

"Ow!" Richard swung at him but missed. He grabbed for his wounded knee. "Stupid bird! I've gotta walk all the way to the damned castle, and you're trying to cripple me first?"

Three of the biggest swans ganged up on the little one, sending him flapping and squawking out of range of a well-aimed kick. The first step Richard took away from the scattered shirts, though, they were all back in front of him, wings spread in blatant challenge.

"Hell," said Richard, and threw up his hands in disgust.

It wasn't hard to dig the sheet out of the muck, but he was damned if he'd touch the nettle shirts. Those he could, he kicked onto the sheet. The rest he pried out of the muck with two sticks—carefully, after another warning dance from his feathered in-laws.

The swans watched his every move like hawks.

"I'm not making any guarantees on their condition," he warned as he gathered up the unwieldy bundle. "You'll have to take your chances or get Goldie to knit you new ones, that's all."

The head swan gave a feathery shake, then launched itself into the sky. Immediately, the other eleven followed in a rush of air and a wild flapping of wings.

"Hey!" Richard shouted after them. "One of you check out the main gate. If it's open, I want to know!"

He kept to the cover of the trees rather than risk crossing open fields. Stray limbs and branches grabbed at his bundle, but he forged on, driven by his growing fear for Goldie. If Archie so much as bruised her . . .

By the time the swans returned, he'd thought of a hundred different ways to punish the archbishop, each of them more horrible than the last.

The main gate was closed, along with every other easy means of entrance. Of course. Archie wouldn't be fool enough to risk a counterattack, not even if he had all the castle guards and knights safely locked up in Avalon's dungeons.

Richard swore under his breath. That left one way in, and he wasn't looking forward to it.

By the time he reached the base of the outer walls, well away from the main guard posts where someone would be likely to spot him, Goldie's brothers had done what he had asked them. One of the swans flew overhead, dipping its wings in the agreed upon signal. A moment later, one end of a long, stout rope tumbled down from the parapets above Richard.

Richard yanked on it. It seemed to be

anchored well enough to hold his weight. He grimaced and gave it another yank, just to be sure. The thought of falling from that height if the rope gave way was even less appealing than the thought of what climbing the rope was going to do to his injured shoulder.

Nothing else for it. He knotted the bundle of shirts to his belt, then gritted his teeth and started up the rope.

By the time he neared the top of the wall his shoulder was in pure, screaming agony. For a moment he hung on to the edge of the parapet, gasping for air, then awkwardly tumbled over the edge and onto the stone walkway that ran along the top of the curtain walls.

It was the swans bursting into flight above him that alerted him to an approaching guard.

Clumsy with pain, Richard fought to free himself from the rope and the bundle of shirts. He wasn't quick enough. One of Archie's hired thugs came around the corner. At the sight of a muddied, gasping stranger where no one should be, he whipped out his sword.

Before he'd gone a step, however, two swans swooped in front of him, distracting him, while another three attacked him from behind. It was the littlest swan that got his shins, tripping him and sending him sprawling. The swan gave a little dance of triumph, then darted in to peck at the man's eyes.

Cursing, the guard flung up one hand to

shield his face, blindly slashing at the bird with
his sword. Richard rolled and grabbed for the
man's sword arm as the swan hastily flapped
out of reach.

If it hadn't been for the swan pecking at the
man's flailing legs and unprotected head,
Richard might not have won. As it was, it took
a dirty, backhanded slam with the butt of the
man's own sword to knock him out.

The fellow flopped back, limp as a dead fish,
sprawling across the walkway and half tangled
in Richard's rope.

Five minutes later, bound and gagged with
strips torn from his own clothing, the guards-
man was dangling over the parapet at the end
of the rope. After a quick check to make sure
the other end wouldn't pull free and send the
fellow plummeting to his death, richly though
he deserved it, Richard thrust the man's knife
into his own belt, picked up the sword and the
bundled shirts, and gestured for the swans to
follow him.

Richard was counting on Archie's not having
enough men, even with his paid thugs, to properly man the parapets or guard the dungeons.

From the bailey, he could hear shouts and
cries from an angry, frightened crowd. Old
Archie was up to something, no doubt.

He couldn't risk checking it out yet. Not until
he had a few more fighters on his side.

For once, things went his way. He was able to

avoid the only other sentry on the ramparts, and with the swans to distract them and harry their heels, he managed to overpower the two men guarding the steps leading down to the dungeons.

Grabbing the keys from the one of the trussed thugs' belt, Richard unlocked the first cell he came to. A dozen angry, swearing guardsmen poured out, fists up and spoiling for a fight.

At the sight of Richard, muddied, bloodied, and battered, they stopped short, astounded.

"Yer Majesty!"

"We thought you was dead!"

"Not yet," Richard said grimly. He tossed the keys to one of the men. "Free everyone else you can find."

"Gotcha!" The guard grinned, brandishing the keys triumphantly, then disappeared in the direction of the other cells.

Swiftly, Richard told the remaining men what he wanted. They were so hungry to strike back at the traitors who had drugged their ale or snuck up from behind and knocked them out that they would have followed him into Hell itself, armed only with their fists and their fury.

It was all Richard could do to convince them to wait until reinforcements were freed from the remaining cells and everyone was properly armed for the fight ahead. Once he was sure they understood his orders and had passed them on to the first of the men boiling up out of the lower cells, he slipped away.

He had to find Goldie. Now, before anything else could go wrong.

As soon as he was sure that she was safe, he'd return to deal with the archbishop and his henchmen. Until then, Archie would have to wait.

He had one unexpected advantage. In his present sorry state, he looked more like a peasant than a king. With a purloined cap pulled low to hide his face and the muddied bundle hiding his sword, he would scarcely be noticed, let alone challenged. If anyone did, the poor fellow would soon have more pressing worries on his hands.

In the confusion of whatever was going on in the bailey, he ought to be able to slip through the crowd unnoticed while his men fanned out through the castle, seeking the invaders and eliminating them, one by one.

When he emerged from the dungeons, the swans were gone, off searching for Goldie. If she was anywhere out of doors, they'd find her faster than he could.

As it turned out, he didn't need their help.

Chapter Eighteen

Arianne had thought she knew what fear was.

She'd been wrong.

Fear—*real* fear, the kind that made your heart shrivel and your bones turn to water—was knowing you were going to die a horrible death with nothing you could do to escape and no one to save you from it.

As she watched His Grace's beetle-browed thugs pile the bundles of faggots around the stake to which she was bound, Arianne fought the urge to scream at the crowd for their blind stupidity. Couldn't they see she was innocent? Couldn't they hear the lies in Archibald's oily voice?

To stop the useless words, she bit her tongue so hard that she could taste blood. Avalon's beloved king was dead, and Avalon's people were determined to see someone pay for the crime. Whatever Archibald might have done in the past was forgotten. She was a silent stranger dropped in their midst, and they were more than happy to throw the blame for their present troubles squarely on her shoulders. If she spoke now, after all these weeks of silence, they'd probably stone her to death before they finished burning her.

Someone would find the nettle shirts, she told herself over and over again. So long as she never broke her vow of silence, someone would find a way to set her brothers free.

She *had* to believe it.

Against the dreadful hammering of her heart, she proudly forced up her chin. She was a queen, after all.

Over the sea of avid faces her gaze locked with Archibald's. His thin countenance was alight with evil, gloating triumph. She met his gaze just long enough to see the triumph turn to resentful anger that he hadn't managed to break her, then she looked away, over the crowd, scanning the bright blue sky for some faint trace of her brothers.

One last glimpse, that was all she asked. A chance to say good-bye, even if she couldn't put it into words.

The sky remained empty.

It was better this way, she told herself. Better

that they not know, that they not be there to see her burn.

But still, she would have liked to see them one last time, white against the blue, blue sky.

As if from a distance, she heard the crowd roar as Archie's henchmen set fire to the faggots piled about her.

Wait for me, Richard, my love, she thought. *I'm coming. Soon.*

It was the smoke that made the tears start in her eyes, she told herself. It was her imagination that made her think she saw him, there at the edge of the crowd. Only her imagination . . . and her love.

The smoke billowed higher, thick and black and choking. She could feel the merciless heat beating against her skin though the flames hadn't yet touched her. Not yet. Dimly, she heard the crowd roar, then a greater roar. Was her hearing failing, or was there a different cry now, rising above the crackling of the fire in a swelling wave of sound?

Arianne blinked against the tears streaming down her face. Smoke filled her lungs, making her choke and cough. A spurt of bright orange-red fire licked at the hem of her skirt.

And then, suddenly, a beloved face appeared in the smoke, flashed past her, and was gone. A moment later, her bonds seem to fall away from her as if by magic.

Was she already dead, then? Was dying really this easy?

The answer came in a pair of strong arms that snatched her off the pyre and dragged her against a broad, hard, familiar chest.

"Goldie. *Goldie!* God forgive me, my love, are you all right?"

She didn't have a chance to answer, for her husband's mouth crushed down on hers, driving away all thought but that he was alive—alive!—and so was she, and that was all that mattered.

She tasted of smoke and life, and for an instant Richard forgot everything in the sheer joy of holding her in his arms once more.

He forgot the fighting that had broken out around the bailey as Harry and his men engaged Archie's much smaller force, forgot the swans who had dive-bombed the guards around Goldie's pyre, distracting them long enough for him to break through the crowd and cut her free, forgot the throbbing pain in his shoulder and the fickle crowd that was even now chanting his name in a frenzy of guilt and relief that their king was not dead after all.

He even forgot old Archibald, who had screeched like a demon at the sight of him, then quickly fled into the crowd.

Harry would take care of Archie. The crowd could take care of itself.

For now, he had Goldie safe, and that was enough.

Eventually, though, even he had to come up for air.

Reluctantly, against her murmured protest, he pulled away, just far enough so he could drink in the sight of her. Despite her tangled hair, despite the smudges on her cheeks and the horror on the gown she wore, he had never seen anyone more lovely.

His brave, beautiful Goldie. His wife.

To hell with Montavia and its king. To hell even with her dozen enchanted brothers. Goldie was *his*, and he'd be damned before he'd let anyone take her from him.

"I love you," he said, and felt the tears he never would own to welling in his eyes. "I've loved you from the moment I saw you standing there in the door of that cottage, gilded in firelight and scowling at me for having pounded on your door."

She gave him a wavery smile. He thought he heard a little chuckle, too, somewhere deep in her throat, but that might have been only his imagination.

"I've been a fool."

Her lips twitched in real amusement this time. She shook her head, then raised a hand and mimed a crown on his brow.

He laughed. "All right, then, I've been a king. Sometimes it comes to the same thing."

Lightly, she touched a finger to his lips.

He claimed her hand and kissed it. When she tried to pull free, he simply tightened his hold.

"I am a king, but I am also a man, and it is the man in me who loves you. Who really, truly loves you." He cocked his head a little wistfully. "You know that, don't you? That I do love you?"

Her lips parted, caught on her breath. He could see the pulse pounding in her throat and the glow of happiness that suddenly shone in her face.

He bent to kiss her again.

A sharp pain at the back of his right calf brought his head up with a jerk. "Ow! What the—?"

The smallest swan of the flock stood behind him, looking quite cross.

With a small, choked cry of joy, Goldie pulled free and knelt to enfold the bird in an enthusiastic hug, laughing and crying and trying to shower him with kisses all at the same time. Like any small boy, the swan tolerated his sister's feminine enthusiasms for a few moments, then wriggled and squawked and flapped his wings, trying to pull free.

Goldie reluctantly let him go, then laughed as eleven more swans settled on the ground around her. They all crowded forward, pushing and shoving, trying to claim her attention.

It wasn't until he got another sharp nip on the shin that Richard remembered the bundled sheet he'd tossed aside in his mad dash through the crowd to reach Goldie and set her free.

"All right, already." He grinned at the little swan, which was hopping from one foot to the other in impatience. "Yeah, I'm glad she's okay, too, but hang on a minute, will you? I can't do everything at once."

He glanced around the bailey. The crowd, shamefaced, was already starting to disperse and slink away. Every one of Archie's men that he could see was under guard or knocked out cold. Archie was nowhere in sight.

His own men had been rather more enthusiastic in the completion of their duties than was strictly necessary, but Richard wasn't complaining. A couple of hours locked in his own dungeon would make any man eager to give his attackers a little better than he'd got.

Richard's grin widened. He wouldn't even have to go looking for Goldie's bundle, because Harry was bringing it to him.

"I'm told you've formed some sort of attachment to this thing," Harry said, gingerly offering him the lumpy bundle.

Richard took it from him without flinching. "Archie?"

Harry shrugged and scowled. The blood-crusted lump on the side of his head made it clear he had a personal grudge to settle with the archbishop and his men.

"We can't find him. He must have slipped out

with the crowd. But we'll get him, never fear! I owe that bastard a good lump or two."

Richard glanced at the far side of the bailey, where his men were herding Archie's defeated mercenaries. "I've a better suggestion."

Harry eyed him with interest. "Do you?"

"First, I'm confiscating all of Archie's land and property."

Harry nodded approvingly. "Confiscation is good."

"Then I'm confiscating all his followers' land and property, including the mercenaries' arms and armor."

"Even better. And then?"

Richard smiled, savoring the thought. "And then I'm going to set the mercenaries free—"

"You *what*?"

". . . and suggest they find His Grace and demand repayment from him."

"Ah!" said Harry, smiling now. "I like it. I like it a lot. But I bet if we put our minds to it, we can come up with a few—what shall I call 'em? Improvements?"

"Suggestions for improvements are always welcome." He glanced at Goldie, who was still trying to sort through the swans crowding around her. "But they can wait. Right now . . ."

Harry glanced at Goldie, then looked back at him. The smile vanished. "Right now I'd say you have some apologizing to do for the mess you've made. And I," he added, straightening, "have some housework waiting. A little matter of mopping up, you know?"

He started to walk away, then stopped and turned back. "Oh, Richard?"

"Yeah?"

Harry grinned. "Remember, there are all sorts of ways to apologize, but some of 'em are a lot more entertaining than others."

Richard laughed. He had a few ideas of his own, but they could wait. For now . . .

He shoved his way through the flock and dropped the bundle on the ground at Goldie's—*Arianne's*—feet. The expression of joy on her face was payment enough for the hassle of having dragged the damn thing back to the castle with him.

Goldie fumbled with the awkward knot in the sheet; then spread the mud-caked shirts out on the ground. One, two . . . She silently counted, then sank back, relieved, when all of them were there.

The swans crowded around her, more eager than ever. Two got into a squabbling, hissing fight but backed off fast enough when she rapped one of them on his tail feathers.

Order restored, she sorted through the shirts, then, one by one, starting with the largest, picked them up and threw them over her brothers' heads.

One by one, the swans and nettle shirts disappeared, leaving twelve dirty, knee-stained, grinning little boys in their places.

None of them seemed any the worse for their adventure. Little Dickie's left arm turned out a little stiff—an unnoticed tear in the sleeve, perhaps—but that was it.

And even that couldn't have been too serious, because it hadn't affected his boyish appetite in the least. Once the thrill of finding himself a human again had worn off, he wormed his way through the crowd of his brothers to tug on his sister's sleeve.

"Please, Arie," he said, "I'm hungry. When are we going to eat?"

Goldie—*Arianne!*—laughed and leaned down to give him a hug and a smacking big kiss on the top of his head.

The other eleven immediately took up the chorus.

"Yeah, Arie! What's for supper?"

"Does the cook here make strawberry tarts?"

"Can we have seconds if we ask politely and say please?"

"Please, Arie?" said yet another. He grabbed his stomach and mimed a theatrical collapse. "I swear I'm going to die if I don't get something to eat soon!"

She laughed. "You boys are *always* hungry. Didn't you get anything to eat when you were swans?"

The one she'd called Jonathan James grimaced. "Yeah, grasshoppers an' bugs an' weeds an' stuff. But not even *one* strawberry tart! Not *one!*"

"Poor things." Goldie laughed and affectionately ruffled the shaggy hair of the boy who was nearest to her. "Well, then—"

She stopped. Richard watched as her mouth dropped open and her eyes grew wide. She stared at her brothers in dawning amazement. Then she stared at him.

Then she threw herself into his arms, laughing and chattering, dragging him about in a clumsy, joyous waltz.

"I can talk! Oh, Richard, I can talk! Really, really *talk!* And *sing!* Oh, I've wanted so badly to sing. You don't know how *much* I've wanted to sing! And tell jokes and cuss over those darned nettles and . . . and . . ."

He laughed and spun her around again. "I suppose this means you'll be chattering like a magpie every waking moment?"

"Of course!"

"And scolding me and never giving me a moment's peace with your nagging?" He wouldn't even mind, not as long as it was Goldie doing the chattering and the scolding and the nagging.

Her smile made the sun look dim. "Absolutely."

A moment later, the smile faded. She dragged him to a halt. "And . . . Richard?"

"Hmmm?" Her lips were *so* inviting.

"Do you know what else it means?"

"Hmmmm." He bent to kiss her, but she pressed her fingers over his mouth, stopping him. His eyebrows arched in silent inquiry.

"It means . . ." She drew an unsteady breath, and Richard felt his heart twist in his chest with sudden fear.

"It means I can say I love you."

Richard blinked.

"I love you, Richard. With all my heart and soul, I love you, and I'm going to go on loving you all the rest of my life, no matter what."

Words failed him.

Which was perhaps just as well, for at that moment little Dickie tugged on her skirt, clearly unimpressed by all the grown-up silliness.

"Please, Arie," he said plaintively. "I'm really, really, *really* hungry. When are we going to eat?"

Despite the day's confusion, Cook proved equal to the task of feeding twelve very hungry little boys. He couldn't manage to conjure a dozen strawberry tarts on such short notice, but the plum pudding he offered in its place was a resounding success.

Arianne watched them eat and happily plied them with extra helpings. In the last few hours her life had been so thoroughly turned upside down that she was grateful for a little quiet and the comfortable task of seeing her brothers properly fed. She'd even relished the familiar argument over whether they really needed to wash their hands and faces before dinner (they did), though one of these days she'd have to have a little talk with Geoffrey about his habit of washing the palms of his hands and conveniently forgetting the backs.

Avalon was slowly settling back to normal. Archie's mercenaries had been booted out with nothing but the clothes on their backs and a stern warning never to return.

The knights and guardsmen who had been drugged showed no lingering ill effects. Archie had been very clever there, setting his spies and servants to doping the wine and ale barrels so that more than half of Avalon had been blissfully unconscious when the village was set afire.

It was hard to tell who was more eager in their efforts to roust out the last of the mutineers—the men who'd been drugged or those who, badly outnumbered, had taken such a drubbing at the hands of the archbishop's thugs. It was unquestionably the latter who were the roughest in their handling of the prisoners, but no one blamed them for it, least of all Richard.

His Grace, the Archbishop of Avalon, was nowhere to be found.

"Find him, Harry," Richard said. "And when you do, I want you to march him to the border. I don't think we have enough horses to spare one for his use," he added thoughtfully, "but the exercise will be good for him. He obviously wasn't getting enough if he had time to plan this little entertainment."

Harry objected, but the objections turned to a grim smile of satisfaction when Richard added, "Tell him he's a dead man if he so much as sets foot in Avalon again."

Thurgood, still fussing and fretting over the bump on His Majesty's head and the damage to His Majesty's clothes, was informed that he was to be entrusted with supervising the bathing, dressing, and putting to bed of twelve rather rambunctious little boys.

"Twelve?" said Thurgood, appalled.

"That's right," said Richard. "Twelve. Princes, every one."

"Princes?" said Thurgood, blinking.

Richard explained. By the time he got to the end of his tale, Thurgood's eyes were shining and the wattles on his scrawny old neck were quivering with determination.

"Of *course* I'll see to their baths and beds, Your Majesty," he said, drawing himself up with dignity. "You may rely on me."

"I do," said Richard fervently. "Believe me, Thurgood, I do."

The last thing he wanted was to find his wife so preoccupied with the care of her flock of changeling princes that she forgot she had a husband who needed her attention, too.

Kate Holmes

But first he needed a bath and a change of clothes himself. To his disappointment, he found that Goldie had already bathed and gone—he'd have been happy to comb the tangles out of her hair and wash the mud and blood off that gorgeous body of hers if she'd have let him.

He didn't dawdle, but between the soothing effects of warm water and the annoying ministrations of Dr. Arbustis, the court physician—a little wrapping of that collarbone and a little ointment on the bashes and bruises and he'd be fine in no time, the good doctor assured him—it was a good three-quarters of an hour before he finished.

When he emerged at last he found that his wife and Thurgood already had the matter of baths and beds for twelve little boys well in hand.

On the next floor down from the royal bedchambers, a small army of maids and scullery boys were hard at work carrying sheets and pillows and buckets of bathwater up and down the stairs. Nelly, the cheerful maid with the bunions, puffed past him, nearly hidden behind a towering stack of pajamas in a variety of sizes and styles.

"Gotcha a whole family all at once, ain'tcha, Yer Majesty?" she said, clearly delighted.

Dismayed, Richard gaped at the organized

commotion around him and wondered if it would be cowardly to run away. "So it seems."

"Good boys, they is," said Nelly, nodding approval, "and pleased we all are that you ain't dead and the missus ain't no witch. Never fancied that notion myself, but there, some folks will believe any fool thing, won't they?"

"Uh," said Richard, and was grateful when she didn't stop for an answer but sailed on into the extra-large bedroom that had been miraculously converted into a dormitory with a half-dozen little beds set side-by-side on either side of the room and a little stool at the foot of each of them.

He found Goldie in the bathroom next door, on her knees and bent over a large tub filled with three squirming little boys who seemed to be splashing a lot more than they were washing. She was wrestling with one freckle-faced urchin, but the urchin appeared to be winning.

"Jonathan James!" she cried at last in exasperation. "*Will* you sit still so I can scrub behind your ears!"

Jonathan James grinned and cheerfully splashed the brother sitting opposite him.

Thurgood was standing in the midst of the confusion, eyes agleam with satisfaction as he ordered everyone about. After a lifetime spent managing troublesome young princelings, he was clearly in his element.

"You there! Master Dickie!" he said. "Stop wriggling, and let Bertha comb your hair. Behave yourself!"

Recognizing the voice of a master, little Dickie reluctantly stopped wriggling. Two minutes later he was curled in Bertha's ample lap, his head pillowed on her bosom, sound asleep.

Bertha gently kissed the top of his head and carried him off to bed. Richard had the oddest urge to take the boy from her and tuck him in himself. He didn't know much about small boys, but it looked as if he was going to learn. For surely these twelve would spend more time with their sister in Avalon than they would with their absentminded father in Montavia, who would be receiving a dispatch shortly assuring him that all his offspring were safe and sound. It surprised Richard to realize that he was rather looking forward to having a houseful of children around.

The oldest boy, Rheidwn, came toward him, chin up in a bold show of confidence despite the green flannel pajamas that were a couple of inches too small in all directions.

"I'm Crown Prince Rheidwn, sir," he said, very formally. "I'm the oldest."

Richard made an encouraging noise in the back of his throat. He hadn't the faintest notion what he was supposed to say.

"I just wanted to apologize for having poked

your shoulder," the boy continued bravely. "I didn't know you were hurt, but I couldn't get your attention any other way."

Richard grinned and started to ruffle the boy's hair as he'd seen Goldie do, then held out his hand, instead. The boy let out the breath he'd been holding, clearly relieved to be treated like a grown-up instead of a stripling.

"That's all right," said Richard. "I survived. I don't want to think what might have happened to your sister if you hadn't poked me."

The boy's face fell. "*None* of it would have happened if we'd been paying attention to our lessons as Arie told us, instead of getting into trouble like we did."

That made Richard laugh. "I'll tell you of some of the trouble *I* got into when I was your age," he said, "but only if you'll tell me about your adventures first."

Rheidwn's face lit up, but before he could launch into his story, his sister called him over to help with a couple of the littler boys.

Richard watched him go. They were good, brave boys, every one, and they'd make fine men once they grew up. The challenge, he was beginning to see, was to make sure they didn't get into too much trouble before them.

He would have liked to talk to Goldie about it all, but she was too busy getting the last boys bundled into their pajamas and into bed. It wasn't as easy a job as it looked. No sooner was one neatly tucked in than another was popping out for one last cup of water or some equally transparent excuse for getting into trouble.

Goldie tucked in the last of the twelve, kissed him good night, then straightened wearily.

Richard watched her, shaken by a sudden mental image of her bending over the bed of another child—*her* child . . . and his. The love and longing that washed through him at the thought was enough to make his knees go weak.

Across the length of the room, her gaze locked with his. She smiled, and Richard had a vision—a glorious, golden vision— of all the years and years that lay ahead of them and all the discoveries that they would make, together.

Slowly, she came toward him, pausing here to tuck in a blanket, there to brush a soft kiss on a little boy's forehead.

Behind her, quiet and sly as a mouse, a boy slid out of bed.

For an instant, Richard wondered if he should say something, but what?

Thurgood proved more than capable of handling the situation.

"*Master* Tryffin," he said with awful emphasis.

The miscreant stopped in his tracks. One glance told him that he didn't have a chance of sneaking past Thurgood's guard. He heaved a sigh, then obediently trotted back to bed.

Then Goldie slid into Richard's arms, her face titled up for a kiss, and Richard forgot all about the boys and the maids and Thurgood. Three minutes later he was dizzy with desire, and twelve small boys were fast asleep.

The maids crept on tiptoe about the room, snuffing out the candles. Thurgood gave a very small, very satisfied smile.

"Your Majesties may leave," he informed Richard and Arianne with great dignity. "I believe we have everything well in hand here."

To his chagrin, Richard found himself blushing under his valet's knowing look. With a mischievous smile, Goldie grabbed his hand and quietly led him out.

The minute the door closed behind them, she let go of his hand and, giggling, darted away toward the stairs that led up to the royal bedchamber.

For a moment, Richard wasn't sure he'd really seen what he thought he'd seen in her eyes. But then she stopped and glanced at him over her shoulder, and if ever he'd seen a come-hither look in a woman's eyes, Richard thought, he saw it in his wife's.

"Wait for me!" he cried, but she was already disappearing around the bend in the stairs above. Her laughter floated down to him, drawing him up after her. Two steps at a time at first, then three.

He caught her in the corridor outside their bedchamber and swept her up in his arms, heedless of his protesting collarbone.

She threw her arms around his neck, half laughing, half crying, saying "I love you" over and over and over again.

He had her gown off by the time he reached the bed. What he'd missed she ripped off while he shed his own clothes as fast as he could.

But before he could make the most of their unclad state, she stopped him with a hand to his chest.

He froze, then watched in delight as her face turned scarlet.

"Now I know the cat's got your tongue," he teased.

She bit her lip, caught between laughing and hiding under the covers.

"Remember that troubadour?" she said. She had a most delectable voice. Like apricots and honey, sweet clear through. "You know. Gregory? The one you banished from the kingdom?'

Richard's smile vanished. He sat up, dreading what came next.

"I remember."

She nodded, then ducked her head, clearly struggling to find the right words for what she had to tell him.

Richard couldn't have spoken if he'd wanted

to. The words were frozen inside him, held by fear.

"I . . . well . . . uh . . ." She stopped, bit her lip, then brought her head up until her gaze locked with his. "I heard him singing a song. It—I made him teach it to me. Every word. I even had him write it down so I wouldn't forget. I—I learned it especially for you."

Richard stared at her, fascinated. His fear had vanished as she'd stumbled through the explanation, to be replaced by awe. When she blushed like this, even her breasts turned pink. So pink, in fact, that they rivaled the rosy perfection of her nipples, which had risen to dangerously tempting peaks.

Richard swallowed. "Go on. Sing it for me. But for the sake of John Paul and me, don't make it too long, will you?"

She giggled—by now, the blush was down to her belly button—took a deep breath, and started singing.

Her voice lifted like a lark's. It was a beautiful voice, the kind of voice that made a man forget everything else but following it.

Because it was so beautiful, it took him a few lines before he realized she was singing a bawdy drinking song recounting the extremely athletic sexual exploits of a king and a beggar maid.

Goldie was on the fifth stanza, the one about the chandelier and the silver chains, before

Richard stopped laughing long enough to grab for her.

She tried to dodge, which threw them both off balance so that they ended up rolling off the bed and onto the floor together. Despite the laughter choking her, Goldie tried to finish the last lines of that fifth stanza.

She never made it to the sixth.

Dear Reader,

Remember the "Fractured Fairy Tales" included in the old Rocky and Bullwinkle cartoon shows? I do. I loved those offbeat stories that put a funny little twist on our favorite fairy tales.

I liked them so much, in fact, that I decided to try writing one of my own.

The original tale of "The Wild Swans"—in all its versions—is about a young princess who is forced to knit shirts out of nettles in order to free her brothers from a witch's spell, which has changed them into swans—and she has to do the painful deed completely without complaint. If she speaks even one word before their shirts are finished, her beloved if boisterous brothers will remain swans forever.

As she's doggedly knitting away, who should ride up on his charger but a handsome king? (Of course! This is a fairy tale, remember?) Smitten by her beauty, the king flings the silent princess onto his horse and promptly gallops off to his castle, where he just as promptly marries her.

Unfortunately, the princess soon learns that marriage to a king—even a studly, good-natured one—is no piece of cake. Especially when she's still stuck knitting those darned nettle shirts, pestered by a villain (there's always a villain), and unable to say a word on her own behalf.

At the heart of my tale is the age-old frustration all women have confronted with the men in their lives—namely, having to explain *everything* to the big lunks. When it comes to communication, even the best husbands, lovers, fathers, and friends can drive a woman to distraction. We remember birthdays; they remember baseball stats. We love romantic little gestures like a single rose or a sentimental card; they think they're being devoted when they remember to take out the trash and check the oil in the car.

I don't imagine things were much different for a princess in her castle, who thought a French ballad sung to her before the fire would be so romantic—while her handsome husband deemed bringing home a couple of dead deer the ultimate gesture of affection. (All right, an adequate supply of venison *was* important, just as trash removal and car maintenance are, but *we* know there's a difference!)

I hope you'll enjoy reading my fractured little fairy tale as much as I enjoyed writing it. And remember—the part about the hero figuring out what the heroine wants without her having to tell him? That's pure fantasy!

Best wishes,
Kate Holmes

P.S. Please don't expect historical accuracy in this story—it's a *fractured* fairy tale, remember?

HEAVEN'S ROGUE

COLLEEN SHANNON

His is timeless perfection, molded by a genius. He stands
magnificently tensed for action, noble, confident, and invincible.
His firm hips cradle superior masculinity. His body reflects the
heroic ideal of an age; once every thousand years such a flawless
man exists. And Honoria Psyche Fitzhugh recognizes in him the
soulmate she'd always pined for and the champion she sorely
needs. Too bad he is a stone-cold statue... a statue on which
Honor has staked her career as a museum curator. But when the
white marble turns to warm flesh under her fingertips, Honor
knows she will risk more than her future in the art world for the
man she has liberated with her touch. At the dawn of a new
millennium, Honor has awakened a true Renaissance man, but
has she found a love to carry her into the next century?

___52340-X $5.99 US/$6.99 CAN

A Faerie Tale Romance

Prince of Kisses

COLLEEN SHANNON

Daughter of wealth and privilege, lovely Charlaine Kimball is known to Victorian society as the Ice Princess. But when a brash intruder dares to take a king's ransom in jewels from her private safe, indignation burns away her usual cool reserve. And when the handsome rogue presumes to steal a kiss from her untouched lips, forbidden longing sets her soul ablaze.

Illegitimate son of a penniless Frenchwoman, Devlin Rhodes is nothing but a lowly bounder to the British aristocrats who snub him. But his leapfrogging ambition engages him in a dangerous game. Now he will have to win Charlaine's hand in marriage–and have her begging for the kiss that will awaken his heart and transform him into the man he was always meant to be.

—52200-4 $5.99 US/$6.99 CAN

The Steadfast Heart

Colleen Shannon

Though it has been nearly ten years since Vincent Anthony Kimball's first and only love, Chantal, disappeared from his life, memories of her sweet face still haunt him. Then he sees her at the ballet, and is engulfed by waves of need and longing. But is she really his long-lost Chantal, or the prima ballerina Papillone? Whatever the case, Vince knows that, like the brave tin soldier of the fairy tale, he will do anything to return his true love to him, give anything to unite their hearts as one.

___52271-3 $5.99 US/$6.99 CAN